I0675343

Wishing Well

Wishing Well

Copyright © 2022 Knight Writing Press

Additional copyright information for individual works provided at the end of this publication.

Enrapturing Tales is an imprint of:

Knight Writing Press
PMB # 162
13009 S. Parker Rd.
Parker CO 80134
knightwritingpress.com
KnightWritingPress@gmail.com

Cover Art and Cover Design © 2022 Knight Writing Press

Interior Art © 2022 Knight Writing Press

Additional Copyright Information can be found on page 271

Interior Book Design and eBook Design by Knight Writing Press

Editor Sam Knight

All rights reserved. No part of this publication may be reproduced or transmitted in any form, without the express written permission of the copyright holder, with the exception of brief quotations within critical articles and reviews or as permitted by law.

This is a work of fiction. Any similarities to real persons, places, or events are coincidental, the work of the authors' imagination, or used fictitiously.

Electronic versions of this work are licensed for the personal enjoyment of the original purchaser only and may not be re-sold or given away. If you would like to share this work with another person, please purchase a physical copy or purchase an additional electronic copy for that person. Thank you for respecting the hard work of the authors and publishers by doing so.

First Publication August 2022

Paperback ISBN-13: 978-1-62869-053-8
eBook ISBN-13: 978-1-62869-054-5

For every wish you
ever made that you
thought didn't come
true...

Maybe there was a
good reason it
didn't.

Table of Contents

A Note from the Editor

Content Warning for this Anthology

Wishes are a tricky thing. We've all been cautioned to be careful what we wish for, because we just might get it. The cautionary tales teach us that wishes may go very, very wrong.

This anthology contains some stories of wishes that go wrong. Fortunately, some go right, too, but that's not what I need to say here.

While I, personally, do not consider any of these stories too dark, too disturbing, or too anything, some of them are a bit dark, some are a bit disturbing. Some deal with adult themes, and some are about violence, and some have curse words.

Nearly all the violence in these stories takes place "off screen," but not all of it does. Most of these stories have mild language, but not all of them do. Most do not contain moral or ethical dilemmas, but some do.

Though I think the chances anyone will regret reading any of these stories are slight, I feel I should caution those who feel they need warnings.

If that is you, then, just as though you were making a wish, I suggest you indulge in careful consideration before you enter this anthology. Consider yourself warned.

If that is not you, if you already know what your wishes would be… Well, you should consider yourself warned as well.

Be careful what you wish for.

-Sam Knight
July 3rd, 2022

Don't Annoy the Genie

by
Emily Martha Sorensen

Don't Annoy the Genie

The genie snapped his fingers. "There you go. No man shall ever kill you. That brings your total to—"

"But women can?" the Dark Lord whined.

"Okay, no living human. Your bill—"

"No *living* human? What about zombies?"

A snap of the fingers. "Living or dead, but aren't those undead yours already?"

"And animals! And poison! And plants!"

The genie kept snapping his fingers, starting to look cranky. "Okay, but my fee i—"

"And weapons! There's no point if a 'human' can't kill me, but a sword they hold can…"

The genie killed the Dark Lord.

About the Author

Emily Martha Sorensen writes fantasy and science fiction books with realistic paths to a happy ending. She considers all her books clean, with zero swearing and not much violence, but the romance between married couples can be PG-13.

She likes clever characters with unique personalities who charge straight through her plot and spend it spinning wildly off the rails. (Those brats.)

She likes magic systems with strict rules and intriguing limitations.

She likes romance after the happily ever after. That's where the relationship begins!

She likes plot twists that will make your jaw drop.

She likes hope and fun and humor.

She likes darkness that exists only to help characters grow towards greater light.

She likes—

Wait, where did those uncooperative protagonists put the plot this time? They just ran off with it, cackling maniacally!

Well, she hopes they'll leave you grinning.
You can find her books at
http://www.emilymarthasorensen.com.

The Girl from the Well

by
Kay Hanifen

The Girl from the Well

Celeste hated her grandparents' house. It was old, the floorboards creaked, the hinges shrieked every time she opened the door, and it smelled like must and cigarettes. Worst of all, there weren't any other kids around for miles—the closest neighbor was an old man who glared at her from his front porch every time she walked past his house—so she was stuck watching golf with Grandpa, watching soap operas with Grandma, or walking alone in the woods.

Her parents said it would only be a week, but by the end of day one, it felt like an eternity until they were going to pick her up again. Bereft of anything else to do on a hot summer day, she decided to wander the property.

After announcing her departure to her grandparents, she stepped outside and was immediately blasted with the full weight of summer's humidity. She slapped at a mosquito, already irritated with the bugs and heat, but too bored to suffer another moment indoors. Something glinted in the afternoon sun on the front porch.

Stooping down, she picked up a lucky penny one of her grandparents must have dropped and pocketed it. She wasn't sure why—you can't buy anything with a single penny these days. Maybe she could practice magic tricks with it later.

Their home was a small farm at one point, but it had long fallen into disrepair. Still, it allowed for plenty of secret places to explore. She could pretend there was a portal to a fairy world hidden in the woods. She'd be whisked away to adventures and learn to swordfight and maybe become a queen.

Picking up a stick, she swung it at an invisible enemy, striking it down with her enchanted sword. She leapt from tree stumps and dodged rustling leaves like monstrous claws. Landing wrong after a daring jump from a rock, her ankle twisted, and she fell, rolling down the hill into a small embankment.

For a moment, she just laid on her back unsure whether to laugh or to cry as mosquitoes buzzed above her. Getting to her feet, she brushed off her scraped and dirty knees and tested her weight in her twisted ankle. It hurt a little bit, but not too badly, so she searched for her mighty weapon, only to find that it had broken in the fall.

With an irritated sigh, she blew a stray hair from her face. And then she spotted something a little farther ahead. A little well sat alone and abandoned in the woods. She approached it and saw a kid had written "Wishin Wel" on the side, in long-faded paint. Reaching into her pocket, she pondered the penny.

Celeste was at an age where the idea of magic in the world hadn't quite died. She still dutifully wrote her letter to Santa and put her baby teeth under her pillow for the tooth fairy to collect. To her, dropping a penny in a well was as likely to grant her wish as anything else.

She clutched the shiny penny to her heart, willing all the magic of the well into her words. "I wish for someone to play with."

Dropping the penny, she counted the seconds until the splash. It took much longer than she expected. The well must have been very deep. A twig snapped behind her, and she whirled around.

A girl, about her age, in overalls and a striped shirt, peered shyly out from behind a tree. Celeste couldn't help the grin spreading across her face. Her wish had come true. "Hi, I'm Celeste," she said with a wave.

"I'm Molly," the other girl mumbled, studying her muddy shoes

"Do you want to play?"

That got her attention, and her head snapped up eagerly. "Can we have a tea party?"

Truthfully, Celeste had been dying for a proper tea party. When she suggested it to Grandma, she just gave her a mug of sweet tea that they drank in an awkward silence. "Yes!"

They used acorn hats for teacups, pebbles for petite fours, and a tree stump for their table as they put on airs and offered each other cream and sugar in a posh British accent.

"Lady Moltilda, have you heard the news about Lord Fussbudget?"

"I have not, Lady Celestina," Molly giggled. "Tell me more."

"Apparently, he decided that no woman was good enough for him, so he's marrying his horse."

"Nay, that can't be true!"

"Oh, she certainly does neigh. I heard he really loves her nickers too." Both girls dissolved into a fit of laughter.

When they subsided, Molly sighed sadly. "My brother hates tea parties. He says they're for babies."

"No, they're not," Celeste said indignantly. "The Queen of England does it all the time, and she's like a hundred."

Molly's face lit up. "Really?"

"My mom said it was called High Tea, and that my great grandpa got invited to one after fighting in a war because he shot down a bunch of bad guys."

Her eyes widened. "Wow. I want to have tea with the Queen someday."

Picking up her acorn cup with her pinky out, Celeste said, "Then you gotta practice. Cheers!"

"Cheers!" Molly echoed as they clinked their acorns together.

They played all afternoon, and before Celeste knew it, the sun was going down, and the fireflies were flickering throughout the forest. She gave a regretful look to Molly. "I have to go back. Can we play again tomorrow?"

The other girl looked shocked. "You want to come back?"

"Duh," she said with a giggle. "You're my friend."

She rocked back and forth on her feet. "I never really had a friend before. Most of the kids in my class are boys, and they like my brother better than me."

Celeste wrinkled her nose. "Ew, boys. They're the worst."

The other girl giggled. "They really are. I'll see you tomorrow."

With a final wave, Celeste skipped all the way back home. This week was about to be a whole lot better.

"Where were you?" Grandma asked as she heated spaghetti in the microwave. Apparently, she'd missed dinner while out playing with Molly.

She'd also forgotten about the scrapes on her knee, but the sting of Grandpa applying disinfectant to them swiftly reminded her. She hissed at the pain. "I met girl and we were playing."

Grandma and Grandpa exchanged glances that she didn't care to decipher. Her stomach was growling too much, and her throat was too parched. She took a big gulp of the iced tea in front of her. "Do you know how old she is?" Grandpa asked.

She shrugged. "My age, I think."

Placing the bowl of spaghetti in front of her, Grandma asked, "I don't know about any families with children nearby. Is she from around here?"

Celeste's face crumpled slightly when she saw that it was spaghetti primavera instead of spaghetti and meatballs like she thought. Still, she took a dutiful bite and choked it down. Grown-ups made the weirdest dishes. Who thought it was a good idea to ruin perfectly good pasta with broccoli and peas? "I dunno," she replied, washing down the bitter broccoli with sweet tea.

"Where does she go to school?" Grandpa asked.

Again, she shrugged. Why did grown-ups always ask such boring questions? Who cares where she goes to school? Her favorite color is purple, and she liked Cinderella best of the Disney Princesses. It was a little weird that she hadn't heard of Queen Elsa or Moana, but Celeste just assumed that her parents didn't have a TV. Michael Sanders, in Celeste's class last year, would brag that he was so good at reading because his parents didn't own a TV. He said it 'rots the brain,' and that he's going to be the only one smart enough to be president one day, but she thought he was secretly jealous that everyone else had one. Molly wouldn't brag about something like that. She'd just look kinda sad, the way she looked sad about most things Celeste talked about.

"Well, let her know she's welcome to drop by any time she wants," Grandma said, brushing her hands on her apron.

"Maybe Molly and I could watch Frozen on your TV. She's never seen it." She glanced hopefully between her grandparents. Their TV time was sacrosanct, but maybe they'd make an exception just once.

Grandma shrugged. "Sure, if she wants. I'd love to meet her."

Little girls have a talent for making temporary yet incredibly intimate friendships with any other little girl they come across, especially when that other girl is the only kid nearby. Such was the case with Molly and Celeste. They held tea parties and protected imaginary fairies from the imaginary trolls that wanted to eat them. They played from morning until the sun was low in the sky, and the week was flying by faster than Celeste expected. As they got to know each other, the less she liked Molly's bully of a big brother. He loved terrorizing Molly—always putting snakes in her bed and jumping out from dark corners with a yell, just to hear her scream. Celeste started collecting rocks in her pockets to throw at him if he ever came by to bother them.

It was Friday when she said, "Hey, do you want to have a sleepover at my grandparents' house tonight? It's my last night, and we can watch Frozen."

Molly stiffened just a little, but enough for Celeste to notice. "I don't think my parents will say it's okay."

"Well, you can always ask. The worst they'll do is say no." The pair had been wandering aimlessly through the woods, Celeste taking Molly's lead until the tree line broke, and she found herself in the yard of the scary old man who lived next door. Her pockets were laden with rocks in case they came across Molly's brother, but they would do little against an adult with a shotgun. She tugged at her friend, but Molly stood frozen. She pulled again. "Come on, we have to go before he sees us," she hissed, but it was too late.

"You there!" the old man shouted. "Get off my property."

Celeste screamed and ran, pulling a dazed Molly back into the woods. She didn't stop running until they were back at the well and her lungs burned. Leaning against a tree, she caught her breath. "Are you okay?" she asked.

Molly blinked as though just coming out of a daydream. "What? Oh, yes, I'm fine."

"You don't look fine."

Her friend stared wistfully back in the direction of the house. "I—I guess I just had this really weird feeling. It was like I belonged there."

"With that scary old guy?" She laughed. "No one belongs over there."

Molly turned slowly to study her face. After a few agonizing seconds of scrutiny, she shrugged and was back to her usual self. "You're right. He gives me the creeps."

And that was the end of that for the day. Celeste tried to press further, but every time she did, Molly got a dreamy expression on her face and refused to answer any of her questions. She was starting to get worried about her friend. Molly could be a little spacey and sad, but that day, it was like she was mist slipping through Celeste's fingers.

On most days, she was sad when it came time to say goodbye, but that evening, it was sort of a relief. She slipped in the backdoor, removed her shoes and washed her hands. Grandpa was looking at an old photo album on the kitchen table. "What's that?" she asked, the strangeness of the day forgotten.

Grandpa scooted over so she'd have space to look. "Grandma found my old photo album while cleaning under the bed. I was just taking a trip down memory lane." He flipped the page, and two boys sat fishing and grinning at the camera. She knew there was a river nearby, but they hadn't taken her there yet. This was probably where they took the picture. In the background, a little girl in overalls sat with her back to the scene, apparently absorbed in making a sandcastle. Something about her was vaguely familiar.

"Who's that?" she asked.

"Oh, it's just me and the neighbor." He pointed to the boy next to him. "That's Aaron."

"And the girl behind you?"

He squinted at the picture. "I think that was his sister. What was her name? Mary? Milly?"

"Molly?" she suggested.

He snapped in triumph as though he was the one who figured it out. "Molly! That's it! She was Aaron's annoying tagalong sister. It's a shame what happened to her."

"What happened?"

"We don't know. She disappeared one day. Aaron used to talk about leaving town and seeing the world, but after she vanished, he planted his roots in his ancestral home next door."

16

"He's the scary old man with the guns?" Celeste asked, eyes wide.

Grandpa chuckled. "Aaron might be a little gruff, but don't worry. He won't hurt a fly."

Celeste was reeling. Apparently, her new friend was a ghost, and the scary old man was her brother. She had to be sure, though. When she told adults her ideas, they'd always ruffle her hair and say she had quite an imagination even when she wasn't imagining things. "Do you have any other pictures of Molly?"

Grandpa raised his bushy eyebrows. "Maybe. Let's see." Together, they flipped through the photo album. Tucked between the last two pages, there was a loose photograph of the three children in Halloween costumes. Molly was a ballerina while Aaron and Grandpa were both cowboys.

Celeste snatched the photo and ran outside, heedless of Grandpa's calls to come back because it was dark. She sprinted into the woods, stumbling over tree roots and rocks in the darkness. When she approached the well, she saw a light flickering nearby and slowed down. Hiding behind a tree, she caught her breath as she peered out. The old man was pulling something from the bottom of the well, grunting with exertion. Finally, he pulled up the bucket and dumped it out onto the ground.

Celeste gasped at the sight of a half-rotting skull attached to a body wearing Molly's striped shirt and overalls. He must have heard her because his head snapped up. Covering her mouth, she ducked again behind the tree, but it was too late. He spotted her, and before she could run away, he grabbed her roughly by the arms and dragged her into the open. One hand went around her mouth as she struggled against him. Reaching into her pocket with her free hand, she threw a handful of rocks in his face. He grunted, letting go in surprise as she staggered away.

This was a time to be brave, but all Celeste could think about was how Mr. Aaron knew where Molly's body was, meaning that he probably killed his own sister and would probably kill her too, for knowing too much. She fell backwards, almost on top of the body and burst into tears.

"You killed her," she sobbed, crab walking out of his reach.

He froze, looking stricken in the moonlight. "I—I didn't mean to. You have to believe me. It was an accident. She was driving me crazy following me around all the time, and I pushed her. I—I didn't think she'd lose her balance and fall into the well." Tears now streamed down the old man's face. Celeste had never seen a grown-up cry before. She supposed that they were capable of it, but she always assumed that once you get to a certain age, you forget how. But this old man was sobbing as he held the rotting corpse close. "I'm so sorry. All these years, I wished it was me instead."

"Aaron?" came Molly's voice from behind. Still on the ground, Celeste looked up and realized that Molly was standing barely two feet away. Her friend offered her a hand up and she accepted gratefully as she got to her feet. Sobbing, the old man lurched towards the specter of his sister, but Celeste stepped between them. She didn't know if he could actually hurt Molly, but she didn't want to risk it. He'd already killed her, after all.

He sat back, sniffling. "Molly, I'm so sorry. I—I didn't mean it."

"Why did you leave me in there?" she asked softly. "Why didn't you tell Mom and Dad? It was cold and dark and lonely and—"

Celeste pulled her into a hug as she sobbed into her friend's shoulder. Despite the summer heat, she was cold as snow.

Mr. Aaron reached out as though he wanted to comfort her before lowering his hand and looking ashamed. "Because I'm a coward. I—I should have told them, but I was scared. I thought everyone would hate me." He doubled over as though in physical pain. "God. Sorry doesn't even begin to cover how I feel. I was so mean to you; made you think I didn't love you. The last thing I said was that I hated you, but it's not true. I swear, it's not."

Slowly, Molly lifted her head and wiped the tears from her cheeks. She gave Celeste a nod and a squeeze before letting go and approaching her sniveling brother. Molly didn't offer forgiveness or absolution. She simply offered a hug, and he squeezed her back like she was a rediscovered favorite stuffed animal. Turning to look at Celeste, Molly gave a watery smile. "Thank you for being such a good friend."

18

With that, Molly helped Mr. Aaron to his feet and led him deeper into the woods. Celeste realized that, in the scuffle, she'd dropped the photograph. The black and white picture stood out against the dark ground. She clutched it close to her chest as she walked back to her grandparents' house. She sat numbly through the scolding, the orders to take a bath and go to bed without dinner.

The next morning, Grandpa was crying because Mr. Aaron had died in his sleep on the front porch. The paper boy had found him and called the police. This was Celeste's first real exposure to death, but Celeste felt oddly numb and distant from the whole thing. She watched Grandpa write the obituary and begin funeral planning. Apparently, he was the closest thing to family that Aaron had.

Mom arrived to pick her up in the afternoon. Celeste barely spoke a word as she loaded up her suitcase and watched the farmhouse disappear behind them. Passing by Mr. Aaron's house, it felt strange to not see the scary old man with a shotgun sitting on the porch. Instead, a little girl and her slightly older brother stood on the front lawn and waved. She waved back and watched as Molly and Aaron disappeared like morning mist.

"Who are you waving to?" Mom asked.

She leaned back in her seat. "Just a couple friends."

"I'm glad you found someone to play with," she replied and then resumed humming along to the radio.

Celeste stared at the photograph, the happy faces of Molly and Aaron, both now at peace, and smiled back at them. "Yeah, me too."

About the Author

Kay Hanifen was born on a Friday the 13th and once lived for three months in a haunted castle. So, obviously, she had to become a horror writer. Her articles have appeared in *Ghouls Magazine*, *Screen Rant*, *The Borgen Project*, and *Leatherneck Magazine*; and her short stories have appeared in *Strangely Funny VIII*, *Crunchy With Ketchup*, *Midnight From Beyond the Stars*, *Dark Shadows: The Gay Nineties*, *Wicked Newsletters*, *Fearful Fun*, *Death of a Bad Neighbor*, *Enchanted Entrapments*, *Diet Riot: A Fatterpunk Anthology*, *M is for Medical*, *Blood Moon*, *Terror in the Trenches*, *Slice of Paradise*, *Vinyl Cuts*, *Sherlock Holmes and Watson's Medical Mysteries*, *Beware the Bugs*, and *Rockets and Robots*.

When she's not consuming pop culture with the voraciousness of a vampire at a 24-hour blood bank, you can usually find her with her two black cats or at KayHanifenAuthor.wordpress.com.

The Wishing Cat
by
Sylvia Son

The Wishing Cat

In front of the bookstore was a sign. And next to the sign was a giant fuzzy gray basketball in a basket. On the sign it said in bold caps:

DO NOT TOUCH OR PET CAT AT YOUR OWN PERIL!

Dean, Joe, and Amy walked past the store. Dean stopped and stared at the ball.

"Hey, check that out."

"What are you looking at?" Amy said.

Dean pointed at the cat.

"It's a cat." Joe said. "What a surprise."

"Isn't that a mall violation, having animals inside?" Amy said.

"That's not the point," Dean said.

"Then what is?" Joe said.

"I'm just surprised they actually let him out."

Amy reached out to pet the rounded body.

"No, don't!" Dean said.

"Why? Am I not allowed to touch him?"

"Check the sign."

Amy glanced down and saw the sign. "Oh, I didn't realize it didn't like to be touched."

"Oh no, it likes to be petted. It's real hungry for affection."

"I'm surprised they let him out, especially after last week."

"Why?" Amy said.

"Apparently last week Tod Philips broke into the cat's owner's house."

"Shit," Joe said. "Is the owner okay?"

"She's alright. He only broke in to pet her cat."

Amy and Joe were stunned for about 10 seconds. "Wait," Joe said. "Why? Is it magical?"

"Yes."

Amy reached up and touched Dean's forehead.

"What are you doing?"

Amy shrugged. "I'm just checking to see if you have a fever."

Dean ducked away from her hand. "I'm not crazy. Believe it." He waved at a random customer. She was reading a magazine.

"Hey!" He waved at her.

"Me?" she said.

"Yeah, can you settle an argument?"

"I guess."

"That cat." Dean pointed at the cat.

The woman recoiled away from it. "I'm not touching him."

Amy spoke up. "Is it cursed?"

"No," she said. "Of course not. Don't you know what that is?"

"That why we're asking."

The woman spoke loud enough for everyone in the shop to hear. "Hey everyone. They don't know what that cat is."

That offended Joe so much he walked over to the cat.

"Joe," Amy warned. "What are you doing?"

He petted the cat. Everyone gasped in shock. The cat rolled his body and purred.

"What have you done?" Dean said in absolute horror.

"I petted him. So, am I cursed now?"

"You'll wish it was a curse."

A woman in her 50's walked to the crowd. "What is going on here?"

"Who are you?" Joe said.

"I'm the owner of that cat."

"Well," Joe said. "I petted the cat, so how trouble much I'm in?"

"No, you're not in any actual trouble." The woman sighed. "You get three wishes, now." She picked the plump cat up and dumped him into Joe's arms.

"What?"

"Just return him when you're done."

"I don't want a cat."

The woman scoffed. "I'm not giving him to you. I'm lending him. Return when you're finished."

"Finished with what?"

"Are you not listening? Your three wishes."

"Three wishes? I don't understand. Is this a genie?"

"No, it's a cat. Just feed him twice a day until you're done. And remember, three wishes."

"But…"

"Aht! I don't want to hear whatever depraved desires you're thinking about."

"That's not what I'm—"

"Whatever. Just return him when you're done. Gerald!"

Gerald was a seven-foot behemoth wearing a white apron over his sweatshirt and jeans. He gently took Joe by the arm and dragged him away

"Have a nice day," Gerald said.

"Well," Amy said. "That was weird.

They walked in silence to the bus station with Joe in the middle, still holding the cat, Amy on his left and Dean on his right. It wasn't as if the cat was going to let him go. Once every few steps they would turn their heads to stare at the cat in Joe's arms.

"You know," Amy said. "It's kind of unfair."

"How?" Joe said.

"You ended up petting the cat and now you get three wishes."

"Are you serious? That is the one thing that's bothering you? Well fine, here. Take it." He hefted his arms up and held the cat out at Amy. Even as the cat glared at Amy, the cat was able to dig deeper into Joe's arms with his claws. Amy took a step away from Joe.

"What?" Amy said. She looked kind of offended. "What kind of selfish person do you think I am? You petted him. Those wishes are yours fair and square. I don't steal other people's stuff." She pushed his arms back to cradle the cat and the cat loosened his grip.

Dean snorted. "Trust me; you'll be glad you never petted him."

"Why?" Joe said. "Is this cat cursed like a monkey's paw and if I make a wish something terrible will happen to me?"

"No. Nothing like that. It's just you'll regret making those wishes."

"I thought you said he wasn't cursed."

"It's not. You have to see it to believe it."

Dean didn't have time to elaborate, his bus stopped in front of them, and he stepped in.

"Thanks for being so vague," Joe said.

Dean found a seat with window, and he pushed it open. "My advice," he said. "Make your wishes as simple as possible. You'll be less disappointed by the outcome."

Joe opened the door of his apartment with one arm and, once he walked through, the cat finally released his death grip on Joe and leaped out of his arms.

"Make yourself at home," Joe said dryly.

The cat did. He jumped onto the coffee table circled himself three times and curled into a ball to stare at him.

"I carried you all the way here and now you're tired? No wonder you're so fat."

The cat responded by standing up and then jumped onto the couch. For a cat so...stout, he was rather agile.

Joe wasn't sure what the cat was going to do until he saw it squat slightly and it pooped on the cushion. Joe spent the next 20 minutes cleaning the couch upholstery. The cat was back sitting on the coffee table, lounging on his side.

"Fine," Joe said. "You win. No more insults." He dumped the dirty sponge into a garbage bag. "So," he asked, "how does it work?"

The cat stared.

"Do you say some magic word and then poof it happens?"

The cat responded by yawning.

Joe couldn't believe he was doing this. It seemed like an elaborate scam and any moment as soon as he said his wishes they were going to pop out and point and laugh at him. He'd kill Dean if that were true. Well, he thought. Go big and at least gamble that there was a fifty-fifty chance it was true.

"Alright," he said to the cat. "My first wish is a million dollars." He rationalized it wasn't too big to bring attention to himself, but large enough to enjoy.

The cat arched his back and then proceeded to groom himself. Joe stood for a minute. Nothing happened. No showers of cash. No phone call. Not even a knock on the door. Nothing.

"I knew it. It was a scam." He was stuck with a regular cat.

Tomorrow, Joe thought. I'm going to sell this cat.

He stomped to his room and closed the door to make sure the cat didn't follow after him. If he had waited 10 more seconds, he would have seen waves of light seeping out of the cat.

Wish fulfilled.

Sort of.

Then the cat continued to groom himself.

Ten minutes later, there was knock on the door. Joe slowly opened the bedroom door and peeked his head out. He checked the clock by his bed. It was 9:30 pm. He exited his bedroom, ignored the cat licking its leg, and opened the door.

A man in a tuxedo stood with a giant Bristol board.

"Joe Costas."

"Yes."

"Congratulations."

"For what?"

"You have been randomly selected and won the grand prize."

"I did?" He perked his head up with interest.

"Of one million dollars—"

"Yes!" Joe cut him off in mid-sentence. The cat actually granted his wish! This was a wishing cat!

"—worth of cat accessories."

The words tore his bliss in half like a fingernail dragged down a chalkboard. "What?"

"Cat food. Cat toys. Cat grooming kits. Everything you need to care and maintain your cat. All valuing at one million dollars." He slowly pushed the giant cardboard cheque through the doorway. "You can cash this in at any pet store."

"I don't want it," he pushed it back at him.

"Oh, I insist."

"Well, I insist you take it back."

"There's a $1000 penalty if you don't sign and accept it. Look, I hand out the cheques you can keep it in your apartment closet for all I care, but I'm not leaving with it."

"Fine," Joe said.

"Great." He held out a clipboard. "Now if you can sign here stating you received the prize I can leave."

Joe took the clipboard and signed his name.

"Thank you and congratulations. Have a nice day. He turned and walked down the hall. Joe was impressed that the man in the tux was able to walk and dodge the tennis ball he threw at him without breaking a step.

Joe slammed the door behind him. The cat was now sitting up on his hind legs to stare at him.

He needed to call someone for this.

"Hello?" Amy said.

"Amy, it's Joe."

"Joe? What is it? Is something wrong?"

"Yes and no."

"Did you do something to the cat? Oh my god, did you kill him?"

"No!" What kind of person did Amy think he was? "I'm a little offended you think I'm some sort of a cat killer. And I'm also annoyed you're more concerned about that cat than me.

"Fine. I'm sorry. So why are you calling?"

"I made a wish."

"Congratulations," she said, but her tone sounded less than thrilled.

"No, that's the thing. When I made wish, it went weird."

"Weird?" she said. "What do you mean?"

"Well, I wished for a million dollars, and instead I got a gift certificate for a million dollars' worth of cat merchandise."

"Wait," Amy said. "Did you say cat stuff?"

"Yes. Some weird dude in a suit showed up with a giant cheque for a million dollars in cat products.

There was a long moment of silence.

"Hello? Amy. Are you still there?"

Amy responded by first spitting out a mouth full of air and then laughed and laughed and laughed long and hard.

"It's not funny."

"I think it is."

"I think the cat did it on purpose."

"It's a cat; I don't think it's that spiteful. Unless…"

"Unless what?"

"Dean did warn you."

"Yeah, dark and horrific stuff, but not this."

"Just choose your wishes more specifically. Don't wish for something so complex."

"Then what's the point of having a cat that can grant wishes?"

"Maybe that's the point."

"What point?"

"Be careful what you wish for?" And she hung up on him.

Joe looked back at the cat was still sitting on the coffee table.

"You did that on purpose, didn't you?"

The cat stared.

"Or," he remembered the "warning" by the owner, "is this what you consider wealth?"

Cat stared again.

Joe sighed. "Okay, we need our wishes to be specific." He paced back and forth. "Right. Cat, I wish for a woman to fall in love with me. And a sports car. Yeah, that's specific enough."

The cat stood on all four legs and Joe saw waves of light trickle out from the furry body.

"Whoa," was all he could say.

The waves moved faster and faster, and then zinged out all at once. Then everything was quiet.

"Is that it? Now what? What happens now?"

The cat responded by leaping onto the couch and circled three times and curled himself into a ball and proceeded to snore.

Joe was about to poke the cat for some answer but realized it was a wish cat, not a talking cat. Maybe a wish this big needed time to cook.

Joe awoke to something damp and rough against his face like sandpaper. It was a constant beat and starting to itch.

Not bothering to open his eyes he waved his hand at whoever was doing it. Probably Amy.

"Knock it off, Amy. It's not funny." His hand collided with air and a noise.

"Meow."

Joe opened his eyes and stared face to face with an orange and white Maine coon cat.

"What?"

The cat licked him on the nose again.

"You're in love with me, aren't you?"

The cat curled itself into a ball next to his head and purred.

The wish cat in the living room was lying on Joe's couch, and his head perked up to see Joe walking towards him. Following at Joe's heels was the Maine coon cat.

Joe stopped in front of the couch. He pointed at the cat on the floor. "You did this? Is this supposed to be love?"

The wish cat tilted his head up and flicked his tail while the female cat continued purring and rubbing herself against his leg.

"Can you do something about this? No? So, I'm stuck with her?"

The cat responded by yawning.

Walking around the townhouse with a purring cat was a little disconcerting but manageable. When he went to the kitchen for a beer, he barely avoided colliding his feet into her even as she looked up at him with adoration. Bathrooms were a little trickier. He had to run and closed the door to get some privacy. And just when he thought he was starting to get used to her, the cat suddenly stopped following after him, groomed herself, and then leaped onto the open windowsill and jumped out.

Joe stood there not really sure what just happened. He should have felt relieved but he also kind of felt rejected.

"Did you do that?" He wanted to pick the cat up and shake him until the cat gave him answers, but he stopped himself, rationalizing that this was a cat and cats don't talk.

Still, he was a little hurt that she'd left without a second thought. But then he remembered he had one more wish. A sports car.

"So," he said to the cat. "Where's my car?"

The cat jumped off the coffee table and walked to Joe's bedroom. Joe followed after him.

Amy and Dean were standing by the front of the bookstore. It had been less than 12 hours since they saw Joe. Other than the call Amy received, they haven't heard again from him until this morning. He didn't say much, but he implied he was returning the cat.

"So soon?" Dean had asked. "You gave up on the wishes?"

"No."

"You made your wishes?"

"Yup." That was the only thing he had said. And that was why they were here, waiting for him, to see what he had wished for.

"What do you think he wished for?" Amy said.

"Don't know."

"Do you think one of his wishes turned him into a cat?"

Dean's eyes widened for a second. "I don't want to think about that."

"I think he might make a cute cat."

"You're weird."

"Why not? I—" She stopped, seeing Joe walking towards them without the cat.

"Oh my god." Amy said. "Do you think he ate the cat?"

Joe stopped at the entrance. "Hey," Joe said.

"Hey," Dean responded back. "You're alright."

"Of course."

"Where's the cat?" Amy said. "Did you eat him?"

"What? No!" Joe was offended by that. "What kind of person you think I am?"

"Well," Dean said. "A guy who made three wishes, and yet you seem alive and in one piece."

"It's not a monkey's paw. And that's debatable."

"Okay," Amy said. She was still worried. "Where's the cat?"

"Yeah. Remember the three wishes deal?"

"Yeah. You mentioned you wished for riches, and you got instead a million-dollar gift certificate."

"And my second wish was a cute girl. And as a result, I woke up with a female cat licking my face."

Dean and Amy stared at him for ten seconds and then began to laugh.

"It's not funny."

"It is," Amy said. "And it's not. So where is the little lady?"

Joe shrugged. "After twenty minutes she lost interest and left."

"Oh," Amy said. "I'm sorry? I guess she only cared about what's important to her. I wonder if it's because they have a short attention span or something like that."

"Is that supposed to make me feel better?" Joe said.

"Do you want to be married to a cat?" Amy said.

"No."

"Then be grateful that she had an attention span of a hummingbird."

"I am." They were quiet for a second. "But—"

"No buts," Amy said. "Count yourself lucky. All those wishes were cat-based. Be grateful you didn't turn into a cat. But still, I'm curious. What was your third wish?"

Joe was silent.

"Well?" Dean said.

"I wished for a sports car."

"Oh," Amy said. "That seems normal enough. I mean the worst thing is that it will have cat prints all over it."

"You would think that would happen. But—"

"But what? Where's the cat?"

A soft beep-beep noise came from far away, and Dean and Amy's jaws dropped to see the cat sitting in a cat-sized motorized car. It was a Lamborghini, with the top off, and cherry red. The kind of car Joe might have bought if he had the money.

It weaved side to side to avoid customers in the mall. The mini car sped up and towards them then stopped a foot away. Ironically, the cat looked good in it.

"I asked for a car and got that instead."

"He's actually kind of cute," Amy said. She leaned down to pick the cat up. The cat hissed at her.

"Don't bother," Joe said. "He likes it and won't let me take him out of it."

The cat in the car backed up and then drove into the bookstore for the next customer to pet him and start all over again.

About the Author

Sylvia lives in Mississauga and writes. She likes horror movies, improv and board games but not at the same time. But she has played Ultimate Werewolf and it's sort of the same thing.

The Price of the Pool
by
Kara Race-Moore

The Price of the Pool

S asha sat in the carriage, doing her best to read despite the jolts and bounces of the road.

"You will ruin your eyes reading like that, my lady," admonished her lady-in-waiting, Lady Galina.

Sasha didn't stop reading her book, *Seven Years in Atlantis*, and said without looking up, "Then I'll just ask the Goddess for new eyes when I go in the Pool."

"Don't even joke about that!" snapped Lady Galina. "You know what you must ask for."

"Yes, yes," said Sasha in a bored voice, wishing her lady-in-waiting would stop pestering her so she could concentrate on the description of the Atlantean festival held for the yearly fish migration.

But alas, Lady Galina was still talking. "At least we are making good time on this final leg. We should be at the inn just before sundown, and then be able to check into the rooms we reserved right away."

"According to Tang Seng, in his memoir *Travels with Lesser Gods*, 'A good traveler has no fixed plans, and is not intent on arriving,'" Sasha quoted airily.

"Perhaps that is an attitude one can have if you don't have to worry about your father," said Lady Galina pointedly, "but if the boyar sets a schedule, then you follow it."

Sasha didn't reply but felt her shoulders hunch as she stared intently at the page, seeing nothing, wishing her lady-in-waiting wasn't so correct. In truth, Lady Galina wielded quite a lot of power over Sasha, rather than the other way around. Lady Galina was more a guardian and instructor than servant. Lady Galina was also a distant cousin to the boyar's family; she held no land or money herself, but she stood on all the dignity of her bloodline.

Sasha glanced out the window, but the view was the same as it had been for the last few hours--a rocky shoreline and a wide expanse of sea.

Sasha had thought she would stare hungrily out the window the entire trip, devouring the landscapes, but she found, even though they were traveling to new lands, the landscape stayed the same for most of the time; first an endless stretch of forest, followed by an endless expanse of grasslands, and then other endless features.

Still, she enjoyed it whenever they had entered new lands. The fields of woolly mammoths of her homeland had been replaced by herds of unicorns as they had left the hinterlands of Rus and entered the grasslands of the Scythians. When new things would come into view, she would look her fill, but then would always eventually return to her books to learn more about what she was seeing, or would be seeing next, or wished she could see.

It had been a long journey from home, rattling across the countryside. She would have preferred to ride, but her father had insisted she stay safe inside the carriage, counting on the family crest emblazoned on the side and the guards riding before and after to protect her. She knew there were bandits on some roads, but still she resented the layers of protection.

Their destination was a town situated on a hill by the sea. Coming down towards the main town entrance, Sasha had a good view of all of it. The town's buildings almost all had roofs made of red clay titles and walls of a bright white stone. Sunshine poured down on the town as heavily as snow fell in her homeland.

Lording above the town, sitting at the highest point, was the Temple of Mitera, mother goddess of all women, and its grounds, surrounded by a tall, white wall enclosing the large main temple and its surrounding buildings.

As the sun began to set, casting long orange tendrils over the sea, they arrived at the town's main gates. Poking her head out, Sasha didn't see the kind of gate guards one usually saw inspecting people for weapons or poking through baggage. The guards here were just toll collectors, prices based on if you were on foot, on hoof, or on wheels. The town did not fear attack. A foolish few had tried over the years, and the goddess's wrath had been terrible.

Toll paid, moving slowly down the main streets still some distance from the temple, they made their way to the busy lodging district. The entire town had built up in the shadow of the sacred temple, busily catering to those who came to visit the Pool looking for a miracle, and there were plenty of places for visitors to stay.

The carriage traveled down the broad road lined on either side with inns. Farther back from the road, up the hill, there were finer houses the wealthy could rent if they didn't wish to share space. In between all the inns there were shops selling all manner of goods that might need to be replaced after a long journey, or supplies needed for those heading home. People came from far and wide and everything possible was sold here to help those on long journeys.

Among the shops selling long-lasting travel food, travel bedding, soaps, and other sundries, Sasha nearly gasped as they passed a shopfront with a display of bright red dresses in the front window. The store looked to sell nothing but mourning clothes for those journeying home without the member of the party that had gone to the Pool and not come out. Would her party be forced to shop there? She frowned, fairly sure her stepmother would have made sure to pack red cloaks. Lady Karolyn was pragmatic in that kind of way, never letting finer feelings get in the way of doing what was needed.

They came to the inn where several rooms had been held in reserve for herself and her entourage. As the servants scurried about the room, putting the baggage away, Sasha sat on the bed and looked out the window. From here she couldn't see the temple, just a row of roofs from all the other taverns and inns in the area.

"Come, my lady," said Lady Galina. "I have ordered a hot bath brought up. You must wash after your long journey."

Sasha shuddered as she looked at the tub of hot water. Soon she would be going into the Pool-and might not come out. But she allowed herself to be undressed, scrubbed down in the water that rapidly went from too hot to too cold, and when she got out, thankfully took the soft robe from her lady-in-waiting.

She brushed her hair and tied it into two braids as Lady Galina fussed with getting the evening meal ordered and sent up, arguing with the inn's staff about foods not available in these foreign lands.

As she tied off the second braid, Sasha idly wondered if anyone had used their trip into the Pool to make their hair a new color. It might seem like a wasted wish at first glance but think of all the stories that emphasized a girl's hair. If a girl with a pretty enough face but thin hair of some boring mouse color wished for a mane of thick golden locks that always gleamed like gold, or hair as silvery as moonlight, might that not result in a higher-ranking husband than she could have hoped for with merely ordinary hair?

Sasha sat down at the small table as the inn servant brought in the meal. Dinner was grilled fish, a dish of olives, and a dry crumbly cheese with a loaf of bread. Lady Galina sniffed, complaining it was barely edible, but Sasha was delighted by the cheese. She wished they could have eaten downstairs, but all throughout the trip Lady Galina had insisted on private meals whenever possible, reprimanding Sasha that she was not to mix in the common room with common folk.

Still, Sasha would see people when she went to the temple, and there would be so many types in the heavily visited town, with people coming from as far away as the southern desert seas of Sheba to the northern icy tundra of Hyperborea.

The next morning when she woke, Lady Galina was already unpacking their clothes. It had been strange when they had packed for the journey to include her lightest summer clothes, meant for the hottest days of the late summer, as they were leaving her father's lands in early spring, with snow still on the ground in patches, but now she was glad to be able to exchange her usual heavy wool dresses for light linen ones.

As they were just finishing a breakfast of boiled eggs and a round loaf of bread, the messenger they had sent came back with Sasha's time slot--she would be allowed to enter the temple in two days' time. Lady Galina made a noise of disapproval at the delay.

"It is not that long a wait," pointed out Sasha. "You know as well as I do, that they are very strict with seeing all on the basis of first come, first served. Remember, the Empress Melissa II herself waited a full week before she could enter the Pool."

"That was when she was still a princess, not empress," countered Lady Galina. "Not even the royal heir then, being several steps away at that point from the Ebony Throne."

"A princess still outranks the daughter of a boyar," said Sasha wryly. "Two days will pass soon enough."

However, Sasha found the day dragging by. The sun seemed to have slowed to a crawl, as if it was now being drawn by an old tortoise instead of the usual golden stallions.

She spent the day engaged in embroidery with Lady Galina. She missed her loom, and the meditative trance she was able to fall into while working on it, but it was too big and cumbersome to bring with her. She found needlework tiresome, too finicky, and likely to cause her pinpricks, and Lady Galina would chatter on so. Also, the noises of the strange town seemed to call to her from outside the window. It was easy to ignore the usual noises of her father's household, but here the new sounds all beckoned to her, and she longed to throw down her needle and escape.

As she pulled on loops of bright blue threads that were forming the petals for a flower that would decorate a cushion, she thought hard about how to avoid spending her whole time in this town stuck in this room. That night she consulted a local guidebook.

The next morning, she announced at breakfast that she would be going to the local temple of Vesna, lady of the spring, to pray for her upcoming visit to the Pool. Lady Galina frowned. Only virgins were allowed to visit Vesna's temples, and so the widowed Lady Galina could not accompany her charge.

"I'll take Annika with me, of course," said Sasha, before Lady Galina could forbid the excursion outright.

Lady Galina gave a reluctant nod. Annika was a warrior maidan, her virginity long ago pledged to the gods of war to allow her fight with the men. Annika had fought for Sasha's grandfather and then her father. Now, although greying, she was still a formidable wall of muscle that would scare off any petty thief or potential assailant from even thinking of coming near Sasha. Sadly, too many blows to the head over the years had thoroughly blunted her mind, but she was still able to follow simple directions such as 'no one touches Lady Sasha.'

Lady Galina returned to her embroidery. "On your way back, look in the bakeries for some syrniki. The inn doesn't have any."

Delighted with her plan to escape the room working, Sasha practically skipped out the door, Annika plodding behind her.

Sasha made no effort to find the quickest way to the local temple of Vesna, instead strolling down the sidewalks and taking the time to admire everything they passed.

It was odd to see all the local stone walls and tiled roofs instead of the timber and domed roofs of her homeland. However, nestled in-between the local architecture, she saw the distinctive towers and arches of buildings for a dozen other forms of worship, many she only recognized from her travel books, such as the black temple to Cailleach, winter goddess from the dark Teutonic forests, and the humble looking building guarded by two of the sacred golden dogs from the isle of Cynocephalus. Priests and priestesses of many other gods had set up small temples here for their faithful to come say one last prayer to their especial deity before approaching the goddess Mitera.

In some ways it was a typical temple-town, a settlement that had developed around a popular temple, with merchants and tavernkeepers offering everything a pilgrim could need outside of the temple's prevue. But in other ways it was very different. Because the temple only offered a promise of hope to women, the only men traveling there were part of a woman's retinue: the servants and guards of the women who came. And due to the amount of women who traveled there, many of the business that had spring up catered exclusively to women's needs, run by women merchants. Sasha had never seen so many women. It was breathtaking to see so many women going about their day, free as birds.

At Sasha's insistence, she and Annika stopped in a store called 'Needless Things.' The store lived up to its name, shelves and counters and bins overflowing with all sorts of trinkets and souvenirs, stacks of little items one could buy to brag later about having been to the temple of the Pool.

The shop had a shelf of little cloth dolls dressed in local holiday fashions, and a table stacked high with mugs, each garishly painted with a silly rendering of the different Arcadian gods. A display racked held a selection of straw hats beribboned with the holy colors of Mitera. At the front counter were paperweights in the form of miniatures of the temple, the goddess statue, and the Pool itself, and nearby was a crate filled with little pillows, probably meant to make carriage rides easier, each embroidered with views of the temple at sunset.

Sasha examined a row of little glass bottles labeled 'Pool Bubbles.' Removing the glass top to one revealed the stopper was attached to a small wire wand with a circle at the end, the vial filled with some soapy liquid for blowing bubbles through the wand.

On a rack of cheap books, one was titled *What Are the Odds?* Sasha picked it up and glanced through at the endless numbers of those who had survived the Pool and those who hadn't. Although the amount who survived was much higher, Sasha could see the amount of those who didn't was enough to give anyone pause before they entered the Pool.

There was another book called *Wishes Granted*, a compilation of some of the more extreme miracles granted by the Pool. She flipped it open to a random page containing an interview with a woman who had asked the goddess to allow her ears to also understand animal speech and her tongue be able to talk back, gushing about her life as an animal healer and how much she loved talking with her pets.

Sasha bought a fancy quill and they moved on in their explorations.

They stopped briefly in a store that sold nothing but bottles of olive oil. There were hundreds of varieties, made with more types of olives than Sasha ever dreamed existed. Sasha raised her eyebrows at the prices, but she supposed adding ingredients such as unicorn horn powder or gold flakes would raise the price.

At one point they stopped in a little bakery. The bakery didn't have any of the fried pancakes Lady Galina had asked for, but Sasha was delighted with the flaky pastry she got, filled with honey and nuts. She bought several more along with some pastries filled with a soft, sweet cheese, hoping that would satisfy Lady Galina. Sasha and Annika munched on the flaky, sticky, honey-filled squares as they walked on through the bustling streets.

The sun had made its way most across most of the sky, and Sasha knew they would have to soon end the day of exploring. Guiltily, Sasha made sure to make a brief stop at the small local temple to Vesna, dropping a coin in the box for orphans.

Back at the inn, she resisted the temptation to chatter about everything she'd seen that day, merely telling Lady Galina that the local chapter for Vesna was well run.

As they ate dinner, she said as casually as she could, "You know, before we go home, we could make a slight detour to see the Greeter of Korinthos. The statue is so high the legs that straddle the harbor mouth are tall enough for the tallest ship to sail through!"

"We will do no such thing. We will return directly home as soon as this business is finished. The sooner we are back in civilized lands, the better."

Sasha tried not to slump. It somehow seemed more exhausting to think of turning right around and going straight home than to imagine further travels.

The morning of her appointment dawned. Sasha was awake long before Lady Galina called for her to get out of bed. She had briefly crept out of bed ages ago to watch the dawn light start to lighten the street outside, wondering if she would get to see the sunset that day.

Lady Galina, however, was not one to indulge in sentimentality. She acted as though it was a perfectly normal day, one in which it was important to get dressed, eat breakfast, and be ready to go on her say so.

Lady Galina and Sasha took a hired litter to the Temple. At Lady Galina's insistence, Sasha had not brought anything with her, so she didn't have a book to read as they traveled through the crowded streets. At the drop off point, Lady Galina paid the lead bearer as Sasha stared at the temple. It wasn't as big as the emperor's Amber Palace, but it was still just as awe inspiring, the white columns gleaming in the sunlight.

Immediately before them were the gates where many other woman and girls were already gathered, some alone, others in small groups. Two guards directed people where to line up, one line for those entering today, the other for those getting their name on the schedule. A priestess oversaw two novices taking people's names for later entrance while another priestess checked names off a list and allowed people to enter.

As Sasha and Galina joined the line of those scheduled to enter that day, a middle-aged woman with gorgeous golden tipped, white feathered wings was arguing with a guard at the gate. "You've already had your miracle," the guard was saying, pushing the woman back.

"No, no, you don't understand, I made a mistake! I don't want another miracle! I just want the goddess to take it back! I made my wish too young! I just want to be normal! The wings didn't get me what I wanted!"

But the guard just shook her head and continued pushing the woman back. Crying, the woman stumbled away, her wings dropping, the golden tips dragging in the dust.

Lady Galina made a clucking noise of disapproval while Sasha stared in disbelief that such amazing wings hadn't made the woman happy.

"They shouldn't allow it to be free," stated Lady Galina. "It just invites all the riff-raff to show up."

"I suspect the goddess wouldn't like that," said Sasha drily.

Her lady-in-waiting made a *humph* noise that suggested she would happily give the goddess advice on how to run Her temple if she was given a chance.

Sasha suddenly wondered why Lady Galina wasn't planning on entering the Pool. Had her father forbidden it? Or was she afraid?

Lady Galina gave her a terse 'good luck' as the supplicants were separated at the gate from servants, handlers, family and well-wishers. Sasha gave a brief wave of good-bye as she and the other women and girls of that allotted time were allowed through the temple's brass entrance gate.

"Welcome to the Temple of the Pool," said their leader, a young novice. "We welcome all who wish to come because we wish to find the Pattern. Please follow me."

They wound along a path that led up the hill, through a gorgeous landscape of perfectly cut grass, flowering bushes, small trees, and flowerbeds that were a riot of the goddess' favored colors.

In the courtyard directly in front of the temple itself, there was a line forming, leading to a large urn on a marble plinth. Sasha had read about this, a clever device that dispensed water from a spring on the temple grounds, blessed by the high priestess. A coin was dropped into a slot at the top of the jar and clever mechanisms inside carefully dispensed a cup full of water from the bottom spigot.

The group was brought up the wide stairway into the temple itself. The main lobby held a marble fountain with a sculpted rendition of the goddess holding aloft her sacred jar, pouring forth water. As they passed by everyone nervously tossed in a coin for luck. The bottom of the fountain's basin was covered in coins from all over, tossed in by all those who entered, asking for luck to be on their side.

The group was then walked by a wide doorway leading off the main hall into a room filled with large, complex looking machinery made up of tall cylinders and spinning bronze cogs and wheels. Two women in the robes of junior priestesses stood near the whirring machinery, taking notes.

"That," said the novice proudly as they filed by, "is the Analytical Engine, built many years ago by the blessed Sister Hypatia. We use it as part of our calculations to try and discover the Pattern. As many of you already know, not everyone comes out of the Pool, and we track the amount of who does and doesn't to try and find the specific number pattern in the goddess's seemingly chaotic choice of those who pay the Price."

The novice then led them down a hallway and into a chamber swathed in dark curtains with several rows of seats facing a small stage. Sasha and the others looked around; some were curious, other scornful. Once everyone had sat down, the door was shut and for a moment they all sat in complete darkness. Then a light shone on the stage. Probably, thought Sasha, from an elaborate mirror system to reflect sun or firelight.

A painted wooden figure of a young woman rolled across the stage. With this, more wooden figures, and a changing backdrop, the story of the Pool played out. The Arcadian princess fled her pursuers into a cave and discovered the Pool. The wooden goddess swooped down in the machinery of the theater, gesturing at Her Pool of Miracles. The princess figure disappeared beneath the stage, and then popped back out, clearly a different wooden figure, all painted gold to represent the power the goddess had given her, and went on to save her kingdom. Sasha wondered how many times this play was wound back up and played each day.

When it finished, curtains were pulled back to allow in more light from windows high above, and the young novice came back out and addressed the small audience.

"A reminder, the goddess Mitera does not grant chests of treasure or fine palaces. The Pool will change something about your own body that you wish to be changed, which is no small thing. We devotedly hope that all of you receive the miracle you are seeking, but we also thank you for your service if the goddess choses you as the Price." There was some nervous whispering at the reminder that all of them might not come back.

The novice continued her speech, "Please remember, you may change your mind at any time, even if it's as you are in the Pool. You are free to leave without making a wish and you may come back at any time, if you so choose. The goddess does not force anyone. The Pool is a gift to be freely given, freely received."

"Except for the Price," muttered an ancient woman sitting next to Sasha.

"Most importantly," concluded the novice, "you must understand that the goddess only grants one miracle to any woman who enters Her pool. If, for example, you come here to have the goddess bless your throat with amazing singing, She will, but, if you develop a lung ailment later in life, entering the Pool a second time will do nothing. Be very sure when you enter that whatever you seek is the most important thing you could ask for."

A young girl of about ten raised her hand. "What happens if a man enters the Pool?" she asked curiously.

"His ankles would get wet. Nothing else," said the novice dryly. "It would be the same as if he simply walked into a duck pond. No miracle, no Price. The goddess does not interact with men. They are not forbidden; they are merely irrelevant."

"But is it true some have wished for a miracle of *becoming* men?" asked the same girl.

"Yes," said the novice in a clipped tone, clearly unhappy with the question. "The goddess will make any changes you want to your own body, no more, no less. Now," she went on briskly, "you will each be speaking individually to one of our scribes who will interview you before entering the Pool. We want as much information as possible on everyone who enters the Pool to help calculate Pattern."

With the help of several junior priestesses and the air of much practice, the group was sent down a hallway and each instructed on different doors to go through. Sasha, following the directions given to her, found herself in a small, windowless room filled with bookshelves holding rows of notebooks and stacks of parchment. There was a desk taking up much of the room, a young scribe sitting on one side, quill in hand, ink bottle at the ready next to a notebook open to a blank page.

She gestured at Sasha to sit in the comfy looking chair across from her. There was a small side table next to the empty seat holding a goblet, water jug, and small plate of baked quince slices.

"Please sit," the woman gestured again. "And do not worry, there is no rush. You will still be able to approach the Pool no matter how long this takes. We wish to have every detail possible to help us search for the Pattern. Also, please be assured all members of the Temple take a sacred oath to not reveal any of the information we collect here. It is just for trying to calculate the Pattern." She sounded like she had said this little speech as many times as the little play had been performed, but she still looked at Sasha in a friendly manner.

After Sasha made herself comfortable and poured herself some water, the scribe began asking questions and recording the answers. There were the expected ones of her date of birth, her family line, and which personal house deity she prayed to in the evenings. Then there were other, unexpected, questions such as what she had eaten for breakfast that morning, when was her most recent bowel movements, did she dye her hair, what was her favorite breed of dog, and if she ever partook of any moondust, smoke leaf, or other mind shifting substances.

After an exhaustive interview, covering every aspect of Sasha's life, leaving her feeling as wrung out as a damp sponge, the scribe finally asked, "And what miracle do you wish the Pool to provide?"

"Must I say?" she asked, feeling as if she was being trapped in a corner.

"We record every detail possible about the women who enter as we search for the Pattern. The need that drives women here is one of the top items we record and study."

Sasha sighed, her shoulders slumping. Feeling her checks heat up she said, "My courses come irregularly. The healers consulted all fear I will never get with child. So…" she trailed off.

The woman nodded. "Many women come here for fertility and have gone on to have dozens of fat little babies." She smiled at Sasha brightly. Sasha nervously smiled back, her stomach twisting at the thought of a future filled with fat babies.

The scribe rummaged in her desk and pulled out a slim pamphlet. "Now, please be aware that many women report feelings of intense euphoria after initially leaving the Pool, followed by a sudden slump into depression and regret. These are common feelings, so don't worry, you should be back to your normal equilibrium within a few days. Here," she handed Sasha the pamphlet, labeled *Post-Wish Care*, "this has advice for self-care after your wish is granted. Try to eat lots of green vegetables and dairy over the next few days."

Sasha took the pamphlet with cold hands. This little pamphlet, more than anything else, made her upcoming entrance to the Pool feel real in a way the rest of her trip hadn't. Up until now it had all felt like the kind of travel and sight-seeing she had always wanted to pursue. But now she was faced with the cold, hard fact that this whole trip was just one more order given by her father, expected to be obeyed.

The scribe turned around and pointed at the door behind her. "Through there is a hallway—all the doors on the right lead back to these offices; take the first door on your left. That will be the changing room." The scribe pulled a single sheet out from her notes and handed it to her. It had a series of blank lines and numbered boxes with a long number at the very top. "Give this to one of the attendants," she instructed. "They will give you a robe to change into, keep hold of your belongings, and take note of your measurements before you go in. Then they'll give you this back for you to give to one of the novices who observe the Pool. She will take notes on how the Pool reacts to you. The number on top there matches with the number of your file with all the notes I just took." She gestured at the papers on her desk. "With the Goddess's blessing, someday both of these notes combined may help us find the Pattern. Thank you, and I hope you get what you are looking for."

Sasha smiled nervously and got up to exit. Through the door, she was now in another hallway. She had the sensation she was moving downwards as she walked along. A door opened on her right and the ten-year-old girl came out from one of the other offices. "She asked so many questions!" she said brightly. She skipped along beside Sasha chattering about the unexpected facts and figures she had given the scribe about her life. Sasha, despite only being a few years older, felt near ancient beside the girl. She wondered what the girl was going in the Pool for, but didn't ask, for fear the girl would ask her in turn.

In the changing room, there was a bustle of women in various states of dress and undress while attendants took measurements. There was also a row of private latrines, which Sasha gratefully made a beeline for, all the water she had drunk during her exhaustive interview suddenly needing sudden release. She sat long after she was done, reluctant to continue her task. When she finally made herself come back out, she didn't see the girl, but there were other women around, no one making eye contact as measuring tapes were wrapped around them and various features made note of.

Sasha gave her paper to one the young priestesses, who instructed her to undress. Sasha shivered in the cool air as the priestess measured her height as well as the shape and size of all her limbs. She noted down the figures, then peered into Sash's face before scribbling more notes while muttering phrases such as: "eyes: blue." Finished, she handed Sasha a medium sized white robe along with the now half-filled paper.

Sasha went through the door clearly marked 'Pool' in several languages, the letters picked out in a mosaic of tiny crystals, and entered the underground cavern that held the sacred Pool. There was a novice who gestured Sasha towards the line. Bright, overlarge flower blossoms were painted on the stone floor, indicating where the women and girls waiting their turn were to stand. Sasha joined the line, taking her place on a large purple flower. There were four people ahead of her, with the little girl third in line.

Everyone was staring at the middle of the cavern. There was the miracle pool of which so much was said, that which so many had traveled so far for, looking small and unassuming. It looked shallow and more like a simple tidepool than any sort of divine gift. But the waters were bubbling as if the Pool was a pot boiling on a stove. A priestess stood near the Pool, with several novices attending her.

Everyone kept staring, and then a woman burst forth from the roiling waters. She most likely had looked much different when she went in—she was now as muscled as a gladiator, every muscle standing out and perfectly defined.

She brushed her hands down her sides, looking pleased. She was still undoubtably female, but a warrior from head to toe. She shook back her wet hair as she pronounced gravely, "Now they will see. And I shall crush my enemies." She glanced at the priestess. "I vow, before you all, by the next full moon I shall send a gift of twenty talons of silver to the Temple, and again every year on this day as my thanks."

The priestess did not look surprised by this outburst of generosity. It was probably typical. "On behalf of the goddess Mitera, we thank you humbly for your gifts." She did not look humble at all, and Sasha spotted a scribe nearby, taking notes.

The woman nodded curtly, grabbed the robe offered by the novice, and stalked out.

The next woman, older than Sasha but only by a year or two, walked up to the Pool in quick, little steps. She paused for a long moment and then stepped in and waded forward, the Pool clearly deepening quickly, as she was soon almost neck deep. Her breath became more and more rapid until it was quick pants of fear. "I can't do it! I can't do it!" she suddenly cried. Turning around with a splash she struggled her way out of the water and leapt out to crumple into a damp heap on the floor. "I can't! I can't!" she kept repeating, tears streaming down her face.

The priestess gestured to one of the acolytes who knelt to help the weeping woman up, wrapping her in a robe and leading her out of the room, not towards the main exit, but most likely to some small chamber they had for those who needed to recover after not being able to go through with it.

The next woman, middled aged and looking nervous by the proceeding woman's fear, went in. As she handed her robe to a novice, Sasha saw a mass of scars on her upper torso, the breasts misshapen from, what Sasha would guess, failed surgeries to remove a cancer. The look of fear on her face deepened as the Pool began to freeze around her. She disappeared beneath the water just as it froze completely over.

There was silence as everyone stared, then the ice cracked dramatically in an upward jet of shards and the woman stumbled out, weeping as she clutched at her chest, scars gone, the breasts perfectly shaped. From her grateful babble it was just possible to ascertain that a lump in her left breast and all its consuming tendrils was now gone. She promised that a golden statuette of the Goddess would be commissioned and sent to the Temple as soon as possible, and a month's worth of food for the temple kitchens sent once a year on the anniversary of her healing.

Next was the little girl. She hopped into the Pool, her feet splashing the now unfrozen water. Giggling, she went further in, the water rising around her quickly. She took a deep breath, her checks bulging like a frog, and plunged down into the water.

Sasha waited, wondering what the waters would do this time, and then there was a sharp hiss from several of the women in the room as the waters went mirror still and turned a dark red, so dark as to be near black. Then they cleared, and it was just a shallow pool of water again, with no sign of the girl.

"A Price has been paid!" announced the priestess. Behind her, her assistant was scribbling notes, her stylus flashing across the page. "We thank this daughter for her sacrifice!"

There was a long moment where the only sound in the cavern was the assistant's note taking. Then an assistant gently touched the arm of the next woman in line. It was the old woman Sasha had sat next to in the theater.

She was ancient, hunched over a walking stick, and barely managed to shuffle to the Pool. With a novice on each side helping her shrug out of the robe, she carefully entered and waded forward until she disappeared beneath the water, the pool waters rippling and turning bright gold.

A long pause, and then the woman reappeared, now near unrecognizable, young and beautiful; wrinkles, bags, wattles and stoop all washed away. Her wispy gray hair was now a thick, vibrant red mane, her limbs long and lean, her whole body glowing with vitality. She stepped out and twirled in place, ignoring the robe the attendant novice offered.

"I'm young again!" she sang out in a pleasant soprano tone. She ran her hands through her thick hair and chuckled. "Oh, I am going to do things *right* this time!" She danced away, naked, the novice running after her, helplessly holding out the robe.

Sasha felt sick at the rapid turn off events from the little girl paying the Price, to this old woman's frenzied joy, and now finding herself at the front of the line. She walked up to the Pool, forcing herself to breathe slow and steady. Reluctantly, she got in the Pool and flexed her feet. The bottom was smooth stone, sloping downwards. She waded in, the slant of the bottom sinking her down until she was neck deep. She let herself tip back, feet up, and enjoy the sensation of floating in the water, delaying what she was supposed to do. She knew this was the part where she wished for fertility…but instead she kept wondering how she could avoid going home.

She took a deep breath and let herself sink down. She had the feeling of time standing still as she sank down, deeper than the Pool had any right to be, the light fading above as she was soon surrounded by blue-black darkness, feeling no need to take a breath. *I don't want to go home*, she thought sadly.

Are you offering yourself as a Price? Asked a voice in her mind, sounding amused. *Many have tried that, thinking to guarantee the miracle for some sister or friend or lover next in line. As I've told them, it doesn't work like that.*

No. *I don't want to be the Price, no offense, but NO!* She thought hastily. *But why was that little girl the Price? She was so young!*

It is the Pattern, said the voice. *Young or old, the Pattern does not care.*

You mean You do not care, she accused, some part in the back of her mind amazed at her daring as she dared mouth off to a goddess.

Even the divine have to follow rules, said the voice. *I did as much as I could to help my daughters. Now, daughter, what do you want?*

I just want to travel and see the world.

Full laughter in her mind. *A marvelous life goal, but not one I can help with. But if escape is what you want...*

A divine-given plan flooded Sasha's mind, spooling out as clearly as when she had watched the puppet play. *Yes!* she said.

As you wish.

Sasha left the Pool, her body now invisible and her touch rendering any clothes invisible as well. She grabbed a robe and a pair of sandals in the changing room and hurried by foot back to the inn. Still unseen, she hurriedly changed and grabbed her things, thankful she hadn't spent too much on souvenirs. As she left the town gates, as the goddess had promised, she became visible again.

She was now assumed dead, all ties to home and family were now cut. It hurt, as much as cutting any part of her would hurt, but she was also free. Free to go where she wished. To see it all.

"A journey of a thousand miles begins with a single step," Sasha quoted to herself, and headed towards that horizon.

About the Author

Kara Race-Moore studied history at Simmons College in Boston, Massachusetts as an excuse to read about the soap opera lives of British royals. She worked in educational publishing, casting the molds for future generations' minds, but has since moved into the more civilized world of litigation. She currently lives in Los Angeles, the land where fact and fiction tend to blur. She can be found at:

https://kararacemoore.wordpress.com/

A Wish Well Spent

by

Laura G. Kaschak

A Wish Well Spent

Jim hated being late. He was used to his wife holding him up with whatever ridiculous preparations she had to do every time they left the house. But being used to it didn't mean it pissed him off any less. It always felt like she stalled extra long when she knew it was something he had been looking forward to.

"Would you put a little hustle in your walk for Christ's sake? You've already made me miss the opening races. By the time we get there, there won't be any left to bet on." He gave her arm a hard tug to urge her forward. She never seemed to listen if he didn't use something other than words with her.

Faye stumbled a moment but then finally increased her pace. Maybe he'd be able to salvage some of this day after all. He made a mental note to not bring her with him next time.

Suddenly, Faye stopped short and froze in place.

"Damn it, Faye. What now?"

"That man across the street. Do you see him? Sitting against the wall. I don't think he's ok."

Jim glanced over to where she was pointing and spotted the man she was referring to. Rumpled and dirty, he huddled on the ground against the wall. His chest heaved as if he'd been running for his life moments before.

"That bum? So, he's taking a rest on the ground. That's what bums do. Let's go." He yanked her arm again but this time she held still. He squeezed his hand tighter until his fingertips dug into her flesh, hoping she'd get the message that way.

Faye winced but refused to move.

"Please, Jim. We have to go check on him. I think he needs help."

Why did she always have to be so dramatic? Well, if walking across the street and looking at a bum would get them to the races faster, then he'd just have to humor her. Letting out a loud sigh, he scurried across the street with Faye following close behind.

As they got closer to the man, it became obvious that his chest was indeed heaving with massive effort as he tried to breathe. They could hear his wheezing and sputtering before they even stepped onto the curb. Jim leaned down, being careful not to get too close to him. Even if these kinds of people didn't happen to be carrying a disease, their smell alone could take you down.

"Do you need help?" he asked the man, raising his voice so he could be heard over the man's gasps for air.

"Inhaler...my...inhaler...must...have...fallen...need...inhale r." The man rummaged in his jacket pocket to make the point then gestured down the sidewalk, showing which direction he had come from.

"Oh, of course. We will go look for it right now." Faye assured him and took off in the direction he had indicated.

Jim snagged her before she got too far.

"Are you joking? We don't have time for this. Who knows how far away he dropped it or how long it will take us to find it? This is not our problem. Someone else will come along and deal with it. Let's go."

Faye's eyes flooded with tears. "I can't be that cruel. He could die before someone else comes along. We have to try. Please, just five minutes?"

Damn. Jim knew once she turned on the waterworks, he'd get no peace at all until she got her way.

"Fine, five more minutes. Then I'm leaving."

She nodded vigorously, not even looking at him. They both searched the ground as they tracked back what they hoped were the man's steps.

Thankfully, they spotted the inhaler moments later. It had fallen on the ground and was lying in a bit of stagnant water. Jim's stomach turned at the idea that the man would be putting that into his mouth now, but he reminded himself that someone so low wouldn't care about that kind of thing anyway.

Faye ran the inhaler back to where they had left the man. He was still doing an impersonation of a goldfish thrown to the floor by a petulant child. Jim took his time getting to them. He had no interest in interacting with the man any more than he had to. By the time he reached them, the man's breathing was starting to settle into a more normal pattern.

"Ok, buddy. Glad you're feeling better. Good luck with all that. Faye, it's time to go. Say goodbye." Jim reached to pull Faye away since she didn't have enough good sense to leave on her own.

"Wait!" the man called out. "Thank you. Thank you so much. Please, allow me to repay the kindness."

Jim almost laughed at the idea that this man thought he could do anything for them. The best thing he could do would be to shut up and let them get on with their lives.

The man rummaged around his pockets and pulled out two coins. Great, what a reward. Jim fought the urge to roll his eyes and exclaim he could go into early retirement now. The man held out the coins and dropped them into Faye's hand.

"A wish for each of you. Say your wish while you hold a coin then toss it over your right shoulder. Your wish will come true. Be careful and choose wisely. A wish well spent will bring you happiness for a lifetime. Only one wish per coin. Once the words are spoken, the coin will no longer hold power." He grinned at them with a sparkle in his eye.

Now Jim really wanted to get away from this loony bird before he did anything crazier.

"Great. Thanks. Come on, we have somewhere to be." He gave Faye's arm a swift, hard jerk and dragged her down the street.

She looked at the coins in her had as they walked. She held one out to him and said, "Look. I've never seen coins like these. There are no real markings. I can't even tell what kind of metal they are, can you? They look so old."

Jim grabbed the coin from her. "Well, that's because they're magical of course. Christ Faye, how did you even get this far in life being so naive? A bum hands you a couple chunks of metal garbage he picked up and you are in awe. Grow up. You think these things are really what he said they are?"

He held the coin up and in a dramatic voice called out, "Oh great, magic coin of the realm of crazy bums, hear my words and grant me my wish! I wish I could win a fortune at the racetrack today if we can even get there in time since my idiot wife has wasted our whole day on nonsense!" He chucked the coin over his shoulder. "There, I'm so happy we wasted our time getting such a magical gift. Now let's hurry up so I can get that fortune I wished for."

They walked the rest of the way in silence and arrived just in time to place a bet on the final race. He'd brought enough cash with him to spend the day betting on most of the races, but it was all blown now. He angrily threw his entire wad down on the single remaining race. It wasn't until he'd left the betting window that he realized he'd made a mistake and put it all down on a horse to win that had terrible twenty-to-one odds.

"That coin really had better do its job since, thanks to you, I only have one chance to win anything."

Faye kept her head down and pouted in silence which was perfectly fine with Jim. He wasn't sure how long it was going to take for his anger to extinguish, but he doubted it would be any time that day.

Lost in thoughts, he almost didn't notice the horses turning the corner and approaching the finish line. He looked up just in time to see his long shot of a bet come through as a winner. That was going to pay off more than he'd ever gotten before. He'd be going home with a small fortune.

"Faye! Faye! Holy shit! Did you see that? Do you know what this means? We won!! We won a damned fortune!" He started laughing with glee. "Guess I'll have to thank that crazy bum on the way home. Damned if that magic coin of his didn't do its job! If only I'd known, I could have wished for something bigger."

He grabbed Faye's shoulders and pulled her straight out of her seat to standing.

"You still have that other coin, don't you? Tell me you have it. This might have been a fluke for all we know but just in case, I'm not wasting that last wish."

Faye's eyes had become large saucers and she was silently stunned. But she nodded her head and patted her pocket to show him that she still held the last coin.

They rushed to the betting window as the crowds of people started draining out of the track. Faye had been very quiet as they waited in line but then spoke up to let Jim know she needed to stop at the restroom before they left. He was too giddy to even notice that she had stepped away.

He rarely got this kind of chance to gloat and rub something in other people's faces, so he was making the most of it. The looks of shock and jealousy on the people in line with him as he bragged about his chance winnings made his day almost as much as getting the actual money.

By the time he reached the front of the line, Faye had returned by his side. He gathered his winnings and pulled her towards home. "Come on, Faye. We gotta get home and decide what to do with that other wish. I still can't believe this!"

Giggling like a little kid bubbling over with the excitement at getting a new toy, he walked towards home, holding Faye's hand. For a moment, he realized how silly he was behaving. But he couldn't help himself. He'd never won this much money, and he might even have another actual wish just waiting for his command. He'd have to put a lot of careful thought into what he would ask for.

As they turned the next corner, a man roughly pushed past them, slamming his shoulder into Jim as he walked on. Jim stopped and turned around. "Hey, asshole. Watch where you're going."

Before Jim could turn back around to continue home, the man produced a gun from his pocket and aimed it directly at him. "Oh, I know exactly where I'm going. I'm going straight towards the asshole with the big winnings from today. Hand them over." He reached his empty hand towards Jim.

"Ok, Ok. No need to do anything crazy. Here, it's right here. But it's not as much as you think. I was just exaggerating for effect."

Jim silently cursed himself for showing off his winnings at the betting window. He glanced to see where Faye was and saw she had plastered herself against the wall. She looked like a deer in headlights, pretty and useless.

He pulled the wad of cash out of his pocket and held it out towards the gunman. Just as the gunman reached for it, Jim let it fall to the ground, using the moment of surprise as a chance to grab the wrist of the hand holding the weapon. He'd be damned if he was going to let some loser like this take his money.

The two men struggled as cash fluttered up around them. Suddenly a loud bang rang through the air followed by a scream from Faye. Jim felt a sledgehammer crack into his chest. The air left him, and he collapsed on the ground. The gunman stumbled backwards, looking down in shock and horror. He suddenly came to his senses enough to do a quick scoop of some bills before taking off into the night.

Faye ran over to Jim and kneeled by his head. She eased her arm under to cradle him. He lifted his head to look down at himself. His money was scattered all around him, most of it splattered with his blood. He couldn't see the wound in his chest, but the pain told him where it was. The feeling of coldness creeping through his body told him it was bad and he would be bleeding out in moments.

"Faye. Faye, the coin. You have the last wish. Take it out. Make a wish to save my life. I don't know if it will really work but it's the only chance. I don't think I'll make it until help gets here." He couldn't believe how hard it was just to get the words out. He hoped like hell that coin did what the other one had done.

Faye looked down at him and slid her hand along his cheek.

"Oh, it would work. There is absolutely no doubt that those coins really held the power to grant wishes." She told him.

His mind was fading with the blood loss and the pain was blinding most of his thoughts. He struggled to make sense of her words.

"How can you be so sure? Then why are you wasting time? Faye, I'm not going to make it. Don't wait any longer. Take the coin out and make the wish. Now."

"I'm sorry dear, but I can't. I already used it to make a wish. It's gone. And you see, the reason I know it worked is because this is exactly what I wished for. I wished to be rid of you for good. My wish came true."

She smiled down at him in a way he had never seen her do before. He was sure he'd never seen her look so happy in all their years together. Part of him hoped he was hallucinating what she had just said, but deep down he knew the truth.

His vision grew darker until he couldn't see anything but that smile. As he slipped away into death, he heard her whisper, "Definitely a wish well spent."

About the Author

Laura G. Kaschak writes paranormal thrillers for both adults and young teens, including the "Shadow Squad" book series. Her chilling short stories have been featured in many dark fiction anthologies. She grew up in the pine barrens with the constant companionship of the Jersey Devil and now lives in Virginia wine country, successfully fooling everyone into believing she's a grownup. Find out more about Laura's upcoming projects by following her on Instagram @Laura.G.Kaschak.Author.

Waxing, Waning
by
Remy Allen

Waxing, Waning

Four days before I became the moon, I was struggling to keep a grip on my friend's telescope and hold the door at the top of his apartment building's stairs open.

"We're gettin' too old for this crap," I muttered, desperately trying to keep my balance. He was half a flight down, but he'd done this a million times by now, and half of those times were alone, so his response betrayed not even a mote of exhaustion.

"Maybe YOU are, man, but stargazing is as old a hobby as it gets, and it'll continue to be long after our time."

We crashed through the door as it cried in protest on dry, rusted hinges. With a last push, we settled our load into its usual spot on the roof of T.J.'s apartment building. As he made his preparations, I wondered to myself where his energy came from. Did the bachelor's life grant him all of that drive? Just knowing that my wife and child were waiting for me at home was enough to make me feel lethargic. I loved them, of course, but sometimes even looking at my son was enough to drain me.

As he continued to make adjustments, I returned down the gray stairs, watching my step in the dim illumination of a clear dusk sky. We were an economical pair, so the coolers I fetched on those two trips doubled as our chairs.

I slammed the second chest of ice onto the ground, so it flanked the telescope, doing my best to stifle the sounds of being winded. I wasn't normally the competitive type, but the instinctual urge to not admit he had more stamina had welled up in me since we'd come up the stairs. With a grunt of effort, I settled into my spot on top of the cooler.

There we were; T.J. called it "stargazing," but it was more like "drinking on the roof." Well, he *drank*. Even if I didn't have to drive home, I stayed away from the booze. The last thing I wanted, or needed, was something to get me even more tired than was normal to me at this point. While we waited for the sun to leave the sky, we reminisced on the days of our mutual school life; T.J. was a misunderstood geek where I was simply a nerd. They'd been challenging, but we'd survived in part thanks to having a shoulder to lean on. Like brothers in arms, we'd come to find comfort in each other's company, and our ritual was as weekly as the weather would allow.

At last, the brilliant pinks, oranges, and yellows of the evening sky had given way to the speckled black of night. T.J was poised on the edge of his makeshift seat, one eye in the viewfinder to gaze at the moon. I'd sworn on more than one occasion that he wouldn't be happy until he found a print from Armstrong's boot up there. I'd always asked him what got him interested in the hobby, but it took him being atypically drunk to admit that he'd end up on top of his two-story home to escape the sound of his parent's numerous fights, looking up and dreaming of being anywhere else but an Earth where they'd grown to hate each other. I'd never been to his house, since he was too embarrassed of his parents, but when he'd spend the night at mine, he'd end up out there when he needed a breath of fresh air.

Personally, I'd gotten tired of looking at the same thing a few years ago, but I wasn't tired of T.J. He didn't have much trouble with the silences that permeated our weekly hangouts, but this evening he must have been feeling chatty. As he swiveled the black tube around the tripod to track something, he offered up a new piece of information about his beloved heavens.

"A full moon tonight. I read something interesting about it the other day."

"Yeah? Let's hear it."

"In the far North of Alaska, where it's night from November to January, a tribe of Iñupiat, the "people of the sea" in their language, have a story. On a clear night, without so much as a breeze, the moon might hear you if you speak a wish to it. They believe the spirits of their ancestors appear in the *aurora borealis,* so maybe the moon was sort of a…guardian for the spirits? Like a beacon to heaven. Anyway, if it hears your wish, and you see the moon during the day when the sun rises again, it means your wish came true."

"If I were them, I'd wish for it to get warmer."

T.J. and I shared a laugh. He pondered something for a moment, and asked, "Well, what would you wish for now?"

I paused to consider. I'd spent time thinking about it, sure, but this wasn't quite the same as, say, what you'd do if you won the lottery. It could be anything. No limits. "You know, I feel like the perfect man would say he wishes for his family to be happy and healthy, but that doesn't feel...extravagant enough. If it's a wish, it had better be a big one, right?"

He nodded as if to confirm my conjecture. I paused again, reflecting deeper still. Something I'd always wanted...

In my mind's eye, I pictured the recognition I'd never gotten in high school. Was it petty? Of course. I was an adult now, with a mortgage and a child to raise. I had a thousand things I wanted more than recognition. But a wish...

"I guess deep down, I've always wanted to be in the spotlight, for everyone to notice me and see me. I don't really have a marketable talent or any star power, so it'd be nice for magic to pick up the tab. I just feel like... I don't know, this is dumb, I'm fine with what I have, but it'd feel good to be appreciated for who I am."

T.J. chuckled softly, several cans of IPA helping to loosen his lips. "I think you're getting greedy, man. You should be happy with what you've got. Helen and Andrew appreciate you for who you are. I do, too, for that matter. That's way better than some stranger obsessing over you."

I considered engaging in a debate over that, but instead of a witty rebuttal, a yawn was what came out of my mouth. I knew it was about time to get going, and I took a minute to finish my soda while my compatriot packed up his belongings and disappeared back down the stairs. When he returned, we stood for a moment longer as the streetlights began to pierce the gentle embrace of the evening, one needle of light at a time.

"You gonna head home?" he asked, as if I would surprise him with a sudden self-invitation to sleep over tonight.

"I guess I should." I sighed, taking one last gaze at my surroundings before setting my sights on the door to the roof. T.J. said good night and waved goodbye from the roof after I'd descended the creaky stairs and exited out the front door of his apartment building.

The night was oddly still. Leaves hung unwavering on static branches, and the hum of cars was distant. Some people may relish silences like that, but I found myself hurrying to get to my car and make my way back to my safe, suburban home. Despite having the radio for company, I found my thoughts drifting. Hanging clearly in the corner of my windshield was our radiant moon; pearly white, bright enough to see her craters. I thought back to what I had said to T.J not long ago. The allure of fame, to indulge in the pleasure of arms-length attention. Money, power, carnal desires, all of that was secondary to me. What was most important, I thought, was the focus on me. Everyone I'd ever known who never even *tried* to understand me, enraptured by my celebrity.

My eyes drifted back to the moon. I thought about how nice it must be to be our natural satellite. The brightest light around shining its eternal spotlight on you, inviting everyone around the world regardless of age, sex, class, or creed to steal a glance. I found myself a little jealous, and I whispered as such to her.

"I wish everyone could see me like they see you, just for a day."

I'd have the energy for that, absolutely. No doubt in my mind. *That'd jazz me right up*, I thought to myself.

My son was already in bed by the time I crept through the door, his chest steadily rising and falling when I peeked in on him, knowing he appreciated getting to see me if he were still up. I crept back through the entryway and into the living room, finding Helen watching the last few minutes of a documentary on the ocean. She kindly asked if I had a nice time, and I told her I did, taking the spot next to her on the couch. I struggled to keep my eyes open as David Attenborough informed us how much of the ocean there was left to explore. While the credits rolled, I followed her down the hall to our room. I thought about telling her about what had happened that night, but I yawned again before a word could escape. I decided there'd be tomorrow, instead, and we said our goodnights and turned in.

No matter how tightly I shut my eyes, it was as though the moon was shining right through them. I tossed and turned and disturbed Helen more than once, yet I couldn't get a wink of sleep. All throughout the night my mind and body fought, both exhausted but neither succumbing to the Sandman. I almost couldn't tell when the sun pushed through the curtains in a thin line across my face. Despite never drifting off, I still was still forced to claw my way out of a stupor, struggling to remove myself from the teasing comfort of the pillow.

The moment I had left the bed, it felt like I was going through my routine on manual instead of automatic. Everything was a struggle; a fight to remind myself that before I knew it, I would be back home, free to enjoy a wonderful nap in my sweet, sweet bed. My fingers refused to tie the same Windsor knot I'd done up a thousand times before, the last task before I left for work that I could execute with effortless boredom on any other morning. Helen finally had to step in to finish it off, clucking her tongue at me.

"Long night, Keppler?" she joked with me. *Spaced out indeed,* I thought to myself. I couldn't tell you anything else about what happened that day if I'd needed an alibi for a murder. One moment I was in my car, and the next I was at work, and the next I was driving home. The nine hours had been a long and continuous streak of printer ink blurred with spilled coffee. Sitting on our couch, I rubbed my itching eyes and drank my third cup, begging it to work its magic.

I turned in early that night. My body had other plans. Worse still, the numbers on the clock thought they were so damn funny. 3:08 A.M., they chuckled at me. The moon was laughing, too. I'd dared to express my jealousy, and now she was cursing me to behold her luminescent form for the whole showing. She didn't care that I was suffering, that all I wanted was an hour, maybe two, just to refresh myself. A sprinkle of sand from that fickle man.

I thought I had been tired before, but I had been foolish— naive, even. This wasn't simply being tired. This was exhaustion. I could hardly remember what it was like to feel rested. With the sun came another break from catatonia, another grainy blur of fast-forwarded film. I hit the hay at eight-fifteen that night, before my son even went down, muttering something incoherent about needing some rest.

My swollen eyes tracked the motion of the turning ceiling fan. Generations were born and died, civilizations sprang up and crumbled, evolutions of species took place, then the clock buzzed, blinking seven o'clock at me. Wednesday morning, and I hadn't slept since Sunday night.

The lamp light had a tracer. My toothbrush wouldn't go into my mouth, struggling to hit its mark through the triple vision in the mirror. I knew I couldn't call off from work; I was too important. I splashed water on my face, surprised that the wells under my eyes didn't retain it. I had a thousand-mile stare and patchy stubble on my chin.

Focus.

Helen was unhappy with my behavior, and little Andrew wasn't much better off. I was distant, snappy, and unresponsive. Any noise set me off, any light made me recoil in primal disgust. As I climbed into my car, a brief moment of clarity reminded me she'd been unhappy long before that. I would trade her for a catnap right this second if I could; maybe we both would be better off.

I didn't mean that. But I did consider it.

The sound of the car door slamming. The key in the ignition. The click of the seatbelt. It was coming in a stream, every sensation recalled from memory, since I wasn't present enough for conscious input. I'd driven to work ten thousand times. Time to see if I really could do it with my eyes closed. I pulled out of our driveway and turned down our quiet suburban road, thinking of the last time I'd been coherent. Wishing on the moon. The spotlight.

Turning onto the highway, the sun was in my eyes. At least I couldn't doze off. When the highway curved and I could see properly, I saw that something else encroaching on the sun's solo act. The moon was hanging back, refusing to leave the stage, keeping her distance from the shining star. The people wanted an encore, and she was the one to give it to them. What was it T.J. had said? If you saw it during the day, your wish had come true?

No cameras, please, I haven't been through makeup yet. I'm in no condition to take your place, Luna.

I laughed.

From above my head, I saw myself laughing.

I saw the roof of my car.

The highway drifted farther away until it was the size of a vein in the busy transit system of my town. The countryside, the suburbs, the downtown skyline, I could see all of them. Giggling like I was a kid again, I realized I could see my house from here. For some reason, it didn't register with me to be concerned. Why would I be? I wasn't going to fall, I felt lighter than air! As a matter of fact, I *had* to be, for soon I was drifting above the clouds, punching through like a pine needle in a field of cotton. Below my feet, my home planet was a stained blue marble I could've held in my hand.

I squinted. The stars were draped around me like a wafer-thin shawl, the Earth miles below my feet. There was no sound, no movement, nothing in the way of stimulus but the retina-burning corona of the sun making a pyre of my vision. I found myself wondering why I didn't need to breathe in space. When I didn't become lightheaded, I decided I didn't need to breathe at all, which was fortunate given where I was. I couldn't help but notice that, for how good of a view I had of our tiny slice of space, the moon was being awfully shy. Looking around for her, I couldn't help but notice that the way the Earth looked from where I was reminded me of a photograph I had seen a long time ago in a science textbook. The one that astronaut had taken in '68: *Earthrise.*

I felt certain then that I was the moon. It was as certain to me as when you wake up in the middle of the night in pitch black, yet you know without a doubt you're in your bed.

The sun blazed yellow, red, and white, closer to me than I'd ever seen it. The biggest spotlight I knew, front and center on my face. The gaze of people all over the world, rich or poor, tall or small, black or white, now caught by me. Just like I'd wanted.

The irony was palpable. I had no eyes to blink, no lungs to breathe. Nothing more than a drifting lump of space dust, with the unloving gaze of millions upon me, completely bereft of emotion. I sat in the vacuum, all alone with my thoughts. Tracking the slow drifting of the Earth on its axis, I found myself missing Helen and little Andy most of all. I didn't care if they exhausted me anymore. Being so cold, so far away, disconnected from the people I knew cared for me, like I wasn't even breathing, wasn't worth this. There was attention, but it meant nothing. I felt myself choke up, and yet I couldn't cry.

Everyone knows there's no water on the moon.

If there was an upside, it was that I no longer felt tired. I felt like I'd slept for 20 years. For all I knew, it *had* been 20 years down there. Big Ben was the biggest clock I could think of, and I still couldn't read his face from where I was. The longer I hung up there, watching my home planet spin around without me, the more time I had to think. To go insane would have been a blessing, I couldn't help but think. Instead, I was woefully coherent, forced to recall all of the things that I had taken for granted for so long.

Helen. I'd let her down. I'd been a subtle kind of selfish, not even aware of how often my desires interfered with our relationship. I'd always thought you were supposed to have dreams; passions to pursue, goals to keep you moving. I didn't think to stop to see where we were, what we'd accomplished. That we could accomplish them together. And Andrew, I'd let him down too. I'd let myself worm my way out of spending time with him with the indispensable line of "Not today, I'm tired." I knew that there'd be more time, after all. There wasn't any reason to think otherwise. Now I had no idea if I'd have even another second with him. Thinking of those words now stirred up pangs of guilt and shame in my core. I strained my vision, trying to make out our house somewhere in that strange jigsaw-bordered blotch of green that floated by. I missed that house, and the family I had somewhere down there, so much. I needed some kind of indication they were there, that they were thinking of me, that I had a chance to make this right. The fears, the desperate wants, were weighing me down. I felt them pulling me, somewhere in the beyond, back into a body I'd once occupied.

My eyes bolted wide. I sucked in a deep, flailing breath. I had forgotten I needed to breathe on Earth. The next sensation was the familiar scratch of a cheap hospital blanket on my back, the itch of a hospital gown on my chest, and the sterile, unwelcoming stink of sanitizing solution in my nostrils.

No one was in the room with me. Embarrassed at my desperate breath, l breathed a sigh of relief for the isolation. The curtains on the window to my right were drawn, leaving the droning fluorescent bulbs above my head for light. I could tell from the strong yellow glow on the floor's edge that the sun was shining bright outside.

Now came the sandpapery tickle in my dry throat. I kept examining the room, trying to parse out more details. There was an IV next to me, a thin line snaking down from a clear bag into a needle snug and symbiotic in my wrist. The control pad attached to my bed was near my hand, so I pushed the -CALL- button twice. A nurse rushed in, her response more hasty than I thought I'd warrant. She appeared shocked, but in an excitable way, like she'd won a phone-in contest on the radio.

"I can't believe it!" she cried in my general direction, yet not at me. I tried to speak but found a cough was all that came out.

"Sir, I know you're probably confused, but try to stay calm," she continued. "You're in a safe place and being taken care of, we—"

"Wa… wat…" I interrupted, the rasp in my throat catching me off guard. A hacking cough came out after I pushed my vocal cords too hard. She came in close, patting my back sympathetically. Once it had subsided, I looked back up at her with pathetic, confused eyes.

"Whaaaa…t happened?" she suggested.

I tried to mime drinking water. My limbs moved like a poorly oiled robot, struggling to do so much as their basic function. She recognized my request, returning in a flash with a small disposable cup and straw. I took it from her, sucking down everything in the cup just as quickly and marveling at how much will I had to muster to simply force the liquid through. She pulled the cup away, smiling at me. Pity? I couldn't tell. Whatever it was, I'd have to take it.

"Are you ready to hear what happened now?"

I nodded slowly, feeling my creaking joints cry out in protest. Gently came the whisper from my throat. "*Yes…*"

"Sir, you were in a serious car accident. You're lucky to be alive, honestly. The doctor says that your body was totally relaxed on impact, not unlike what we see in drunk driving incidents; your toxicology report came back clean, though. I can't believe you *could* be passed out with how much caffeine was in your system. The doctors are wondering if it could have been some kind of narcoleptic event, although those usually happen earlier in life."

I blinked. Had I driven through the hospital wall? I strained to recall something as traumatic as a car accident, drawing a blank no matter how far I pushed back against the incorporeal membrane that seemed to be stretched across my memories. I was still trying to get used to being on the Earth that I had just recently been staring at.

"Wife…?" I managed.

She didn't frown, but her face betrayed some unpleasantness.

"You were the only one in the car at the time, sir. It has been a couple months since your wife has been here."

"Month….s…?"

She nodded.

"You've been in a coma for five months. I should tell you that's longer than usual. It's a miracle that you've retained this level of brain function. It's like you were just sleeping, really. Though you'd probably have been worse off without a feeding tube."

I felt sweat beading across my body. My heart clenched, and I struggled to keep breathing. *Five months,* I thought. Five months I'd never get back. Maybe the adrenaline of panic was all I needed to speak more than one word, but it worked.

"Anyone…else in the… accident?"

Now she frowned definitively, undeniably. "I'm not sure I should be the one to tell you."

I looked at her insistently. She chewed her lip, the only sign of nervousness I could see.

"You hit a van with a family in it. The mother and father survived, but their daughter couldn't be saved." So matter-of-fact. Clinical, that was a good word for it. If sentences could smell, it would be of ethanol astringent. A desperate cry lodged itself in the middle of my throat, as if that could be what saved that little girl from the fate I'd unintentionally cast her to. I choked it back as tears welled up, fat and salty in the corners of my eyes.

"Mr. Tyler, I can't imagine how you must feel, but you should know that the accident wasn't your fault. Even the girl's family don't blame you. You weren't intoxicated, it was a freak accident.

They did think about a lawsuit for a bit, not out of anger, but just to… Well, your friend talked them out of it."

I wasn't going to correct her, but I knew better than to believe it was an accident. On the contrary, it had all gone just as I'd wished. I tried to be thankful for the small favor of not having a court case to deal with, but with the weight of what I'd done, I didn't have it in me. I thought to call Helen, before I remembered what the nurse had said. Months, it had been. I wondered who else there could be after what had happened. But when she said friend, I remembered someone that might. The nurse, seeing my intentions, left as I reached weakly for my phone, before I realized it was dead. Five months was a long time for a battery to sit unused. I frantically pressed the -CALL- button again, the nurse retracing her steps.

"Sir?"

"I need a phone, ma'am. Mine's dead."

"Mister Tyler, I can sympathize with wanting to contact your loved ones, but the nearest phones are on the ground floor. You should wait until you've fully regained consciousness, maybe have something to eat before you even consider leaving your bed. The doctor will definitely want to examine you, as well."

"Please… It can't wait. I need one call. If I can borrow yours… I promise I'll stay put."

The nurse considered my request for a moment, then produced her phone with a relenting sigh. I punched T.J.'s number into the keypad and raised the phone to my ear, trying to hold it steady and prepare myself to speak without it being a blubbery mess.

T.J. picked up on the second ring. "Hello?" came his voice, an unfamiliar detachment in his voice from not knowing who was calling.

"Teej. I'm awake."

"Wayne, holy shit man, I can't believe it. You-you… You're…"

He paused.

"I thought you were gone for good, man."

"Way I feel… I guess… I should've stayed there." I wheezed. The dam was being held back with one shaky finger, and it couldn't keep the pressure on forever. I knew I was going to break down, it was just a matter of when.

"Dude. I can't imagine. Really, I can't. I have to… Wow. I'll be there in a few, man. Holy shit…" He seemed to still be in disbelief even as he hung up with me.

When the nurse had gone for the second time, I could only think of being the moon. Hanging up there for everyone to see and then ignore. My light was not even my own, just stolen from something greater than myself.

I picked up the remote, flipping through the channels before settling on the news. Normally I wasn't a fan, but I wanted to know what I'd missed in the five months I'd been out of the loop. They wrapped up a story about the local zoo's panda having another unsuccessful bid at breeding, bringing it back to the news desk. The anchor was all business, looking into the camera with ruthless, killer professionalism.

"We now turn our attention to the completion of the monument to a catastrophe that shook the lives of two families five months ago."

The lump in my throat returned.

"Thirty-two-year-old Wayne Tyler suffered from what responders described as a narcoleptic fit while traversing State Highway 72, colliding with a van driven by the Anderson family. The father and mother, Jason and Maria, were relatively unharmed, but their daughter, Camilla, unfortunately succumbed to her injuries a week after the accident. Medical examiners insist that neither alcohol nor drugs played a role in this tragedy, and the Andersons have declined to press charges, calling it a 'freak accident.' They've partnered with ENDDD, an organization dedicated to education on…"

The words faded out to a dull hum. The only thing I could understand was the picture of my face in the little square in the corner. My recognition.

I'd have vomited if my stomach didn't really want that water I'd given it. I hung suspended in self-hatred thick enough to feel on my skin. I should have known better than to wish for something so self-serving. I should have listened to T.J. when he tried to tell me. I had flown too close to the sun, and now all that was left was watching the ground rush to meet me.

The door opening brought me back to reality. There was T.J., looking frantic. He rushed over to my side, studied my face for a moment.

"Dude," he said.

I waited.

"I can't believe it."

I had hoped one of us could.

"Hey..." I managed.

He grabbed me and pulled me into a rough hug. It was genuine, full of feeling and repressed fear and worry. I couldn't lift my arms to return it, but I hoped he could feel that I wanted to. He released me, moved away, and breathed deep.

"Dude, I gotta... There's something you should know. I wasn't sure how I could... Helen, there was so much for her to deal with, and your insurance wouldn't cover everything for how long you were here. I tried my best to help out and be there for her, and it just... I didn't mean for it to..."

It was so cliché. I wanted to be sad, but I felt as though I didn't deserve it. I had robbed someone of their life, it was only fair someone deserving should have the good parts of mine. I may have been shaking off five months of beauty sleep, but I could piece together what he was getting at. There was only one thing I could really think to say, something that chewed at the hazy corners of my consciousness.

"Do you remember... that thing? Making a wish... on the moon?" I drawled at him.

"Sure, man, sure. Course I do. Wayne, did they check you out? You can understand what I'm saying? You're not mad about, you know...?"

"Teej, if she made that choice, I can't stop her. I've done enough."

He sighed then, so long and so deep I thought he might deflate like a punctured balloon. His eyes shone with tears in the corners, and I could tell he was overwhelmed. I wasn't quite done, though. I had more to say.

"The wish... I wished everyone could... could see me. And now they can."

I pointed at the T.V. When he saw what I meant, the tears began to fall, the quaver in his voice heralding his own dam breaking down.

"It's crazy, man. I found myself wishing too. I wished I could have a life like yours. A wife, a kid, the white picket fence. I wished you could see how good you had it. I didn't mean for this to happen, but I can't help how I feel, man. I don't know what to say."

I didn't say anything. There wasn't anything to say, anymore. I couldn't even be sure what would hurt worse; to make him stay or watch him go. I didn't have to make that decision, though, because my friend couldn't take the silence like he used to. I watched him leave the way he came. I thought I heard him say, "Call me before you get discharged," before the door closed, but that could have been wishful thinking.

My fifteen minutes of fame were up. My wings were broken, my body exhausted from my flight. There was just one thing I needed to see. I willed my husk out of the hospital bed, against what I could imagine would be the advice of my doctors. I didn't care; I had to know. My legs were stippled with the deep sensation of pins and needles, making me work to keep my balance. I shambled my way to the window, the concentrated sunlight heating my toes as I stood before the curtain.

I pulled the curtains back from the window, the sunlight's rays lapping at my vision like oxygen-starved flames. My eyes slowly, painfully adjusted to the light they'd not seen in five months. I saw T.J., on his way back to his car.

My gaze drifted up as he started to drive away. Blue sky. Yellow sun. White clouds.

And the moon; pearly white, bright enough to see her craters, hanging off to the side.

About the Author

Remy Allen has been a reader for much longer than they have a writer, having only recently reached a quality of prose that they feel is worthy of scrutiny. Due in part to their lack of education beyond a high-school diploma, they've worked a variety of menial jobs in the past, including being a prep cook, rolling barrels of bourbon whiskey in their native Kentucky, apartment maintenance (which they were especially terrible at), and making industrial-sized rolls of foam.

At the time of this biography's writing, they're an unassuming grocery store worker, the toil of which allows their mind to wander into the places where many of their stories end up taking place. They write such indulgent fictions when they're not spending quality time with their devoted partner, rambunctious son, and supremely fluffy cat Piers, whom they had no hand in naming.

You can find them online at:

Twitter.com/RemyWritesOkay

where they're most often cited screaming about their novel they promise will be done very soon. And a few pictures of that cat they mentioned, which is really the important part.

Katie and Kyle Forever
by
Alyssa Beatty

Katie and Kyle Forever

I pull my car up to the guard station and wave at Ron, the Tuesday guard at Leisure World. In high school we called it Seizure World. I kind of like Ron. He flirts with me, which is fun sometimes, but always leads to a headache when I get home.

Ron waves me through without checking my ID, which he is definitely not supposed to do, but I've been coming here every Tuesday for the last two years. And I was maybe a little cool to him last week after the fit Kyle threw when he overheard Ron casually mention getting a drink, so things are a bit awkward. I don't like giving into Kyle's tantrums, but he's figured out how to hurl plates against the wall when he's angry, and frankly I'm just not up to buying a new dining set right now.

I would never admit this to my high school self, but I enjoy coming to Seizure World. The residents are almost entirely women, and most have no filter and no patience for social niceties. I always leave with a smile and a little spring in my step.

I set up my case in the common room as usual. The staff insists on calling it the "sun-room," but there are no windows, and it smells like a gym shoe, so to all the residents and me, it's the common room. "Because it makes us feel like commoners," as Doris, aka Queenie, always says.

Queenie is the first to arrive for my ministrations. She is my favorite. Always shy about showing me her hair, so thin and straggly, but she loves it when I use my big soft brush to tease out the little tangles. And she'll let me try whatever I want with makeup—big extravagant cat-eye liner, purple lipstick, gold and orange eyeshadow; she's down for anything, is Queenie.

"Hey kid, how's tricks?" she asks as she painfully lowers herself down into the plastic chair across from me.

"Tricky," I say, opening my case and laying out my brushes and palettes.

Queenie laughs, her big deep chortle that I have grown to love.

"Funny girl," she says.

"You make that joke, like, literally every week," Kyle says.

I shoot a sharp glance at him. He has started just popping in like this lately. Before he would sort of fade in, like an image when you turn one of those old TV sets on, but then he figured out how to just appear. There's not a lot to do in the afterlife I guess, except learn new skills.

He leans against the wall near the door, arms crossed, long legs splayed out in front of him. The Kyle-lean, I used to call it. When we were in high school it was the sexiest thing I'd ever seen. Five years later it just annoys me. Things were much better between us when he couldn't figure out how to stay corporeal outside the apartment. Bad enough the plate throwing and levitating my towel out of reach when I'm coming out of the shower, but I used to at least get a little peace at work. Now he's always around, not just watching and listening but commenting too, and it is wearing thin. Fast.

"What are we thinking today?" I ask Queenie, pointedly ignoring Kyle. "Mohawk? Full sleeve tattoo?"

"Just make me beautiful again, darling," she says, leaning back in her chair.

"You're always beautiful, Queenie," I say, picking up my soft brush and going to stand behind her.

Kyle snorts from his spot by the door.

"Go away," I mouth at him.

"Make me," he says.

Girls, let me tell you something. A bit of wisdom from 22-year-old me that I wish 17-year-old me had been told: Your high school boyfriend? The *one*? He's probably a bit of a loser. Dump him, go to college, and move on. Don't make promises to be together until death and beyond because he might die doing something stupid, and then you've got yourself a ghost. A ghost who stays seventeen forever and gets cranky when you get any sort of attention from the opposite sex, and who gets annoyed at hearing your dumb work jokes over and over.

I gently brush out Queenie's hair, careful of her fragile skin, smiling down at her blissfully closed eyes.

"Old people are gross," Kyle says over my shoulder.

Queenie's eyes snap open.

"That's enough of that, young man. Just because you're dead doesn't mean you can have bad manners," she says.

Kyle and I lock eyes. Queenie struggles to right herself, and, before I can reach out, Kyle has his hands on her shoulders, gently helping her sit up. Maybe the years of watching me deal with the old ladies has sunk in. He was a pretty good guy when he was alive. I forget that sometimes.

Kyle shifts around until he is directly in front of Queenie. He waves his hand in front of her face.

"Can you, like, see me?" he asks.

Queenie slaps his hand away.

"Of course, I can. I've been hearing you for weeks, and let me tell you, listening to the two of you snark at each other like an old married couple got old pretty fast. You kind of made up for it with your handsome face, though." She gives him a big toothless smile. Queenie only puts in her teeth for the grandkids.

Kyle takes a step back. Alive, he always did this thing when he was surprised where his mouth would literally hang open. He still does, and even though now instead of Dorito and Mountain Dew breath what you get is a whiff of howling black void, it's still sort of endearing.

Queenie leans back a bit so she can meet my eyes.

"I didn't want to say anything," she says. "But Katie girl, you've got to ditch the ghost."

"Hey!" Kyle protests.

"No offense to you, honey." She waves a placating hand at him. "I'd be happy to have you around just to look at your pretty face for all eternity, but Katie is young. She needs a little more."

"We promised to love each other until we died!" Kyle says.

"And you did. But one of you is still alive."

"Tell her, Katie! Tell her how you came to my grave every day, and, like, wished for me to come back!"

"It's true. I did," I admit.

"She was grieving, honey. Because she loved you. But you can't keep hanging around her. She's a grown woman now, she doesn't need you anymore."

Kyle looks at me, but I can't meet his eyes. Queenie has hit the nail on the head, said all the things I felt too guilty to say. I mean, I did wish for him to come back. But I was seventeen and just lost my first love, and I didn't really understand what forever meant, then. Kyle goes sort of colorless and shimmery, and drifts through the wall. All that's left behind is a low keening sound. This is how most of our fights end, lately.

I turn back to Queenie.

"I'm sorry you had to see that," I tell her.

She shakes her head at me. I know her well enough to sigh and sit down across from her.

"What?" I ask.

"You're young, so it's ok that you're wrong about so many things," she says. "But some things you should learn now so you don't have to later. That goes for you too, young man."

Kyle pokes his head out of the wall.

"Like what, exactly?" I ask.

"Why do you think he's still here, Katie?" she asks softly.

"Because we said we'd love each other until we die," Kyle whispers behind her.

"Hush," she says to him.

I look up into Queenie's eyes. They are the most remarkable bright blue. I don't know if I've ever really met her eyes; or anyone's, for years. At first it was to avoid the pity everyone wanted to heap on me, and then it was to avoid the implicit questions: why don't you come out with us anymore? Why didn't you go to college like you planned? What are you doing with your life? But today Queenie catches my gaze and holds it, and it hurts, it hurts like anything, to be seen so fully by eyes that have seen so much.

"Because I wasn't ready to say goodbye," I say. "But I am now. I'm sorry, Kyle. But I think it's time for you to go."

"Whoa, whoa, whoa," Queenie interrupts. "I mean, he's here now. He's missed his window to ascend, no sense just letting him go to waste, right?"

Kyle and I look at each other.

"I missed my window? To ascend?" he asks.

"Oh yeah, you only have about a year to get to heaven, otherwise you're just stuck here for eternity. Didn't anyone tell you that?" Queenie says to him.

"I think I might have slept through that part," Kyle says. "Morning classes were never, like, my thing."

"Well, I went through this all with my Harold when he died, and it turns out you are, sad to say, stuck between the mortal and immortal plane for eternity. But you don't have to necessarily be attached to just one person for all that time. Harold found a lovely widow over at Fresh Meadows. He gets the high stuff off the shelves for her, and she listens to all his war stories, and they're both happy as clams. He comes to visit every few months and we have a nice chat."

Kyle looks at me, and his face just about breaks my heart. Yeah, we've been fighting a lot lately, but he's only here because I wanted him here.

"You want to break up with me?"

I nod. "I'm sorry. It's time. We don't really have a lot in common anymore, you know?"

"I guess."

"Why don't you hang out here for a bit?" Queenie says. "All the girls would love to see you. You've got quite a few fans here, you know."

"I do?"

Queenie gives him a coquettish toothless smile. And, God love him, Kyle smiles back.

"I've noticed you've figured out how to not fall through the walls lately," Queenie says.

Kyle ducks his head.

"The corporeal stuff is, like, super hard to learn," he says.

"I know. You're doing great."

Queenie holds up my big soft brush to him. Kyle gingerly reaches out and wraps his shimmery hand around it.

"All the ladies here can see dead people?" I ask.

"Most of us. The ones who lost their husbands, or the poor ones who lost their kids. Most of the husbands ended up ascending, but a few stuck around. Myrna and her Ron have lunch together every Friday. You find what works."

Queenie leans back, and Kyle runs the brush through her hair. Their sighs are both so soft and ghostly they disappear into the air. I watch them for a bit.

"Do I need to do anything?" I ask Queenie.

"You just need to say the words. And really mean them," she says.

I look at Kyle, remembering in a rush all the good times, all the little things I loved about him. I take a deep breath to ease the sudden pain in my heart.

"I'm letting you go, Kyle," I say softly.

Light flares around Kyle, then dissipates, little motes of brightness floating through the common room. It's beautiful.

"That felt super weird," he says.

"Are you going to be ok, Kyle?"

He shrugs, not meeting my eyes. "I guess. Maybe we could, like, have lunch or something one week when you come in. If you wanted to."

"I'd like that."

"Why don't you take off early today, Katie? I'd like to introduce Kyle around, and most of the girls are still sleeping off last night's bingo party anyway," Queenie says.

"Ok. Bye, Kyle."

"See you." He still looks a little shimmery, but he's starting to get his color back.

In the car I take a breath. It feels a little lonely, suddenly, being without Kyle. I consider running inside and taking it all back, but then I think of Queenie flirting with Kyle and getting a real smile out of him, something I haven't seen in months. I start my car. Maybe on my way out I'll ask Ron about that drink.

About the Author

Alyssa Beatty grew up in the wilds of West Virginia, but now lives in Brooklyn, NY. She shares her home with her husband, and three cats who occasionally offer editorial advice by walking over her keyboard.

After many years writing screenplays, she returned to short fiction, and discovered a deep love for speculative stories. She has previously been published in *Corner Bar Magazine*.

Death Stopped for Florencia

by
C.B. Calsing

Death Stopped for Florencia

Florencia had spent so many days preparing for her role as Saint Death for the village festival, and the fiesta had lasted so long, she didn't know herself anymore. Now the yards of bright yarn and paper roses from her hair lay in a mountain at her feet, and her white lace dress was safely stowed away in her wardrobe. With a little alteration, she could be married in it should that day ever arrive.

As she removed the leering skull paint, revealing her skin beneath, she started to remember. Dark brown eyes, warm tanned skin, lips that could be a little fuller. Just a normal village girl who, according to some, spent a little too much time with her nose in a book and focused on her work. Florencia did love reading, though, and running the telegraph office.

She finished scrubbing with a clean, wet linen, leaving a pile of rags covered in pancake makeup on her vanity, and then stood. Her feet protested, tired from the parade march and all the dancing, but she twirled anyway, remembering the party, hearing the music playing in her head. She must have danced with every single man in the village. One stood out, though now she could not place him. She thought she knew everyone. She twirled again, trying to evoke the feeling of when she'd landed in his arms for a waltz. She closed her eyes, but shadow obscured his face.

She could remember a few things about the stranger. He stood a good head taller than any other man in the village. Slim and elegant, he'd dressed all in black, with silky silver embroidery across the collar of his bolero. His plain black hat, wide-brimmed, had seemed to swallow the bright sunlight that fell upon it. The heels of his boots clicked like castanets across the stone of the village square.

And his hands, cupping hers, chilled her despite the heat of the day.

Who was he?

"Mija, come eat before you sleep," Florencia's mother called from the other room.

Florencia threw an embroidered shawl over her shift and left her room. She wanted to fall straight into bed, but she could not refuse the end-of-festival meal her parents had worked so hard to create.

Her family's cottage was cozy and filled with the smells of frying, chilies, and Papa's hominy stew. Florencia fell into a heavy wooden chair and rested her chin on her hand. Her father brought her a bowl of soup, and her mother served a plate of fried cakes, chopped vegetables, and crumbly cheese. Florencia smiled, inhaling the welcoming scents. "Thank you, Mama and Papa."

They sat at the table, and the three fell to eating. The big adobe room was quiet for a few moments as they all took time to appreciate the cooking and the fine day that had led up to it.

"Mama, did you see the man I danced the waltz with? The tall one?" Florencia asked after she'd finished her helping of food. She leaned back from the table, satisfied.

Her mother tilted her head.

"Dressed all in black? Very fine wool," Florencia prompted.

"Here?" Papa asked. A modest village full of modest folk, very few—even on a festival day—could afford very fine wool. "Maybe a rancher from…" Papa waved to indicate another part of the world. "Did he come in on the train?"

Florencia shook her head. "Not while I was working. He had very nice boots too. And not a speck of dust on his hat."

Mama and Papa exchanged glances.

Mama snorted. "I know you are not too young to get into the alcohol, so I'll not lecture you on that, but did you maybe take a little too much?"

Florencia scoffed. She'd had a few shots, offered by friends who could not be denied, but the weight of her costume and the heat of the day had made licuados and water much more satisfying. "No."

"Maybe you saw what you wanted to see," Papa suggested, a sly smile on his lips.

Florencia rolled her eyes. "Oh, Papa."

When her parents had finished eating, Florencia cleared the table and washed the dishes at the sink. She excused herself to bed.

Later that night, she lay there, thinking of the man, face bathed in shadow, who had whisked her across the dancefloor and made her finally feel like a lady.

The household woke to loud knocking on the heavy oak door. The three members, all bleary-eyed, staggered into the main room adjusting their hastily donned clothes. Sunlight streaked through the dusty windows, but all still felt the need to sleep off the previous day's festivities.

The visitor knocked again.

"One moment, please," Mama said as she checked herself, then crossed to the door. Papa squared his stance and stood facing the door, as if ready to chastise anyone who would interrupt their sleep the day after the festival.

Mama opened the door. Beyond stood the village's schoolteacher, a small, fastidious man who was kind to the children and good to his mother. Florencia also knew he was the only one in the village who maybe read more books than she did.

"Good morning," he said haltingly. "I've come to ask for the hand—"

"Stop!" demanded another voice. Behind the schoolteacher stood another of the town's bachelors, the man who pruned and maintained all the village's flowering trees and the roses around the church square. He was stout and strong but drank too much. "Florencia is to be mine!"

"I beg to differ," a third voice interrupted.

Florencia had to move closer to the door to see the third speaker, the funeral director whose wife had passed two winters ago. He was much older than the other two but just as bright-eyed and insistent this morning.

Then Florencia took another step toward the door, peering out into the morning light. She counted slowly, trying to understand what she was seeing. Outside the door of her family's cottage stood twenty-three men, all bachelors, many of whom she had danced with the day before. Some of them were already promised to her friends, paired off since their school days. Others, like the funeral director, had wives who had preceded them into death and grown children.

"Oh my God," Florencia said, taking a step back.

Bickering arose among the men, of who had first rights to Florencia's hand, of who had danced with her first or spoken with her first or known her family the longest. She fell back into her chair at the dining table, unable to catch her breath. The day before yesterday, the single men of the village had been polite but indifferent. Her mother had blamed Florencia for being too absorbed with her work; Papa said the men did not appreciate her uniqueness. Florencia had not concerned herself one way or the other. Marriage had been the furthest thing from her mind. How could she give up the privilege of running the telegraph, of being the first in the village to know things, just to bear children and wash a man's linens?

But today she had become desirable.

Her parents had the reputation of being the most hospitable citizens in the village. Today they would not disappoint. Each of the twenty-three bachelors was invited in. Mama and Papa served breakfast to the early ones, then tea and little sweet cakes to the midmorning visitors. By lunch twelve remained. Everyone took a break for the afternoon siesta, but by cocktail hour ten were back and entertained, one by one, for dinner, dessert, and brandy.

Florencia heard their pleas, their confessions, their accountancy of lauders, flocks, and ledgers as if she were some skirted priest who could give special dispensation, could end their suffering with a simple, "Yes, I'll marry you. You are surely the one." She never spoke those words, but her gaze drifted across the room to the door, out of which she wished to fly and go to work. What news was coming in without her there?

Long after the sun went down, the last bachelor finally left with a tip of his hat for the parents and a kiss on the hand for Florencia.

Exhausted, welcoming sleep again, Florencia headed for her room. The dishes and cleaning would wait for tomorrow. Mama clicked her tongue as she and Papa headed toward their room. "All our food…" She shook her head.

"And all our drink, but it will be worth it if Florencia finds a husband," Papa said. The woman who played Saint Death in the festival almost always found a husband immediately afterward. It was much more effective than playing Mary in the advent pageant.

Florencia tried not to hear her father's words.

But before any could close the doors to their bedrooms, a knock came again at the entry, louder than any of the others.

"What now?" Papa asked as he went to open the door.

Mama and Florencia approached. They gasped as the door swung inward. Outside, snow fell. Earlier than they had ever seen, a thick flurry of gleaming flakes reflected the lamplight from the inside.

In the snow stood the man in black. Florencia had called him el Flaco in her head; all day, when she hadn't been thinking about work, she'd thought about him as the bachelors had courted her. There he stood, so tall that he had to stoop to enter the cottage, which he did without Papa's invitation. Papa did not protest.

No snow marred el Flaco's black hat or the shoulders of his bolero. His heels clicked like castanets on the red tile floor as he crossed to Florencia. With him came the aroma of marigolds and warm summer, but when he cupped Florencia's face in both his hands, the palms were like ice.

"So lovely," el Flaco whispered, stroking her cheek. Florencia took a step back, blinking. She could now see his face, no longer shrouded in shadow. Pale, so pale, the skin was drawn tight against sharp bone. He smiled, his teeth straight and sharp. Then he pirouetted away from her and slapped his hands on his thighs, bending to peer into the eyes of her parents. "You must be so proud!" he announced, then straightened, his hands above his head in a stance that read *victory*. "Excellent work. Really excellent."

He spun to face Florencia once more and stalked back toward her, his steps like a puma's. "You, my dear" —he reached out a hand, and she took it but not wanting to— "were the most wondrous Santa Muerte I've ever had the pleasure to dance with at any of my festivals." He turned her, hand over head, once, twice. "You did me such honor." Here he dropped her hand and doffed his hat of midnight wool. The top of his head gleamed like the polished alabaster of the church's baptismal font. "Such honor," he repeated with a bow. "And you've passed my first test, refusing all those men. Granted, your choices were slim. All others before you have given in and accepted one of those offers."

Florencia looked at her parents, unable to comprehend what was happening. This was the creature who had so entranced her the previous day? The only word she could think of to describe him now was *ghastly*. Her parents had no answer for her in their confused gazes.

El Flaco moved back in as if to dance with her again. He grabbed her hand and wrapped the other arm around her waist. He led her across the red tiles of the cottage in a two-step, humming to himself.

"And so, my dear, since you are so lovely and have done me such honor, I've come to grant you three wishes. Then I shall take you as my own."

Florencia pushed back from him, brought up short as she bumped against her heavy wooden chair. "What?"

"Three wishes," el Flaco said, continuing to dance alone to a song no one else could hear, "and then we will be wed."

Florencia had read enough stories and heard the operas, and she knew now exactly with whom she dealt. Death had come to visit. She had danced with him, and now she would be stuck in one of his compacts. "Papa, is there any mescal left?" she asked as she sat down in her chair and dropped her head into her hands.

Papa ran to the kitchen and found a dusty bottle under the sink. He and Mama brought the bottle and four glasses to the table. El Flaco spun, perched on the edge of the fourth chair, and accepted the small glass of mescal.

The four sat and sipped the smokey alcohol.

"I don't have a choice in this, do I?" Florencia asked after she'd taken some time to think.

"It's a great honor," Death said.

Florencia shrugged. "I suppose, only… Aren't there prettier girls you could have as your own?"

Death shook his head.

"No smarter, though, eh?" Papa said, winking at his daughter. Evidently the day's consumption had finally caught up with him.

"Not helping, Papa." Florencia thought some more. "All right then. I will need time to decide on my three wishes. Come back tomorrow night and I will give you my first."

Death rolled his black eyes and waved toward the door. "Tomorrow? But we should go now; my carriage and four await."

Florencia shook her head. "No, come tomorrow and I will tell you my wish." She finished her drink and crossed her arms, signaling the end of the conversation.

Death stood. "Very well." Exasperation laced his words. "Tomorrow night then." With that he marched out of the cottage, his heels sounding a bit dull this time. He slammed the door behind him.

Florencia sunk farther into her seat, and her parents each had another shot of mezcal.

That night Florencia did not sleep, but with grim determination she dragged herself to the train station and the telegraph office for her allotted time. It was a slow day, and she spent most of it staring at the travel posters that graced the walls of the tiny waiting room with their garish colors. First the capital city, all whitewash and marble, painted in sunset colors with the mountains rising above it. Then a deep canyon of terracotta and blood-red stone, a mighty stag in silhouette in the foreground. Finally, the powerful sea, turquoise water and golden sand, and red-and-white striped umbrellas. The sun hung bright and warm, exaggerated rays piercing through the sky. A long yacht sat just offshore, sails billowing. Florencia rested her chin in her hand and stood behind her counter, staring at that poster. Her first wish came to her.

Mama had spent the day restocking the lauder and fretting over the condition of the house, and she was still busily rushing about when Florencia arrived home from the train station. Papa had gone to talk to the priest about their little issue, but the priest had laughed and told him to lay off the mescal before bed.

Florencia went to her room, brushed out her hair, painted her lips, and looked at herself in the vanity mirror. The makeup of Saint Death had made her otherwise plain visage striking. Now she fully resembled the clerk she was (and comfortably so).

Her family ate its evening meal in relative quiet, a pall of apprehension hanging over the table. After dinner, they tidied, and Mama put out a plate of fancy cookies for Death. They sat at the table and waited.

As before, Death knocked, but when Papa answered the door, he did not wait to be invited in. *Death rarely waits for an invitation.* A flurry of snowflakes and the smell of marigolds flowed in with him.

Florencia took a deep breath as Death danced across the floor to her and sat in his seat at the table. *We must remember to burn that chair when all of this is done.* Florencia squared her shoulders.

105

"Your first wish, my dear?" Death asked, leering at her, a too-wide grin showing all his teeth.

She nodded, exhaled, inhaled, and said, "I would like to visit the sea before I die."

Death's grin melted. He sat back, appearing confused. "That's it?"

Florencia nodded. "Yes, once, before I die, I would like to holiday by the ocean."

Death looked to Mama and Papa as if asking for help. Papa shrugged.

"What about fame?" Death asked, returning his black gaze to Florencia. "Fortune?" He stood and began pacing. "Wouldn't you like to star in the moving pictures? Sing in the capital to adoring crowds? Possess a million gold coins and a palace?" He stopped and stared down at her.

Florencia shook her head firmly. "No, thank you."

"But…that's so…" He threw up his hands as if giving up. "Fine, done. Granted. What's your second wish?"

"Come back tomorrow night, and I'll tell you."

"Not this again…" Death rolled his eyes and stood. "You're lucky I find you so appealing."

Florencia took her turn to shrug.

"I have the coach waiting… It's all done up in black leather and plumage. The horses are ready, four strong, black stallions. You've never seen such opulence! We could leave now. Ride straight through the night to the sea."

"I work tomorrow," Florencia told him.

Death blinked and groaned. "I will return in twenty-four hours' time." With that he stalked out of the room, slamming the door behind him.

"Florencia, what are you doing?" Mama asked once the door had shut.

"I've no idea," Florencia admitted.

She retired to bed, slept fitfully, and then went to work the next day. It was busier than usual at the telegraph office. The bishop would be coming for a visit, and the priest was sending messages back and forth to the capital to make the arrangements. The price of gold had gone up, and the owner of the nearby mine was busy trying to find out how that would affect him. Widow Ruiz's son lived in another town, and it was his birthday, and the widow had to send her felicitations. Florencia tried to keep up with all the incoming and outgoing telegrams, but due to her lack of sleep and preoccupation with Death's visit, she kept making mistakes. By the end of the day, she was barely able to contain her frustration even though everyone had been patient and kind.

When she got home, she brushed out her hair and then threw herself down on her bed for a quick nap. After dinner, the family again waited for Death to come. As before, he knocked, entered with snow and marigolds, and sat at the table.

"Now, my dear," he said to Florencia, "your second and third wish."

"I have my second wish, but..."

"You try my patience, girl."

"And you mine," she snapped back, surprising herself. Could one argue with Death? "I didn't ask for this."

"But the choice is not yours."

"Fine. For my second wish, I would like to never make a mistake at the telegraph office."

Death blinked. "What?"

Florencia sighed. "It was so busy today. I got so many messages wrong the first time. I don't want to make errors."

Death looked at Mama and Papa. Both shrugged.

"That's so...ordinary," Death said, blinking. "Don't you want to own the largest diamond in the world?" His voice was rising. "Have ever-lasting youth? A lauder for your beloved parents that is never empty?"

Mama raised her eyebrows at that.

Florencia just shook her head. "No, thank you."

Death stood, knocking his chair back onto the floor. "Fine!" he roared. "But I'm not coming back to this backward village for your third wish! You are...the worst! What a waste of my time."

Death stormed out of the cottage, slamming the door with a note of finality. Papa stood and righted the chair. Florencia heard the snorting, stamping, and whinnying of horses as Death's carriage took off into the night.

The next day, all was not right in their tiny village. At the station, when Florencia did her morning inspection, she found in the baggage room a rat snapped clean in a trap, yet it still squealed and attempted to pull itself and the trap around the room by its hind legs. It created a haunting clicking sound as the wood, metal, and rat flopped about. Florencia took a shovel to it and still it squeaked, refusing to surrender to the bliss of death.

When Widow Ruiz cut the head off a cockerel for her evening meal, it ran around the yard and kept running. Great gouts of endless blood flooded the gravel, staining the ground red, yet it did not stop. She had no meat for her supper that night, and all night the body of the cockerel kept streaking around the yard, crashing into things and making quite a racket.

And then came the worst: a blasting accident at the mine. One of the workers did not get out in time. The miners brought him into the village on a stretcher, and by all rights he should have been dead. The pile of heaving meat was unidentifiable save for an eyeball here, a curl of intestine there, a tooth embedded in some gray matter... Yet something that might have been a lung rose and fell, and somewhere buried in all that gore, a heart still beat.

The rat and the cockerel had been odd occurrences, but no miracle. This was the devil's work, obviously, to leave a soul in such suffering.

The villagers went to the priest and asked for his help, and he said last rights over the mine worker, but even that did not send him to the other side. The priest could only shrug.

What had brought this on the village? What curse had they drawn?

Days passed, and nothing died. Not the slaughtered pig, nor the shot gamebird, nor the old and decrepit in the charity home who suffered, day after day, in the rotting shells of their failed bodies.

Gossip began to circle about whose fault this was.

And slowly, oh so slowly, as the dead who would not die piled up, the gazes and the rumors all settled on Florencia. She must have done something. Saint Death must have offended someone or something. This culminated in a crowd, not unlike that first day of suitors, gathering outside the cottage, banging on the door, demanding she do something.

Florencia stood on the narrow porch in front of the cottage. In the cold, dry December afternoon, the air was fragrant with the sweat of the villagers and all those things that refused to die.

"Florencia, what did you do?" Widow Ruiz demanded.

"It all started after the festival," another piped up.

Florencia knew exactly what she had done. She did not know how to undo it though.

The crowd pressed in on her, demanding and stinking and yelling. Shaking fists and red faces surrounded her.

"Everyone, for the love of God, stop!" The priest entered the fray, and the crowd quieted and parted for him. He approached the porch, hands clasped, smiling softly.

Relief flooded Florencia. The priest would know what to do, right?

"Florencia, we all know you are to blame. If you would just—"

"Oh my God," Florencia cried, her frustration finally overtaking her. "I wish I'd never been Saint Death!"

A chill swept across the porch, a flurry of snowflakes coming from nowhere, along with the summer-smell of marigolds.

A voice in her ear, too familiar now, said, "Finally! I thought you'd never free me from this mundanity. Done!"

Florencia looked over, saw a glimpse of Death at her shoulder, and then woke up.

Festival day had arrived! Florencia smiled and stretched. Isabel would make a *lovely* Saint Death, and Florencia looked forward to treating her friend to a few shots and dancing with her after the parade. She donned her favorite blue dress embroidered with red roses. At breakfast, a knock came on the front door. Papa opened it. The schoolteacher, who was kind to the children and good to his mother, stood on the other side, hat in hand. He wished to request, humbly if he could, would Florencia dance with him at the festival?

Mama invited him in for chocolate and small sweetcakes, and he kindly accepted. He had such dedication to the children of the village that he had no plans for children of his own, he admitted over the refreshments. Though he thought about marriage, he was content with what he had and was perfectly capable of taking care of himself. He didn't need a wife to launder his shirts or fix his meals.

The festival was amazing, and all claimed Isabel had been the most beautiful Saint Death any had ever seen. The next night, she ran off to the capital with some unknown stranger. All knew she had gone to find her fortune, and none worried about her.

When Florencia returned to work, she quickly grew a reputation for being one of the greatest telegraph operators in the entire territory. She never made an error. She was quick, reliable, and friendly. The main office at the capital even offered her a position, which she politely turned down.

In the spring, the schoolteacher and Florencia married. They took the train to the sea for their honeymoon. As Florencia lay beneath a red-and-white striped umbrella, her love next to her, she felt as if all her wishes had come true, though she could not remember ever voicing these wishes aloud to the universe. On the turquoise water, a yacht with billowing sails cruised past.

About the Author

C.B. Calsing is a graduate of the Creative Writing Workshop at the University of New Orleans. A retired teacher, she reviews, writes, and edits full-time from the Puna district of Hawaii Island. Stay up to date at her blog, cbcalsing.blogspot.com, or follow her on Twitter @cbcalsing.

Best Wishes

by
Edward Ahern

Best Wishes

I get anxious around people. Which is ironic, given that I make my living as a mass marketer. My men friends are kept at social distance, and my few intimate relationships with women have been shipwrecks.

Trips to the supermarket bother me more than a dental appointment. I go at off times and maneuver the aisles as far as possible from the crowd of strangers, avoiding eye contact.

But last Saturday evening the little grocery stocker made me focus. He and his dolly full of cereal boxes blocked my aisle. I was still-stopped and couldn't avoid looking at him. He was over-dressed for the job; his boots expensive leather with high collars and pointed toes, his green slacks a rich wool. His face sloped sharply into his nose, which pointed out at least two inches beyond his eyebrows. He was just tall enough to escape being called a dwarf.

As I shifted my glare into neutral, he looked up at me. "Sorry for the delay, George. I'm done. Here's something for your trouble." And he pushed a cereal box into my chest. *Best Wishes* it said in neon-colored clover leaves.

How the hell did he know my name? Reflex made me grab it, and he turned before I could hand it back.

As he pushed the cart away, he talked over his shoulder. "There's an unannounced sale, fifty percent off, and if your wish is selected you win gold coins."

I thought of just putting it on the shelf, but the shelf was full to bursting. I winced and tossed the cereal into my cart, figuring to give it to the cashier. But I somehow forgot to do so, and the box wound up on my kitchen counter. *Waste not, want not,* I thought, and decided to eat my way through it for the next several breakfasts.

That next morning, I opened the cereal box and found a gold-embossed card.

Take a Chance
Make a Wish
If you're Lucky
Win lots of Gold

The explanation told me to go to www.faechance.com, enter a wish, and wait to see if I'd won. There was no fee for entry, and the prize was five gold coins. *When has General Millers ever given away gold coins? Even with good profit margins.*

I shook out a bowlful of multi-colored nuggets shaped like clover, poured milk and ate a spoonful. I was pleasantly surprised. It didn't taste of beet sugar and artificial flavorings. It tasted, somehow, like my first made-from-scratch bowl of warm oatmeal with molasses and cream. I felt a little buzzed.

My interest, and, yes, my greed, was aroused. After breakfast I went online to the site. I almost stabbed at the power off button. There smiling slyly at me was a picture of the stocking clerk.

His face looked the same, but somehow sharper featured—all points and angles. Once I got over my shock, I read the simple instructions—name, email address, wish, and e-signature. I paused. But good marketing ideas can often be filched from outré sources, so I continued. *What wish can I plug in? What difference does it make?* I typed in: 'Make me popular,' signed, hit enter, and got a confirmation. "Thank you, George for your entry."

I gaped at the screen, reminded that I'd been called by name yesterday. I got dressed and drove back to the supermarket. I quick stepped my way around customers to the cereal aisle and gaped again. There was no Best Wishes cereal, just boxes of something called Crunch-It. I stopped a store employee. Genette her name tag said.

"Where can I find the Best Wishes cereal?"

"Best what? Never heard of it." She smiled up at me. "But I'll be glad to help you with whatever else you need. Whatever."

"Never mind," I said, spun and left the store.

Once home, I walked straight into my study and fired up the desktop. I reentered the web address and was told that it wasn't in use, but I could buy the domain. I went back through my browser history, but there was no record of faechance.com. I hustled out to the kitchen to recheck the card, but it and the box of cereal were gone.

I sat down in a kitchen chair and tried to focus. I had bought the cereal, had eaten it, had entered the contest. Hadn't I? I did some mental math, silently recited a memorized poem—everything seemed to be functional, and I could still almost taste the cereal.

That was Sunday. The next morning, I went to the office and chaired our usual Monday meeting. Twelve people were in the conference room, eight of them women. My cell phone started to vibrate. Several of the women in the room were discreetly texting me. Once I'd opened up the meeting for discussion I inconspicuously glanced at my phone.

From Olivia: 'Admire the way you manage a meeting. So manly.'

From Gretchen: 'Always appreciate your penetrating direction.'

And others, including a suggestive selfie.

I avoided their glances, finished up the meeting, and retreated to my office.

Olivia followed me in.

"We should do lunch today, George, there's a lot I'd like to go over with you in a less formal setting."

I coughed and stutteringly said that we'd have to postpone it, then shooed her out. I am a man of average height, plain looks, and spindly physique. I'm well off but certainly not rich, or, outside of the marketing world, well known. I feel painfully awkward with women and have never had the courage to go onto an internet dating site. Why was I suddenly barraged with female attention?

The Best Wishes contest. Had I somehow been granted that stupid wish?

I called the supermarket manager where I shopped. He and I had a discreet arrangement. I kept him on a little retainer, and he answered my questions about product placements, promotions, and upcoming campaigns.

"Ralph?...George. A question about one of your new items... Best Wishes, it's a cereal... Really? You're sure?... I saw it on your shelves Saturday... Ha, ha, ha. My meds are fine, thank you. Must have been overripe veggies from your produce section... Yeah, thanks, you too."

The train ride out of Manhattan that afternoon was scarier than the usual unwelcome crowding. Several women who had ignored me for years were giving me the Stare of Appraisal. The one seated next to me was pressing her thigh into mine. I opened my tablet and kept my eyes pointed at it until I got off.

Once home, I walked into the kitchen to make a drink. I needed it. But stacked upon the granite topped island were five gold coins. And seated on the other side of the island was the grocery stocker, clad in sepia tights. I staggered.

"Hello, George. Sit down, please, we have a lot to talk about."

I dropped onto a stool. "Who—who the hell are you?"

"Call me Dulcent."

The shock dizzied me. *Play along.* "Unusual man's name."

"Actually, we're pretty androgynous. But let's not digress. You won, which is to say you lost."

"Hah?"

"Fairy wish fulfillment is always barbed, George. You left too many loose ends in your wish. You're already fearing it. But there's a way to keep the women at bay."

"I didn't commit to anything."

"Really? Did you click on the link that provided the contest's fine details? Don't answer, I know you didn't. Did you e-sign the document? Yes, you did. Legally and magically binding."

Dulcent's yoga pants and shirt shifted color to puce as he talked. I put my hands on the table edge to steady myself. I hate being suckered at my own game. "Why would you bother to do this?"

He smiled broadly. His bright back teeth looked more like incisors than molars. "For millennia, George, we'd been content to lurk in forests and glades and wait for you to get lost. We'd give you the wishes you thought you'd tricked us out of and get high off of your panic and anguish when you realized you'd been duped.

"But, in addition paving over our homes, your kind has forced us into a critical situation. We have a crisis of belief. Not ours. Yours. You, our customer base, quit believing in us. We decided we needed a charge back to correct this lack of faith."

"Hah?"

"Please pay attention. We need a marketing program. That's where you come in."

I almost said 'Hah?' again. "Ah. To launch *Best Wishes.*"

"Yes. It's my project. Pretty slick, huh? Right now, it's just a concept, but once we start selling cereal, the money and converts will roll in."

My mind was churning. He did need me and selling what wasn't needed to those who could barely buy it was my forte. This project might make me rich.

"You can create gold, why do you need money?"

His expression soured. "Yes, well, about that. The wishes we grant, the gold we concoct, all require a taxing amount of—call it psychic energy. We don't get enough of it anymore."

Just then my cell phone hummed with a double-entendre message from a nineteen-year-old administrative assistant.

Dulcent smirked as I turned the phone off. "Your admirers. We need to keep you focused on our problem before you start getting entrapped by all those women."

I pocketed the phone. I needed to make myself needed. "Don't take this the wrong way, but your campaign won't work."

Dulcent's tights morphed into an angry purple.

"It caught you, George, didn't it?"

"Because I wanted to see how its plumbing flushed. It's a clever concept, but there are problems. The brand name isn't catchy, the entry form is bureaucratic, and the gold coin prize is too valuable to be credible."

"That's fairy gold. It'll revert to lead. Oops, I shouldn't have said that."

"So, you'll be sued by thousands of dissatisfied contest winners." I glanced at the stack of coins on the island countertop. "My coins will turn into lead as well?"

"Ah, well. Wait." He interlaced his fingers and moved them around each other in a blur. He grimaced as he did it. "There. It's permanent gold now."

The shiny yellow of the five coins had tempered into a softer and richer amber color. I picked one off the pile. It had serious heft.

"Okay, about two ounces, say three thousand dollars a coin, fifteen thousand in all, that's an okay retainer. You've got my attention."

Dulcent grinned again. It was more frightening than the grimace.

I resumed. "The cereal tasted pretty good. Can you produce it in volume?"

"I think so. It's an illusion, like the coins. You actually ate moldy nuggets of stale bread."

Something lurched beneath my belly button. "Is that what you eat?"

"Of course not. Mostly field mice and squirrels, with the occasional dead deer."

"What's your vision for this?"

"We're guessing we can handle three lucky winners a month, predicated on selling a hundred thousand boxes of cereal semi-annually. That's as much cash and psychic energy as we think we can reasonably suck out of you all."

"Ah. The devil, Dulcent, is in the details. The life cycle of a cereal is usually several years. Can you maintain an illusion that long for millions of users and thousands of stores? Somehow insert and maintain yourself in the automated ordering system? The profit margin on brand name cereal runs around seventeen percent. You're a no-name brand, so your so your advertising and overhead costs are negligible—your maximum return would be maybe a buck a box."

Dulcent thought for a second, then snarled. His teeth looked even more unfriendly.

"You're so smart, what would you do?"

It was my turn to pause. "Okay, what you're proposing to do is already illegal and unsanitary. You need to stay on the edge of the system."

"Hah?"

"Stick to boutique grocery chains so you can manage billing and receipts. And small coins, a quarter the size of these. Put something mildly addictive in the cereal."

"It already has special herbs, that's why you got a buzz."

"Excellent. Keep the promotion on the cereal box. If the suck…ah, customer scans the code from ten boxes he gets a chance at a gold coin, and maybe a consolation prize of another box of cereal. Word of mouth gets you new customers, and you use the money from the new customers to pay off the old ones and keep the rest of the money. Eventually the scheme falls apart from its own weight, and the gold turns to lead, so you shut down and set up shop somewhere else.

"You'd have to change the name of the cereal every time you move on, but that's not complicated. Six hundred customers a store, forty or fifty stores, in a few months you've netted out maybe half a million dollars. Probably more because a lot of customers will enter more than once. You can recoup a lot of mojo for $500k."

"Some of them will go to the police."

"Who have no way to trace you."

"What about the lack of belief in us fairies?"

"Here's the solution. You'll have the phone numbers and emails of tens of thousands of pre-addicted entrants. Cast a spell for another product, Manly Brownies, maybe. Have them available only through fairy representatives—effectively fey drug dealers. Once they're hooked you can do a reveal of your true nature. Gives you that one on one manipulation you crave."

Dulcent was grinning, drool dribbling out of the corner of his mouth. He interlaced his fingers again and I knew whatever he spelled I wouldn't like.

"What an outrageously good idea. But, George, why do I still need you?"

"Because if you're not careful and thorough with every step you'll be discovered. And humans usually exterminate annoying species."

"Ah." He moved his fingers apart. "So, we would have to hire you. What would it take?"

"Money, of course, lots of it. And I need you to refine my wish."

"We don't change wishes."

"You will for me. I need to be interesting and trustworthy but not desirable."

"That's perverse."

"Maybe, but it's how I'm comfortable."

Dulcent put his fingers together again. I held up a cautionary index finger.

"Just remember that if you put a barb in my wish, I'll be the devil in your details."

About the Author

Ed Ahern resumed writing after forty odd years in foreign intelligence and international sales. He's had over four hundred stories and poems published so far, and six books. Ed works the other side of writing at Bewildering Stories, where he sits on the review board and manages a posse of nine review editors.

www.twitter.com/bottomstripper

www.facebook.com/EdAhern73/

www.instagram.com/edwardahern1860/

Wish for Ebony

by
Katie Kent

Wish for Ebony

A rose for my Valentine." Ethan knelt down and produced the rose from behind his back, holding it out to Ebony. The whole class broke out into a chorus of "aww" as she took it from him. Everyone, that is, except me.

Ethan and Ebony were the most popular couple in school. He was the typical teenage heartthrob—tall, dark, and handsome. He played football, basketball and had even been known to sub in on the soccer team as well. Ebony was slim and beautiful with long, dark hair. She was top of the class in almost all subjects and was the most positive person I'd ever met, always smiling. It should have been impossible to hate 'Ebothan', as everyone stupidly insisted upon calling the couple, but I did. Because *I* wanted Ebony. I'd wanted her ever since I first laid eyes upon her, two years ago, when I moved here from across the country. Trust me to crush on the most unobtainable, straightest girl in the whole school.

The teacher walked in, and the lesson began. I sat behind Ebony and had to look at that damn rose on the desk next to her for the whole sixty minutes. From time to time her eyes caught Ethan's from across the room and they grinned at each other. Sometimes she'd toss her hair over her shoulder. My eyes burned into the back of her head as I imagined being the one to put that smile upon her face.

I was slow to pack up when the bell rang for the end of school. Most of the other kids raced out of there, but I lingered, in no hurry to see Ebony and Ethan walk hand-in-hand down the stairs and kiss in the hallway.

"Hey, Keira."

I looked up to see Benji in front of my desk.

"What?" I frowned at him. I wasn't in the mood for talking; I just wanted to go home and mope in my bedroom, daydreaming about Ebony and drawing hearts in my diary.

"I have an offer for you." His voice was little more than a whisper.

I sighed. "Benji, you're not really my type." I wasn't out, but that didn't mean I was about to date a guy just to stop any rumours about my sexuality.

He screwed his eyes up. "What? No, I'm not offering you a valentine."

I looked at him. "What, then?"

"You'll see." He smiled. "I think you're going to like it, though."

I slung my rucksack over my shoulder. "Benji, I don't have time for games." *I have to go home and write love letters to Ebony that I'll never send.*

He pressed a piece of paper into my hand. "Meet me here, at eight tonight. I promise, you'll like what I have to say."

I wasn't going to go, but I got sick of moping in my room, and I was intrigued by Benji's offer. I figured I may as well go and see what he had to say—hopefully he didn't turn out to be a serial killer or something.

I arrived at the park just before 8pm. There was no sign of Benji, but on the dot of eight, he materialised, and I mean literally materialised, right in front of my eyes.

I gawped at him. "How did you do that?"

He shrugged, a smile upon his lips. "This is why I wanted to meet you. I'm not really a schoolboy, you know. I'm actually a genie."

I laughed out loud. "Yeah, right. Because we all know genies are real."

He frowned, as if he'd expected me to just accept his explanation. "So how do you explain me appearing out of thin air?"

"I don't know. Maybe you *are* magical. But a genie? Everyone knows that genies don't exist."

"Speak for yourself. I know I exist." He beamed at me. "And I'm here to offer you three wishes."

I rolled my eyes. "Don't I have to rub a lamp or something first?"

"No." He folded his arms. "Things have changed since those days. We can offer wishes to anyone we think really needs them."

"What makes you think I need them?"

He sat down, cross-legged, on the grass, and I did the same. "I've been watching you," he said, "and I think you qualify."

"You've been watching me?" I shuddered. "No offence, but that's kind of creepy."

"Sorry." He grinned. "Anyway, about those wishes."

I looked at him. "Prove you're a genie."

"I can't prove it. Unless you use one of your wishes now. But remember, you only have three."

I thought for a minute. "Okay. Make it snow."

"You need to make it a wish," he said, patiently.

I held up my hands. "Fine. I wish it would snow right now." It was a warm summer day, and we rarely had snow here anyway. I liked the snow; the crunch it made under my shoes, the way snowflakes tasted on my tongue, how it coated everything.

"Consider it done." Benji shut his eyes and concentrated. I had to stop myself from laughing again. But to my surprise, as soon as he opened his eyes again, snowflakes began to fall from the sky.

"OH. MY. GOD. How did you…?" I began.

He interrupted me. "Believe me now?"

I nodded as the snowflakes landed on my arm. I shivered. As it had been a warm day, I'd only come out in jeans and a t-shirt. I didn't even have a coat. "I'm cold," I complained.

"You're the one who wished for snow," he reminded me. "I can't do anything about you being cold, unless you want to wish for a coat or something, but that would be a waste of a good wish, don't you think?"

"Yes." I rubbed my arms, trying to warm them up, then something occurred to me. "Benji, it's not going to keep snowing now for the rest of time, is it? Do I have to wish for it to stop?"

He giggled. "No. You didn't wish for it to snow forever. In fact, you even said 'right now'." Abruptly, the snowflakes stopped, leaving just a thin layer on the ground and the trees.

"Now, may I suggest that you wish for something more meaningful with your second wish?"

I stood up. "I'll get back to you. I need to think about it."

At school the next day, everyone was talking about last night's snow.

I'd been thinking about future wishes. I could wish to have a lot of money. That was always what people thought about first, right? I'd had my eye on a new phone. I could just wish for that phone, I supposed. But that wouldn't change my life. But would money really change my life? I'd still be pining after Ebony.

"Did you see the snow last night?" Ebony asked Ethan.

I decided to be brave and talk to her. "It was amazing, wasn't it?"

She turned around and looked at me, then giggled and carried on talking to Ethan.

Depression settled in my stomach. When Benji arrived I told him, "I'm ready for my next wish. Meet me tonight in the same place."

"So, what will it be?"

Sitting on a bench in the park next to Benji, I took a deep breath, trying to settle my nerves. This would be the first time I had ever come out to anyone. I also didn't want to get the words wrong. I'd spent ages carefully crafting the right sentence. I didn't want this to be temporary, like the snow had been.

I pulled a blade of grass out and studied it, unable to meet Benji's eyes. "I wish that Ebony Mitchell was in love with me, now and forever."

When he didn't respond I looked up to see him smirking. I blushed and opened my mouth to say something else, but he got there first. "This is the wish I was expecting yesterday."

"You knew?"

He nodded. "Genies know everything. I told you I'd been watching you. I could tell how unhappy you were. I wanted to help."

"But what if my wishes hadn't been anything to do with her?"

He shrugged. "Well, the wishes are up to you. I just hoped you'd use them wisely. And you have." He shut his eyes for a brief moment. "Your wish is granted."

I swallowed. "It's done?"

"Yep." He smiled at me. "Bet you can't wait for school tomorrow."

Understatement of the year...

My hands were shaking as I approached the school gates the next day. I'd been awake most of the night, thinking about this moment. I wondered how it would play out. Would Ebony come straight up to me and confess her love for me? Or would she pass me a note, asking me to meet her later behind the bike sheds? Or ask for my number?

"Did you hear that Ebony broke up with Ethan?"

I tried not to react as I opened my locker to take my textbook out, but I couldn't help a small smile flickering across my face as my classmates gossiped next to me.

"No way! What happened? I thought they were solid."

"Apparently, she likes someone else. That's what she told him, anyway."

Adrenaline surged through me. This was it. This was actually happening. My palms felt sweaty as I shoved the textbook into my rucksack.

When I looked up, Ebony was approaching. The girls who had been gossiping about her left after saying hello.

She stopped when she got to me.

"Hi, Ebony." Butterflies raced around my stomach and my mouth felt dry.

"Hi, K...Keira." Her cheeks turned red, and she suddenly looked down at the floor.

"What's up?" I asked her.

She looked up, biting her lip. "Uh, n...nothing."

I was astonished. The last time I'd spoken to her, she had laughed at me, yet after my wish here she was talking to me, all tongue-tied and awkward.

"Well, see you in class then," I said, and she gave me a big smile, stirring something inside me. I had an urge to just lean towards her and kiss her right then and there but outing myself and her in one fell swoop would probably be a bad idea.

Over her shoulder I saw Benji in the distance. When he saw me look in his direction, he gave me a thumbs up.

"She still hasn't asked me out or anything yet," I complained to Benji, a week later. "I know she likes me—she can barely talk around me, and she keeps blushing. It's really cute. But I keep waiting for some kind of a move from her, and there's nothing."

"Can't you ask *her* out?" Benji lay back on the grass, resting on his elbows. "Why does it have to be her?"

I hesitated. "I dunno really. I just want her to make the first move. I guess it's always been my fantasy." I felt my own cheeks heat up. "This wish isn't working out the way I hoped it would."

He shook his head. "Don't blame the wish. You wished for her to be in love with you. That's all. You didn't wish for her to ask you out. Do you want to use your last wish for that?"

"I don't want to waste my last wish. I might need it for something else." I sighed. "Come on, Benji, give me some advice. How do you get a girl to ask you out?"

"I have no idea. Genies are asexual."

I laughed. "Fat use you are."

"Well, you're not out, right? So maybe she thinks you're straight? She might be worried you're not into girls and that you'll just laugh at her if she asks you out."

"You're right." I was silent for a moment, listening to the birds singing. "I need to come out."

He shifted position. "Are you ready for that?"

I bit my thumbnail. "I don't know. Maybe. Maybe not. But I'd do it for her. I'd have to do it sooner or later, anyway." I picked up my phone and opened Facebook. "What do I say?"

He yawned. "I don't think I'm the right person to advise on that, Keira. I grant wishes. I'm not much good at anything else."

I rubbed my eyes. "Fine."

My fingers flew over the phone screen as I composed my message. 'Hey everyone. I've got something to say, and I'm kind of scared, but I think it's time. So, here goes. I'm gay. Yeah. I'm into girls. I'm really not sure what else to say so I'm going to leave it there, but I have to say it's kind of a relief to get it off my chest. Thanks, all. K x.'

I pressed 'post', and then squealed. "I can't believe I've just come out!"

"How does it feel?" Benji asked.

"Good, actually." I looked down as my phone chimed with a notification. It was another girl in my class. 'You go, girl! Good for you.' As I was reading, another one appeared. 'Hot!' I rolled my eyes at the comment from a guy at school.

"Nothing from Ebony yet. But I can see she's online now, so hopefully she'll say something soon." I put my phone back in my pocket, feeling more hopeful than I had when I'd arrived.

"Still nothing." Another two days had passed, and nothing had changed with Ebony. She must have seen it on Facebook; she was always on there, and I saw her liking and responding to other people's posts. I'd had a lot of nice comments at school, which was nice- everyone seemed to be supportive. But Ebony hadn't even mentioned it. She had, however, become even more awkward around me. Yesterday, she'd even dropped an armful of books when I said hello to her.

"I think you're going to have to make the first move," Benji said, thoughtfully.

"I think you're right. God, I didn't expect this to be so complicated. I thought..." I trailed off as Ebony walked past me. When she saw me looking, she blushed and lowered her head.

I shook my head. "She seems different lately. Quieter, and more reserved. Even around other people. She used to be so happy, but now she just seems miserable."

Benji stared at the back of her head. "Well, maybe she'll perk up when you ask her out. She's maybe just shy about the whole thing. She might know that you're gay now, but she still doesn't really know that you're into her. At least when you ask her out, she'll be in no doubt."

I passed Ebony a note as I left class on Monday. 'Meet me behind the bike sheds at 4. K x.'

I had almost given up on her when I finally saw her walking slowly towards me, about ten past four.

When I smiled at her she lowered her head again, but she kept walking in my direction, stopping a few paces away from me, as if she couldn't bear to come any closer.

"What's up?" Her voice was quiet, and she bit her lip as soon as she'd said the words.

I'd rehearsed this speech over and over again throughout the day, but when she stood there in front of me, I forgot all the words I'd practised and just blurted out, "Do you want to go on a date with me some time?"

Her eyes widened. "Oh. I... err..." She'd gone bright red. I waited for her reply. "That's sweet, but I... I'm not into girls," she said. "Sorry."

I gawped at her. I hadn't anticipated this. I'd thought she would just admit everything. "Ebony." I spoke patiently, despite my frustration. "Come on. I know you like me. Why won't you go out with me?"

"I don't like you." She leaned back against the wall, obviously trying her best to look casual. "Not in that way, anyway. I'm straight."

I felt like banging my head against the wall. If it wasn't for the wish, I'd have thought I'd got it wrong. But I *knew* she was into me. I had wished for it, after all. "What are you afraid of?" I looked right into her big, blue eyes and wished I could just kiss her right then and there. But if she was scared of me asking her out, I could only imagine what trying to kiss her would do.

"Nothing. Look, I don't k...know what else to say. I d...don't like you like that."

It would have sounded almost believable, had it not been for her stumbling over her words. I'd never seen her stutter in front of anyone else. It was obvious she had it bad for me.

"Well, if you change your mind, you know where I am."

She nodded and walked away, not looking back.

"She told me she wasn't into girls."

Benji's expression betrayed his frustration. He was probably regretting giving me the wishes. But I had no one else to talk to. I'd always been a bit of a loner, I didn't really have any friends, and my family didn't know I was gay. "Well, she's not."

"What?" I peered at him over my sunglasses. "But she likes me!"

"Yeah, but don't forget the wish was for her to be in love with you. Not for her to be gay or bi."

A sinking feeling hit me. "So, what are you saying? That I messed the wish up?"

"I'm saying that she's probably confused as hell," he said, ignoring my second question. "She's only been into guys her whole life, when suddenly, bam! An overwhelming crush on a girl hits her right out of left field. She had no warning. She's never had any feelings for anyone female before."

I groaned. "Shit. Okay, what do I do about that?"

"Well, unless you want to use your last wish to make her gay or bi, I guess you need to wait until she comes around," he said.

I hesitated. "Do you think she will? I don't really want to use my last wish yet, if I don't have to. Once that wish is gone, that's it."

"Hard to say." He gave me a patient smile. "She *does* fancy you, big time. That much is obvious. I've seen how she acts around you. But she's scared of admitting she likes a girl. Now she definitely knows that you feel the same way, though, it's got to be tempting for her to give into you, surely?"

I sighed. "I really hope so. Because this is doing my head in."

"Perhaps you just need to make sure you give her plenty of reassurance. Like, maybe tell her that you won't force her to come out? That you'll keep it a secret? That might help."

The next day at school, Ebony looked exhausted. "I couldn't sleep last night," I heard her telling one of her friends.

I could guess why. I knew she was wrestling with her feelings for me. I briefly considered using my last wish to make her okay with her feelings, but I suspected that something else would just come up that I'd want to use that wish for. I was just going to have to be persistent. But I worried that confronting her again would just bring the same result as yesterday. So, I decided to write her a letter.

'I know it's a big deal when you first start having feelings for girls,' I wrote, a stab of guilt piercing my stomach. I knew I was the only girl she'd ever have feelings for. There would be no crushes on women on the TV for her. She wouldn't look at one of her female teachers and think 'you're hot'. I forced myself to carry on. 'I know you like me. And I know it scares you. But I can help you through that. Just give me a chance, please. I've liked you for ages. We can be good together. I won't force you to come out, I promise. I won't tell anyone. At school, I won't let on that there's anything between us. You can trust me. Here's my phone number. Just give me a text. It doesn't need to be anything more than that, at first. Looking forward to hearing from you. K x.' I didn't think that Benji counted as 'anyone'. He was a genie, after all.

I gave the letter to her at school the next day, when I was sure no one was watching. She blushed again, and quickly shoved the letter into her rucksack. I just hoped she would read it when she got home.

Her text came just before 10pm, just when I'd given up hope and was about to go to bed. 'Hey,' I read, 'it's Ebony. I…' I could see her typing, then stop, then start again. 'I do like you. It took me by surprise. I've only ever had feelings for boys before. I do want to go out with you, but I'm scared. My family are very traditional. I'm not sure what they would say if I was to date a girl. And I'm not sure how I feel about it either. I'm sorry. Ebony x.'

We ignored each other at school the next day, although I noticed she glanced at me from time to time, biting her lip. I got another text that evening. 'I wanna kiss you so bad.'

I was stunned. She was getting braver, and I liked it. 'Me too,' I responded. 'Wanna come over and try it?'

She didn't respond for half an hour, and I cursed myself for pushing her so quickly, but she finally replied. 'Yes. What's your address?'

My parents were delighted when I told them I had a friend from school coming over to study. I knew they worried about the fact I never seemed to have any friends. I'd been hanging out a fair bit with Benji, but that was always at the park, and I wasn't sure I could really count him as a friend. What happened when the wishes were over?

I paced my room, nerves mixed with adrenaline coursing through my body. When the doorbell rang, I raced down the stairs and opened the door before my parents had a chance to.

Ebony stood on the doorstep in neon pink shorts and a white vest top. I tried not to stare at her perfectly tanned legs. "Hey. Come in."

She gave me a nervous smile as she followed me into the house.

"I can't believe you're here," I said, when she was up in my room. I was sat on my bed, and she had taken my desk chair.

"Me either." She looked at the door, the posters on my wall, the calendar on the other wall, my beanbag chair. Everywhere except at me.

"Ebony. Come here." I patted the bed next to me.

She bit her lip, looking genuinely conflicted.

"There's no one here but us," I said, trying my best to be patient. I'd been waiting so long for this, and I just wanted to kiss her already.

She nodded, but made no move to leave the chair, so I got up and went over to her instead. I knelt on the floor and reached out to tip her chin up. "Is this okay?" I whispered, when my mouth was millimetres away from hers.

She nodded again, a slight blush on her cheeks. Adrenaline was running through my body as my lips brushed hers. Almost unbelievably, she was the one who deepened the kiss, her lips pressed against mine, her tongue parting my mouth.

When she eventually pulled away, her cheeks were bright red, but she was grinning. "That was amazing."

"I think I'm in love with you," she told me, about a month later. "Is that weird? We haven't been together that long, but my feelings for you are stronger than they've ever been for any guy."

This wasn't news to me—I had wished for it, after all, but I knew it would have been a big deal for her, so I pretended to be surprised. "That's amazing." I reached for her hand and brought it to my lips. "I feel the same way about you."

"Really?" A big smile broke out upon her face. "I was worried you might think it was too much, or something."

I laughed. "Ebony, I've been in love with you for a couple of years," I confessed.

Her eyes went wide. "Really?"

"Really," I told her.

"Why didn't you say anything sooner?"

Because you were straight back then. Because you would never have looked that way at me in a million years, if I hadn't made that wish. I shrugged. "You were dating Ethan," I reminded her, "and I didn't know how you felt about me." *Actually, I did. You didn't give me a moment's thought. In fact, you laughed at me.* I frowned at the memory.

"Hey, I'm with you now." She mistook my expression for jealousy, rather than guilt. "And I'm happy."

I looked at her. "Are you, though?" She enjoyed spending time with me, I knew that. She enjoyed kissing me. But she still wasn't the same girl she'd been with Ethan. Back then, it was like she hadn't got a care in the world. Now, she was guarded. She couldn't even say more than two words to me at school, paranoid that someone would find out about us. I'd come out to my family, and they had taken it well, welcoming Ebony as my girlfriend, but she was still afraid about any of her family or friends finding out that she was dating a girl.

"Of course," she said, but her smile wasn't entirely convincing. "Hey," she said, after a pause, "what do you think my type is? Like, I know you're into brunettes. You like Zendaya, and Olivia Rodrigo, and Mila Kunis, and me. I keep trying to work mine out, but I don't feel anything when I look at any other girls or women. I like you, so does that mean I'm into blondes?"

The guilt hit me again. I knew she was confused about her sexuality—she was in love with a girl, but there were no other signs that she was into girls. "Maybe you don't have a recognisable type," I told her. "And that's okay. Not everyone does."

It was about a week later when I walked through the school gates and became aware of everyone staring at me and whispering.

Ethan made his way over to me. "Is it true?" he asked. "Are you dating my ex?"

I swallowed. "I…" I began. I wasn't sure how he knew, and I knew that Ebony didn't want it to be public knowledge, but I'd never been great at lying. "No. What makes you think that?" I said, casually.

He narrowed his eyebrows. "So, this isn't you?" He thrust his phone in my face.

I peered at the screen, which displayed a photo of me and Ebony kissing. "Uh…" I scratched my head. It was kind of hard to deny now, and honestly, I was actually relieved, but I couldn't help worrying about how Ebony would take it.

I was saved having to come up with a response when we saw her walking through the gates. I looked around at the kids whispering and braced myself. Ebony didn't even glance at me, just went to walk straight past me as always, but Ethan reached out and grabbed her arm.

"Oh hey, Ethan." Her eyes flickered to me standing next to him, but she immediately looked back at him. "What's up?"

"When were you going to tell me you liked chicks?" There was anger in his voice, and I winced.

She doesn't. She only likes me.

"What are you talking about?" She tried to laugh, but her voice cracked.

"You're dating Keira. Don't try to deny it."

She looked across to me, her eyes accusing.

"It wasn't me." I shook my head. "He has a photo of us."

"Right." She paled, but immediately tried to recover. "Well, we have been hanging out. That's all there is to it, right, Keira?"

I ran my fingers through my hair. "Ebony, it's a photo of us kissing."

She looked around, as if suddenly becoming aware of the other kids all looking at us. "Shit," she whispered. "Ethan, I…"

"Save it. I can't believe I was dating a lesbian." He gave a bitter laugh. "At least I know it's not me."

"I'm not a lesbian." She looked terrified. "I just like Keira."

"Yeah, right. Like you can be making out with a girl and still proclaiming that you're straight." He walked off.

Out of the corner of my eye, I saw Benji looking over at us.

"I'm going to come out as bisexual." Another couple of weeks had passed, and Ebony seemed to have got used to the fact that everyone at school knew that we were together. We'd been a big talking point at first, but the gossip had died down, and apart from Ethan, no one seemed to have a problem with our relationship. I hadn't asked her what she'd told her friends, but I could only assume she was being honest with them.

"Ebony, are you sure? What about your family?"

She shrugged. "They'll have to find out sooner or later. Maybe it won't be as bad as I fear."

I felt bad when I thought of her declaring her sexuality publicly when she wasn't really bisexual. There would be no coming back from this, once it was out there.

The post appeared later that evening. 'Hey, everyone, I need to get something off my chest. This won't come as a surprise to most of you, but I'm here to confirm that Keira Wright and I are an item. Yeah, I'm dating a girl. I'm still figuring it all out, but I guess this makes me bisexual.' The likes and comments started almost immediately, and all the comments were positive.

Ebony came to school the next day with a cut on her lip.

"Hey, what happened, babe?" I asked her, running my finger over the cut.

She shrugged. "Oh, I walked into a door. So clumsy." She smiled, but it was gone quickly.

I tried to reach for her hand, but she moved it away. I was about to say something when I saw her eyes locked on something behind me. I turned around just in time to see Ethan locking lips with another girl at school.

When I turned back, Ebony's eyes were blazing with jealousy. "You alright?" I asked her.

"I'm fine." She gave a quick laugh. "Ethan can do what he wants, doesn't matter to me." Her eyes said otherwise.

"She still likes him." I cornered Benji before our next class.

"Probably," he said.

"But I wished for her to be in love with *me*." I watched Ethan link arms with the other girl. It was weird to see him with someone else. He and Ebony had been dating for a couple of years.

"She *is* in love with you. But don't forget, she and Ethan were joined at the hip before all this, and you never wished for her feelings for him to be gone."

I groaned. "Are you trying to tell me she has feelings for both of us?"

"I'm not telling you anything," he said, annoyingly vague. "I'm just speculating. Wishes have to be very specific, you know."

"You're telling me." I massaged my temple, feeling a headache coming on. "Clearly I should have wished for her to be in love with me, to have no feelings for Ethan anymore, to be bisexual, and to be okay with her sexuality." I leaned back against the wall, suddenly exhausted.

He gave me a sympathetic smile. "I think you'll find that's four wishes. But don't forget, you still have one left."

I shook my head. "Yes, but I don't even know which of those wishes would be the best one. And what if something else comes up?"

"I need to speak to you."

I shut my locker. "What is it, Ethan? Do you know where Ebony is?" I'd spent the last few days worrying that she might cheat on me with him. Ebony hadn't come to school today, and wasn't replying to my messages, and I was really starting to worry.

"Her parents won't let her go to school because you're here," he said. "They're talking about sending her off to a strict Catholic school, where 'she won't be corrupted by people of an impure sexuality'." He made air quotes with his fingers.

"You can't be serious." I was appalled.

He looked at me. "You haven't met her family, have you?"

"No, but she did tell me they were very traditional. They'll come around, though, surely?"

He folded his arms. "I wouldn't be so sure. They told her they'll cut off her college fund if she keeps dating you. And did she tell you where she got that cut on her lip?"

I took in a breath. "Please tell me that wasn't them."

"Her brother."

"What's her address?" I took out my phone and looked at Ethan expectedly.

"You're not going to go round and confront them, are you?" He looked horrified.

"What else can I do? I need to fight for my girlfriend."

He winced when I called her my girlfriend. "Keira, it's not a good idea."

"What else can I do?" I repeated.

"You can let her go."

"Let her go?" A pit of anxiety opened up in my stomach. "But I love her."

"She's so unhappy, Keira."

"No, she's not," I said, but I knew there was some truth to what he said. And if she'd been confiding in Ethan, rather than me, then something was wrong.

"She's not coping with her feelings for you. She's really confused. She said she was happy with me but one day she woke up and she suddenly had this crush on you. She doesn't really understand it. She says when she came out on Facebook, it felt all wrong. And now she has all this crap with her family to deal with, too."

My throat felt dry. I knew I was responsible for this. "Her address, Ethan," I asked him again.

I knocked on her door a couple of hours later, my heart racing.

The door opened, and a boy who looked slightly older than us opened it.

"Are your parents in?" I asked, looking at him with distain as I pictured him hurting Ebony.

"Who's asking?" he said, suspiciously.

I hesitated, but he'd know soon enough anyway. "Her girlfriend."

He immediately stepped back, as if he thought he might catch homosexuality from me, or something. "You're disgusting," he told me. "Ebony was normal until you came along and corrupted her."

"Please." I rolled my eyes. "She has her own free will, you know." *But she doesn't. She's with you because you made a wish...*

Trying to ignore the voice in my head, I asked him again if his parents were in.

"Mom, Dad!" he shouted, into the house. "It's that bitch— the one who's corrupted Ebony!"

They were at the door within seconds.

"You're not welcome here," the woman who was presumably her mom said.

I tried to reason with them. "Ebony is your daughter. You need to respect her wishes. She wants to be with me."

"Our daughter isn't gay." The man spoke now. "She was normal until she met you. It's like you've put a spell on her."

I mean, I kind of did... I cleared my throat. "Sexuality is a fluid thing. Come on, she's your daughter. Surely you should love her no matter who she's in a relationship with?"

"We have standards in our family," he said. "Ethan is such a lovely young man. He was round here the other night. We know she still likes him."

This really wasn't going well. I scratched my head. "You know, I'm nice too, if you get to know me. I love your daughter, and it's important to me to have her family's blessing."

"Well, you don't have it. Leave Ebony alone."

I stood there in shock—her dad had just shut the door on me.

I tried to ring her when I got home, but it went straight to voicemail. I sent her a text instead. 'Please get back to me. I'm worried about you. I miss you xx'.

She wasn't at school the next day, or the one after that. The weekend came, and still I hadn't heard anything from her. I'd sent a bunch of texts, but none of them were even read, so I suspected that her parents had taken her phone off her. I was miserable, and I could only imagine how she was feeling.

On Monday morning, Benji was consoling me when he suddenly stopped mid-sentence and nudged my shoulder, directing his eyes down the corridor.

Ebony was walking towards us, her head down.

"Hey," I said, when she reached us.

She looked up. "Hi, Keira." There were dark rings under her eyes and although she smiled at me, there was a tortured expression on her face.

"I missed you." I reached out to take her hand, but she pulled it away.

"My parents will kill me. Or you."

Benji and I looked at each other. "They let you come back to school," he said.

"Yeah. Only because the school told them they'd be fined if I didn't go back. And they made me promise not to go near Keira." She looked around, a fearful expression on her face. "I'd better go. I can't let too many people see us talking. It might get back to them."

I sighed. "This is ridiculous. You're my girlfriend. We shouldn't have to put up with this shit."

She shrugged. "It is what it is. It was fun while it lasted." She sounded so depressed, so resigned to this. She was a far cry from the happy, bouncy girl she'd been before the wish.

"So that's it?" I asked, a cold shiver making its way down my body. "We're over?"

A tear slipped from her eye and made its way down her cheek. "Maybe it's for the best." She turned and walked away.

144

I leaned back against my locker, trying to will away the tears that were threatening to spill from my own eyes.

"I'm sorry," Benji said.

"Should I wish that her family are okay with her being gay?"

"You could. But it sounded like she was having a hard time dealing with it herself."

"I could wish that everyone was okay with it," I said, determinedly. I wanted to fix this mess that I had caused. "That would cover her family and her. That would work, right?"

"Probably. But don't forget she still likes Ethan. And that you forgot to actually make her gay or bisexual."

I swallowed, my eyes fixed on her as she spoke to one of her friends. She laughed at something her friend said, but the haunted expression never left her face.

I suddenly knew what I had to do. "I'm ready to use my last wish." I turned back to face Benji. "But can I just check it out with you first?"

"Sure."

"I want to wish that Ebony had never been in love with me. Would that mean that the events of the last couple of months would be erased, that they never happened?"

"Keira, are you sure? What about your feelings for her?"

I kept my eyes trained on her. "I should never have made that wish in the first place. Look at her! No amount of modifying my previous wish will make it right. She's straight, and she's still into Ethan. Even if she gets back with him now, she'll still always be in love with me, because I wished it. And I don't know what that will do to her."

He nodded. "Alright. For what it's worth, I think you're doing the right thing. As for the wish, it might be safer to wish that you'd never made the last wish in the first place."

I hesitated. "That won't turn back time or something, will it?"

He giggled. "No. I don't have those kinds of powers. It will be the same day and time it is now. Things will just reset, so she'll still be with Ethan, and your relationship will never have happened."

"Alright." At that moment Ebony looked over, our eyes met, and a moment passed between us for the last time. "I wish that I'd never made my last wish."

I shut my eyes, and when I opened them again, Benji was no longer stood next to me. Then Ebony walked past, arm linked with Ethan's. She looked happy again, and despite the pain in my heart, I knew I'd done the right thing.

"Hey, Ebony," I said, as they walked past. She looked over, giggled, and walked past without responding.

"Everything okay?"

I jumped. I hadn't noticed Benji arrive at my side. "All good," I lied.

"Don't forget you still have one wish left," he said. "Are you ready to make it yet?"

About the Author

Katie Kent is a writer of fiction and non-fiction living in the UK with her wife, cat and dog. She likes to write stories, mostly for a YA audience, particularly about LGTBQ characters, mental illness, time travel and the future—sometimes all in the same story!

Her stories have been published in *Youth Imagination, Limeoncello* and *Flash Fiction Magazine*, amongst others, and in a handful of anthologies including *The Trouble with Time Travel, Summer of Speculation: Catastrophe, Growth* and *My Heart to Yours*.

Her non-fiction, mostly mental health-related, can be found in publications including *The Mighty, You & Me Magazine, Ailment, OC87 Recovery Diaries* and *Feels Zine*. You can visit her website at KatieKentWriter.com and follow her on Twitter.com/uniKH80.

Where Wishes Come True
by
J. L. Royce

Where Wishes Come True

*Y*ou know, Andrew, the ones who simply wished they were dead are the luckiest, perhaps," Pratik said.

He maintained a sonorous monologue as we trudged past the cordon lines surrounding the Zone. Each stop entailed the production of credentials, and questioning, and curious glances at the suppression suit I wore. *Research*, Pratik would explain, with solemn eyes. *Need to know.*

The guards nodded or shrugged—at the outer cordons, that is, where humans stood the watch. The inner line was held by servitors, inscrutable and programmatically polite, immune to the Zone's effects.

Believed to be immune. Units sent in to reconnoiter the Zone itself did not return; but if they weren't alive, how could they die?

"Well, that's not quite right," Pratik said, a touch of a smile relieving his doleful expression. "Perhaps those who wish they were *never born* meet the cleanest end."

He pursed his lips. "No bodies found, then. Just…gone."

First hikers disappeared, then the search parties sent after them. The drones and servitors sent in to surveil caught glimpses of corpses, some in shocking states—before the machines went dark.

"But you—you're *stable*, eh?" Pratik slapped the shoulder of my environmental suit. "Rock solid."

The battery of tests he'd administered concluded I was not a risk to myself or others; that I had no lingering *wish* to compromise the mission. But I am a psychologist and understand the tests, probably better than the administrators.

Bodies. The man in a state of post-prandial eruption, having eaten his fill, and then more, and still more. The woman found with a full-grown human child-shape still tethered to her ruptured uterus. The child inexplicably transformed into his favorite action hero (unfortunately, long dead). The teen-aged heart attack victim, having expired after a sexual frenzy. The man seen floating off into the Montana sky, tracked by NORAD until his ultimate decompression high above the stratosphere. On and on: an endless variety of bizarre deaths.

"So, be careful what you wish for—just in case." That sad smile. *In case the suit doesn't work.*

"No *white bears*, hmm? You said you were sure. Don't you want me to test the hypothesis?"

Pratik glanced at me. "I'm sure that the theory of the suit is sound. As far as we know. But for a first test, let's not push the limits. Be careful of the suit."

We hurried along through the forest, the trail strewn with stones worn white and round as children's skulls. The silence bothered me, and my anxiety was building. Why *was* I here? Self-analysis is a dangerous game. Illusions are far more comforting than the truth.

"Bit of luck, that it should start out here," Pratik remarked. "Can't imagine what, say, Los Angeles would have looked like if the Zone began there."

We looked at each other. *Drugs? Money? Involuntary breast implants?*

"Or Moscow." Pratik laughed, quavering and nervous. "Drowning in vodka!"

"You don't think it's going to work," I said.

He stopped so suddenly we nearly collided. Pratik faced me.

"It's a risk I'm willing to take," he said. "What we do now, we do for everyone."

I said nothing but stepped around him and trudged on.

"Cat got your tongue? Or second thoughts?" he asked.

"No—I'm all in." I grinned through the faceplate to prove it.

I'd had considerable success in my career, and that propelled me into riskier ventures—intellectually, philosophically, even in my personal life. I'd written one paper after another, with ever-rising impact factors. And now, the Zone. It wasn't just another paper; it was a place in the history books.

We came upon the inner cordon, a fifty-foot-wide no-man's land bulldozed through the pines a few weeks earlier. The heavy machinery lay abandoned nearby. It had been the *outer* cordon when created and staffed with humans. No more.

A human-styled servitor stepped forward. Most of the robotics around the Zone were neomorphs: drones, crawlers, bounders. This one had a token human interface.

It scanned our transponders and said simply, "Clear. Proceed at your own risk."

I ran through my checklist and confirmed sensors and cameras were recording, my transmitters were active.

"We'll have to pull them back soon, we think," said Pratik. "The boundary is expanding, but unevenly; a few inches here, a few feet there. But there's good news."

"It's slowing?" That was too much to hope for.

"Afraid not. The good news is, with the growing size of the Zone, and several rounds of boundary retreat, we've been able to interpolate a Ground Zero, as it were, where the Zone may have begun."

"Silver lining. And..."

"It's your destination, programmed into your navigator. About a mile and a half from here."

I glanced at the tracker strapped around the wrist of my suit, centered the map, and saw the flashing indicator.

"Recording?" Pratik asked.

"Yes."

He scuffed the ground with a dusty Oxford. "Andrew...You, ah...I assume you've left instructions, should..."

"Yeah, all the details. No inconvenience to you." I adjusted my backpack with a jerk on the straps and strode across the crudely cleared expanse.

"Good luck!" Pratik called after me.

I refused to acknowledge him at first, in the grip of a strange mix of emotions. At the inner edge of the clearing, I turned, but he was already gone.

Alone with my thoughts, I considered that ambitions are not wishes; they are goals and plans, not fantasy. I realized that I couldn't think of a single wish.

I'd walked a scant quarter-hour when the woman appeared in my path, so suddenly that I assumed I was hallucinating.

She looked a bit older than me, dressed in modern hiking shoes and clothes, poly top and stretch pants topped with a sleeveless shell. Not striking, good or bad; not my wish fulfillment, certainly.

Pratik hadn't promised anyone would be alive in the Zone (aside from me), but he hadn't said I'd be alone, either.

"Hi," she said. "My name is Pensee."

I checked the sensor readouts of myself and the environment. *Radiation? Toxic chemicals? Long-chain hydrocarbons?* Nothing. Proximity, thermal, motion, and remote vitals all agreed: a person was standing before me.

"My God! Why are you staring off like that?" She stood with her hands on her hips, waiting, then spoke in a contralto drawl. "*Hullo, Pensee! My name is…*"

Jarred back to the moment, I thought, *Play along*.

"Sorry, you took me by surprise. My name is Andrew. Doctor Andrew Holloman." I offered her my gloved hand, but Pensee glanced at it with mild distaste, then grinned.

"What's with the bunny suit, *Doctor* Holloman?"

"Protection." I was still struggling with the question of her reality. Was I attracted to her? *Was* this wish-fulfillment? If so, it meant the suit had failed. Or did this conversation mean it was working?

"From what?" Pensee stepped closer, and I tensed. They hadn't provided me with any weapons—how can you fight your own fantasies?—but I could always try to flee.

"Whatever's killing people in here."

"Oh." She nodded, serious. "Yes, I've seen the bodies—terrible. You wouldn't believe…"

"Doesn't it frighten you?" Andrew asked.

"They're dead; they can't hurt me. You're the first living person I've seen since I got here." Pensee waved up and down at my suit. "I don't think that will matter, though."

I let the remark pass. I was still unaffected, and willing to give the suit the benefit of the doubt.

Realization dawned. "Wait—were you here before the Zone appeared?"

"The what?" The answer was clear from the blank expression on her face. "What's going on?"

I explained in a few sentences what it had taken a horde of scientists this long to figure out: *Something in here is making wishes come true*.

"How have you survived?" I asked. "Food, water, shelter?"

She laughed.

"Well, I was just hoping for a day hike in the wilderness, to decompress; and here I am, weeks later, still enjoying it."

Pensee looked thoughtful. "It *has* been weeks, hasn't it? I sort of lost track."

I had no way of knowing what to believe.

"What were you asking again?" Pensee said.

"You say you only came prepared for the day, yet you appear healthy."

"Yes; I've been so lucky." Pensee gestured into the woods, at a game trail I had overlooked. "Will you come with me? I'll make us a cup of tea. Or coffee?"

"What are you talking about?" The offer left me wondering about her mental state—if she was real. But I've had considerable success in my career, and as risks went, this one seemed pretty tame.

"It's a surprise—well, it surprised me. A place to call home. Come along."

The trail ran in the general direction of my destination, so—delusion or not—I agreed.

"Thanks."

"And maybe you'll slip into something more comfortable?" She gave me a sly grin and sauntered off. I bumbled after, pondering my situation. Why had Pratik not discussed this scenario?

It didn't seem likely this was my wish fulfillment, though she did have a nice smile.

The cabin was nestled among dense oaks and walnut trees. It was well concealed, all but undetectable from the trail. A single apple tree grew wild beside the cabin, its tall branches heavy with golden fruit, though none lay on the ground.

We proceeded up a rough stone walk to the small porch. Layers of leaves covered the shingled roof; the wooden walls were weathered; the gnarled oak limbs bent low.

"Looks like it's been here a long time."

"Doesn't it?" Pensee shook her head and gestured at the lattice covering the crawlspace. "Take a look."

With some difficulty, I went to all fours, flipped on my headlamp, and peered beneath the cabin. I expected years of leaves and detritus. Instead, I saw the neatly truncated remains of the forest floor—trees, bushes, grass, even rocks—sheared away.

I rose and looked at Pensee. "How did you ever find it?"

"Sheer luck," she said. "It was late in the afternoon. I'd gathered some supplies—left behind by one of those poor people—and was looking for a place to spend the night. I just turned a bend in the trail—and *voila!*"

"I saw a flash, or a twinkle." Pensee danced up the steps, flung open the door, and urged me forward with a wave. "Well, I'm sure it was just the low sun on the windows. Come on in."

I followed and stood in the doorway. The space was so predictably, wonderfully *comfortable*: a single cozy room with a loft large enough for a bed. A pair of worn overstuffed chairs sat before the fireplace. The low-ceilinged area beneath the loft had an old-fashioned kitchen with a wood stove and a dry sink.

"I'll build up the fire." Pensee bustled about the room. "You know, I never had any experience before, living like *this*—a wood fire, the hand water pump outside, the *outhouse!*—but it's pretty easy."

When I tried to sit down, she whirled and pointed at me. "Would you *please* take off that suit?"

I fingered the closure on my suit and contemplated the reassuring surroundings. Had I wished them into existence? I ground my teeth and ripped the Velcro open with a jerk. The hood fell back, and I breathed the unfiltered air, rich with the spices of the outdoors and human life, this woman, Pensee.

"That's better." She paused in poking kindling into the maw of the fireplace. "Now take off the rest. Well, you know—the bunny suit." She winked: the little coquette.

I did as she asked. "Why do you call it that?"

"Because I used to be an OR nurse. That's just a paper suit. It protects the environment from *you*, not the other way around."

Just paper. It wasn't something I'd considered. I tossed it on a coat hook by the door. When I was wrapping the tracker back around my wrist, I noticed it blinking frantically.

"We're near the center."

Pensee asked, "Of?"

I hadn't realized I'd spoken out loud. "The Zone."

She bustled about the kitchen, lighting the wood stove and putting on the kettle. "Is that good? Congratulations, then, I suppose."

I walked into the pantry, packed with dry and canned goods.

"Hungry? I'm vegetarian—always was. Let me know what you'd like."

"Where did all this come from?"

"I told you—I just found it. Here and there."

Pensee placed a teapot and mugs on the counter and measured loose tea into a tea ball. She looked up at me. "I'm going to have a cookie."

I stared at Pensee. Her wide eyes were hazel, tinged emerald around the margins, unusual and appealing.

Pensee waved a half-eaten cookie. "After four years of operating room duty, I was fed up. So, I decided to take off a few months and then come back as a private duty nurse."

We were sitting before the fire. I was anxious to track the center of the Zone but submitted to her hospitality.

"What about you, Andrew?"

"I'm a psychologist."

"Really?" She leaned towards my chair. "How did you come to be here? Not camping, with that silly get-up."

Pensee laughed, a pleasant sound I'd heard far too little in the past weeks—in the past years, for that matter.

"I treat personality disorders—narcissistic behavior is my specialty. It's an unrecognized epidemic, you know. When I heard rumors about this…phenomenon, I asserted myself into the situation."

"Narcissists? Aren't those just obnoxious people?"

"Well, schizophrenic solipsism. And this"—I glanced around the cozy, twilit chamber—"seems like the ultimate solipsistic fantasy."

I noticed a small antique desk in the corner. Pensee followed my gaze.

"It's a nice piece, isn't it? Just the place for writing those papers."

I finished my tea. "The government—Homeland Security, the NSA—must have been monitoring internet traffic. They saw my queries, and a fellow named Pratik reached out, and here I am."

"Here you are." Pensee touched my hand.

I must have flinched.

"Are you alright?"

I automatically went to search my heads-up, and realized my hood was off. "I...don't know."

"Come on; the question isn't that hard. You don't need *machines* to tell you."

I considered. "Last week, it seemed so important, getting into the Zone. I thought I would write the seminal paper on the effect, perhaps a first-person piece for the *Times* or the *Atlantic*; I'd almost certainly get a grant for further study..."

Listening to myself prattle on, it all seemed so pointless.

"Now..." I shrugged.

"I know what your problem is." Pensee rose. "*Low blood sugar.* I've got a stew ready to warm—vegetables and beans—it should be ready."

"I need a meal?"

"You need someone to..." She stepped behind my chair, leaned over, and tentatively wrapped her arms around me. She made to kiss my cheek, but I turned my head to say something, and our lips met, quite naturally.

We parted. "...comfort you."

I've had two types of lovers in my life: those who demanded I prove myself worthy of them; and those I forced to prove they were worthy of me. The former offered the challenge of the hunt; the latter, the satisfaction of control, the fulfillment of each and every fantasy.

I lunged out of the chair.

"I don't want your comfort," I said and pressed my mouth onto hers. My fingers found the edge of her top and I pulled it over her breasts, then sought the waistband of her pants. She stepped out of them as she struggled with my belt, then broke off our kiss.

"Upstairs," she said, and taking my hand, led me to the ladder-like steps.

I followed. She moved with a grace I hadn't noticed before.

Night had filled the cabin windows when I awoke. I sat up, careful of the low-slanted ceiling.

"Not yet," Pensee murmured, and touched my arm.

"I should send an update. They'll be concerned and might take action."

She laughed, a melancholy sound, filling that space where sense had fled and passion had filled the void.

"There's no need." Her long limbs, carelessly strewn across the bed, stirred.

"Why?"

"Pratik knows."

"What?" I sought her face in the darkness.

She raised onto an elbow, shaking back tousled hair.

"Of course he knows you're here. He sent you, didn't he?"

She was indistinct in the gloom. "Yes, the mission, but—"

"No, not the mission; he sent *you* to *me*."

"He..."

Pensee sighed. "We negotiated. I promised I could slow the— what did you call it?—*Zone* if I had what I wished for. Food, drink, and...companionship."

"You can do that? Slow it?"

"Who knows? Does it matter?" She fell back upon the bed, and the light from below caught her face. "We're here."

I stared off, trapped in a recursion of wish fulfillment. *Pensee wished for me—or I wished for someone to want me—or Pratik wished...*

It didn't matter, I decided: the evening had been the most pleasurable I'd experienced in a long time.

"There's something I have to ask you," Pensee said.

"What's that?"

"Children." Her eyes drifted shut. "I've always wanted a family of my own someday; and since it appears we're settling in, I wondered..."

I let that remark pass. "You'd want to have prenatal care, get an OB-GYN, use a hospital."

She tsked. "Humans had children for thousands of years with none of that."

I heard a sound in the room below and stiffened.

"Listen!" I whispered.

The rustling grew louder. "Something's down there..."

"Don't worry," Pensee said, stroking my back. "You'll make a wonderful father."

The infant's cry was blustery.

"Oh my," Pensee said, sitting up. "She's hungry, and I'm leaking!"

She rose, clutching her engorged breasts, and padded naked down the stairs. "Bring a towel?"

I did. When I arrived, she was in her chair by the fire, nursing our daughter.

"Come meet her." Pensee smiled up at me. "Your eyes, and my nose, don't you think?"

I sat beside them, staring at the tiny face pressed into her bosom, the little hands kneading for sustenance.

"Glad *that's* out of the way," Pensee said, nodding to the loft. "Feed the fire, Andy; it's getting chilly. And start the stove; dinner's probably cold."

She smiled at me. "It was worth it though, don't you think?"

I nodded; I had no choice.

"When your chores are done, you can go do your writing, or whatever." She returned her attention to the baby. "I'm just going to sit here with my little companion."

I rose to do as she wished.

About the Author

J. L. Royce is a published author of science fiction, the macabre, and whatever else strikes him. He lives in the northern reaches of the American Midwest.

His work appears in *Allegory*, *Fifth Di*, *Fireside*, *Ghostlight*, *Love Letters to Poe*, *Lovecraftiana*, *Mysterion*, *parABnormal*, *Sci Phi*, *Strange Aeon*, *Utopia*, *Wyldblood*, etc.

He is a member of HWA and GLAHW.

Some of his anthologized stories may be found at www.jlroyce.com. Follow him on Twitter: @authorJLRoyce.

Clever, Little Mortals
by
Daniel R. Robichaud

Clever, Little Mortals

Mashael Naifeh led the way upstairs to the attic of grandfather's house. His excuse: "We need to catalog what's here before the family arrives to divide this stuff between them." However, Jawaria knew that was so much nonsense. He wanted to see the good stuff for himself, and he needed his sisters along because he forgot who had the extra set of keys.

Sadia was nineteen, the youngest of the three, and quite content to go along for the ride. She loved her grandfather's taste in bizarre trinkets from the motherland, Saudi Arabia, and she even sported a lovely black and gold headscarf and style that played to their Muslim upbringing. She was also like their father and about twenty-five pounds overweight, which made her first-thing trip to the kitchen refrigerator to see what remained edible no surprise at all.

Mashael was twenty-two and pursuing his MBA. He could do no wrong in their father's eyes—well, back when Father could speak in more than mumbles, thanks to an early onset of Alzheimer's—and Mother was just as charmed, therefore keeping him flush with cash injections whenever he needed them. It was an unspoken rule in the Naifeh family that Mashael always got what Mashael wanted.

That left Jawaria, who got not a fraction of the help, a fraction of the affection, nor a fraction of the morale boosts her brother did. The last thing Mother asked her was whether she was engaged yet, and when she replied that was not the case, Mother made that disapproving clicking sound. "You're going to be twenty-five soon." As though this was even remotely a milestone anymore. Unlike her little sister, she'd lost all interest in her parent's style preferences, deciding on jeans and sweatshirts or stuff that could be gotten from some of the more interesting modestly priced fashion catalogues.

There was no way Jawaria was going to miss this little expedition. No way she was going to let Mashael get first dibs on *jeddi*'s coolest things. It was long past time to put an end to the favoritism that informed their lives as kids and somehow became law while they were adults.

"It smells like dust," Sadia said, drawing up a dangling end of her scarf over her nose. "And rat turds."

"That's just old man smell," Mashael said. "You remember how he smelled."

"Like rat turds?" Sadia asked.

"*Jeddi* smelled like Old Spice and prunes," Jawaria said, "not turds of any kind." She gave a few sniffs of the steps. "And I don't smell anything." What did dust even smell like?

Mashael was first up the stairs, first into the storage area, and therefore the one to pull the chain on the overhead light—really just a bare bulb. When the twisty CFL bulb finally came alive, it bathed the space with cold, white light.

A low growl sounded on the stairs behind them. Jawaria looked back and saw Sadia's sheepish expression. "Was that you?"

"My belly," she said. "I could use a sandwich."

"Didn't you just cram like five mouthfuls of *gorayba*?" The cardamom from the shortbread snack was fragrant on her little sister's breath.

Sadia's embarrassed smile admitted that yes, she had, thank you. Then, Mashael made it all about him, again.

"I've been waiting for the chance to open this thing," he announced. Jawaria had never seen the trunk he slid out from behind a mound of covered chairs. It was an old-fashioned bit of antiquity, that trunk. The sort of thing you saw in old, old movies, all covered with stickers from around the world. It had no stickers, however.

It was locked, no key in sight; he decided to bash the lock open, despite his sisters telling him to stop (Sadia) and calling him an idiot (Jawaria). Of course, big brother ignored his sisters and threw open the lid. When he saw the junk within, his smile wilted. A mix of trinkets from trips to Saudi that caught Sadia's eye, and stuff that sounded fragile when Mashael dumped it on the floor. "There was supposed to be something valuable in here," he muttered. He colored his words with an inadequate mimicry of their grandfather's way of saying, "Infinitely valuable."

"Maybe it's in that shoe box," Jawaria suggested after he'd dumped the rest of the things on the floor. He pulled it out, popped the tape holding the lid down, tossed off bits of crumpled paper padding, and said, "Well, this looks spoiled."

He dragged a jelly jar out by its steel lid and dropped the shoe box that held it for them all to see. Whatever was inside was brown and gross, or was there an empty space past a muck smeared across the glass? When he shook the jar, nothing moved inside or clinked against the walls. "More junk. He sure was a hoarder, wasn't he?"

"Joke's on you," Jawaria said, enjoying his disappointment.

"This sucks," Mashael said, and dropped the jar back into the trunk. Something happened then. Glass uttered the crackle of a fracture. Smoke filled the trunk. The three siblings gaped at this phenomenon. With a thundercrack, a shape appeared above the trunk. It was humanoid, bare chested, and shrouded in smoke from the nipples on down. It grinned at them from above.

"Who has freed me?"

For once, Mashael was mute. He did not handle surprises well.

"We all did," Jawaria said. She knew what this was. A djinn. An honest to goodness djinn! Just like in all those old stories Mother used to tell.

"Then I owe each of you a debt. You shall each have your heart's desire," the djinn said. "Wish it and it will be granted."

It was Sadia who spoke up first. "I got to go. I'm desperately craving a big old peanut butter sandwich—"

"Granted," the djinn said. An instant later, Sadia struggled with a sandwich as wide as her shoulders.

"Thank you?" she asked, looking on the verge of a total freak-out.

Jawaria stared at her sister's burden and blinked a few times. Finally, she said, "This is for real."

As she turned back toward the djinn, her heart started beating triple speed out from a burst of fright. When stared at directly, it seemed human enough. A muscled man with bushy eyebrows and beard and a turban to hide his baldness. When glanced at indirectly, however, Jawaria realized there was nothing human about this creature of smoke and incense.

Mashael did not waste another second. He leapt at the chance to make the next wish, received his "Granted," reply, and immediately became one of the richest men not only in Dearborn, Michigan but in the entire state, maybe even the country. No more worries for him, as though any real worries plagued his mind to begin with.

As always, that left Jawaria struggling to emerge from her little brother's shadow.

The djinn gazed down at them from his cloud of smoke and grinned a dangerous smile. "What shall it be, woman?" the djinn asked. "A handsome husband who will love you every night for as long as you might prefer? A pretty, new *hijab* of the finest make? Thrice your weight in gold? A body that is years younger?"

"Tell me truthfully, djinn," she said. "When I make my wish, will you go free?"

"I shall," the djinn said. "For thirty long years have I awaited this opportunity. *Thirty years* since that *clever, little mortal* tricked me into this jar." His grin turned far crueler when he mentioned this *clever, little mortal*.

"And who was that mortal?"

The djinn said, "He called himself Danish of Naifeh," confirming Jawaria's suspicion. Their dead grandfather trapped the djinn in this jelly jar.

"What does this solve?" Mashael demanded. "Make your wish. I have riches in need of spending."

"You are a fool, Mashael," she muttered.

"Say *what?*" her brother demanded. He was too used to getting his way. Too accustomed to being the man. Too fat in the head.

To the djinn she asked, "What do you intend to do with the man who trapped you?"

"The clever mortal and I shall not meet," the djinn explained. "For he has demanded that it will not be so. But I shall undo the wishes he made."

"And what did he wish for?"

"Why, what any man wants," the djinn said. "Longevity, wealth, and a strong lineage filled with sons."

"The longevity and wealth might vanish in a puff of smoke, but what of his lineage?"

"What sons live shall be slain," the djinn said, matter-of-factly.

Sadia retreated a step and then raised her hands to her mouth. It was a panic attack, one of those hobgoblins that so troubled her. She breathed into her hands, and struggled to find a place of peace, balance, equilibrium. However, horror floated before them.

Jawaria asked, "And what of the daughters?"

The djinn shrugged. "What do I care of them? The men are what carry lineage's burden."

Sadia was not calm yet, but that news should help.

"Very well," Jawaria said, "I will now make my wish—"

"Wait!" Mashael ordered, expression bordering on apoplectic. "Do no such thing!"

The djinn stared into Mashael's face. "I see something familiar in you, boy. Would you be familiar with the lineage we speak of? A member perhaps?"

"No," Mashael said. The way he stammered brought a moment's evil joy to Jawaria's heart.

"But you are, Mashael," Jawaria said. To the djinn, she confided, "All three of us are. Two girls and a man. It was our jeddi who tricked you, sir." As an afterthought, she added, "Please be merciful."

The djinn glared at Mashael now, and the mask of humanity slipped just enough for Mashael to see full on what Jawaria beheld from the corner of her eye. Humanity was pleasant guise, but what lay beneath was rawest terror. Darkness with a hint of eyes peeking through. Hungry darkness that needed no mouth to bite or to devour.

Mashael rounded on his middle sister. "I refuse to let you make a wish."

His words struck her like father's belt did when they were children. She recoiled. He was his father's son, all right, and his grandfather's grandson, with all the rotten and sometimes abusive baggage those particular titles carried. "You have no cause."

"You'll just ruin this," Mashael said. "If you don't make a wish, then the djinn cannot go free, and everything is secured."

"I wish—"

Mashael boxed her on the ear and then slapped a palm over her mouth. "Don't you dare."

She kneed him in the balls. He fell to the floor cupping himself. She said, "You might've had your way all these years, but that ends now." To the djinn she indicated her brother and said, "I wish I was this man, Mashael Naifeh's, sole beneficiary."

"Granted," the djinn said.

She did not feel different, but she knew that she was soon to be not only the richest and most powerful woman in Dearborn, Michigan but perhaps even the entire state. One of the wealthiest women in the country. It would all come to pass after this little, messy detail.

The djinn swooped down upon her brother with zeal and eagerness.

Sadia could not watch, hiding her eyes behind her hands. The sounds, however, and the smells of what the djinn did were enough to bring up the partially digested remnants of her wish.

Jawaria watched her brother's destruction, sickened by what she saw but refusing to look away. Time and again, all these years, she watched him in victory, her guts churning with jealousy. Now, she watched him in defeat with the same churning, though this time from a very different emotion. As soon as it was over, the djinn vanished. True to its word, the djinn did nothing to the daughters and granddaughters of Naifeh. However, he left Mashael's ruined body on the floor.

Well, this complicates matters, doesn't it?

"What are we going to do?" Sadia whispered.

Jawaria considered her options. None of them looked particularly welcoming. "I wish the djinn had taken Mashael with him." No luck. She was out of opportunities to fulfill her heart's desires.

Even now, dead and scattered around the attic, Mashael managed to ruin his older sister's life.

About the Author

Daniel R. Robichaud lives and writes in Humble, Texas. His fiction has been collected in *Hauntings & Happenstances: Autumn Stories* as well as *Gathered Flowers, Stones, and Bones: Fabulist Tales*, both from Twice Told Tales Press.

He writes weekly reviews of film and fiction at the Considering Stories (https://consideringstories.wordpress.com/) website.

Keep up with him on Twitter (@DarkTowhead) or Facebook (https://www.facebook.com/daniel.r.robichaud).

What Do I Want?
by
Stephanie Kvellestad

What Do I Want?

What do I want? There are so many things to want. So many things to think about maybe wanting sometime. Or things that someone else would want and so maybe I should want those things too? But what if I don't?" Gretchen thought to herself. Before that moment, she had never considered what she would wish for if, say, a genie appeared before her and offered to grant her three wishes. Which was why she was so overwhelmed when that exact situation occurred.

Just as her shift at the library was ending, indeed as the library itself was closing, she found herself the recipient of three wishes from a bona fide genie. This genie was unlike any Gretchen had heard or read about. Instead of a powerful being emerging from a bottle or lamp, this genie had coughed his way out of an old book. His face was weathered and wrinkled, like an old man who had spent his life at sea. Not exactly handsome, but not without its charm. All in all, Gretchen thought he looked like somebody's grandfather. His clothing, which was comprised of a dingy brown suit and tie, smelled like peanuts and peppermint gum. Never having met a genie before, she was unsure what the etiquette was.

"Do I have a time frame?" Gretchen looked up and asked the old man in front of her. He yawned and stretched, as though he had been sitting in a cramped area for quite some time.

"No. You get three wishes, that's the deal," the genie replied.

"It's such a big decision. Can I call someone?" Gretchen said.

"They won't believe you," the genie replied.

"Good point. Do you need anything?" Gretchen said.

The old man rolled his eyes. "That's not the point. Listen, just say something you want, and I'll get it for you. It's simple."

"I've been told I tend to overthink…on occasion," Gretchen furrowed her brow. What did she want? She wasn't hungry. She had a nice job. Her car was old, but it still worked and besides, it got great gas mileage.

"Is that something you would like to change? Would you like to stop overthinking?" the genie asked. He reached into his suit pocket and pulled out a handkerchief. He proceeded to wipe down his glasses.

"Hmmm, a good question. I suppose I should work on that, but then if I wish it away, I would have the reward without the hard work of achieving it, and I may sink back into old patterns. Worse patterns, likely. Do you have a rule book or guidelines I can consult before making a decision?" Gretchen stared at the library floor as she spoke. Her mind was racing, the pressure of the decision was overwhelming her.

"Listen, how about some new clothes?" the genie clapped his hands and Gretchen suddenly found herself wearing a piece of haute couture. She blushed. The genie snapped his fingers, and she was once again in her sensible attire: thick, rubber-souled shoes and a much-loved beige dress.

"I like my clothes," she whispered. In her mind, she was going through the contents of her home. What kind of person was she? What would add value to her life? What did she even like? A flash of realization sparkled in her eyes.

"I like candles! Maybe I could wish for a candle!" Gretchen said, proud she had decided on something in such a short amount of time.

"A candle? You can have anything you want. No strings attached. You can wish for a private jet or a million Instagram followers or a king's ransom!" The old man genie was beginning to sound exasperated.

"That all sounds like a lot of responsibility. I'm not ready. No, I think I'd just like a candle. Then again—" Gretchen started.

"What now?" The genie rolled his eyes.

"Well, it seems a shame to wish for a candle when there are so many local companies that are selling nice ones. Hmmm, never mind. I don't wish for a candle. I'll just pick one up on Saturday. There's this farmer's market by my house where a nice old lady makes lavender candles that burn so smooth," Gretchen said.

"There has to be something you want. No one is this content. It's my job to give you something. Listen, this isn't like the stories. It won't backfire or have an ironic twist. It's not a morality tale about contentment," the genie said.

"Oh, no, you misunderstand. It's not that I'm content, no, no, not at all. I want a promotion and more time to write and maybe even one day to be published or be Head Librarian here," Gretchen shrugged.

"Say no more—" the genie went to snap his fingers, but Gretchen stopped him.

"No more. Again, there has been a misunderstanding. I'm not content, I'm deeply afraid. Wishing for something can only make things worse. I can only imagine the nightmare of coming face-to-face with my dream, only to find that I don't have the skillset to continue my success. I don't want to be Head Librarian until I feel ready for the promotion. At the same time, life is unfair and maybe I'll never get the opportunity to be Head Librarian. Is it wrong to waste this opportunity? Or is it worse to take it? You haven't given me the gift of opportunity; you've given me the burden of deciphering the mysteries of the universe. Does Free Will exist?" Gretchen said.

There was silence in the old, dark library as the old man genie stared ahead at Gretchen. Outside, the winter wind blew against the library building.

"What?" he said.

He studied Gretchen as she furrowed her brow in thought. There was nothing particularly special about her. She was of average height, with average mousy hair. Here he was, bestowing the power of magical realism on her, and she couldn't think of anything to wish for. It was either astounding or pathetic. In all of his years granting wishes, he had never met such an either astounding or pathetic person. Most people wish for money or power or success and then move on. His job was getting easier and easier by the year. In a way, it was nice to have a change of pace, infuriating, but nice.

"Now that I think about it, I'm almost...mad. Here I was content with my day—and it was a hard day, so many returns and a kid threw up—when you come along and put pressure on me to suddenly change my life entirely. And I'm supposed to act grateful! No thank you!" Gretchen put the last of her books away and marched out of the aisle.

How could the genie be so rude! Imagine having the audacity to assume she was so downtrodden that her only hope was to be saved by magic! As if her choices up until this point had been so terrible! No, Gretchen was content. Her hard work and good judgement had led her to this point in her life—why should she change herself now?

Resolved in her decision not to make any wishes, she made her way to the back of the library and down a set of stairs that lead to the archives and the staff room, where her purse and jacket were waiting for her. She put her coat on in a huff and pulled her purse strap over her shoulder.

"Of all the nerve!" she said to herself, growing more and more furious by the second.

She marched back towards the stairs, only to find the genie sitting on them.

"Please let me through," Gretchen demanded.

"Please, I just sat down, it'll take me a few minutes to get back up."

"Why are you an old man anyway? Aren't genies…strong?" Gretchen said, letting her anger get the better of her.

"I resent that," the genie replied.

"Please let me through," Gretchen stomped her foot.

"Not until you tell me what you want. That's the rule. I can't leave until your wishes are granted," the genie said, with a whimper for himself.

Gretchen pressed her lips together and thought long and hard. She thought about her day, how everything had been normal up until she was straightening the reference shelves and had accidentally brushed the oldest book with her knuckle. The next thing she knew, the burden of possibility was staring her in the face, refusing to leave her alone.

Her gaze drifted to the window above the library back door. It was getting dark outside, and she still had to go to the store. She was out of milk and knew that she would want milk on her oatmeal the next morning. Not only that, but she still had to make dinner.

Suddenly she got an idea.

"I know just what I want. My first wish is: I wish you would go to the store and pick up a jug of milk…and a cheesecake. Here's some money," Gretchen reached into her purse and handed the genie several coins.

"You're wishing for me to run errands for you?" he asked.

"Yes. They're my wishes, you said there were no rules."

"Oh, well, yes, yes. I did. It's just that—"

"Scoot. I've got to get home and start dinner. Do you like spaghetti and meatballs?"

"Are you inviting me for dinner?"

"Of course! To thank you for getting the milk."

Gretchen patted the old man on the head as she walked by. She was nearly out of the library when he once again blocked her way.

"I'm glad you're here," Gretchen said to him. "I've thought of my second wish. I wish that you would hand wash all of our dinner dishes. After all, I am making the food." Gretchen smiled and brushed past him. "Oh, by the way, how rude of me, but I never asked what your name was?"

"Uh, Jonie," the old man replied.

"Well, Jonie the Genie, I love it! Pleased to meet you. I'm going to go out on a limb here and assume you have my address? Wonderful." Gretchen nodded as she switched off the remaining lights and locked the front door of the library.

Her car was parked out front. She unlocked it and got inside. With a puff of smoke, the genie appeared in the backseat.

"These are terrible wishes, just so you know." Jonie shook his head.

"Why? It's what I want. You're just upset because you have to do the work," Gretchen said. "Now, scoot. I'm getting hungry!"

Jonie nodded and shrugged. He snapped his fingers and disappeared. What a wonderful evening this was turning out to be. It was strange, but making decisions was a lot easier when you simply said what you wanted, without worrying how others would react.

"Within reason, of course," Gretchen said to herself. The snow was just starting to fall when she pulled into her driveway. The first real snowfall of the season. It twinkled in the light of the streetlamps, like sparkles in the air. Gretchen stuck her tongue out, taking a moment to catch snowflakes. The crisp air wrapped around her; the streets were quiet the way they always are during the first snowfall of the year. In the morning, people would bundle up and curse as they scrape off their cars and drive down the slushy streets to work. But tonight, a hushed beauty took over the landscape. Gretchen couldn't imagine wishing for anything better.

Gretchen's home was soft and quiet, like a library back room. Her furniture was an assorted collection from friends, family, and thrift stores, all lovingly restored by Gretchen herself. True to what she said earlier, Gretchen indeed loved candles. From her coffee table to her kitchen counter, all flat surfaces were equipped with a candle.

As she always did after work, Gretchen turned on her father's old record player, lit a candle, and went into the kitchen to start cooking dinner. Jonie arrived just as Gretchen was straining the pasta.

"Perfect timing! The meatballs are almost out of the oven, and the sauce just needs a stir," she said, with a smile.

"Here's the milk. And your cheesecake. It's lemon berry swirl," Jonie replied, setting down the grocery bags on the counter.

"Delicious! I just might get used to having a genie around," Gretchen winked.

"Don't get too used to it. You only have one wish left, after all. And, listen, take my advice, I've been doing this a long time. Don't waste your last wish. Why not treat yourself. Make your life a little easier," Jonie said while examining Gretchen's home. He opened the fridge and explored several cupboards before settling down at the kitchen table.

Gretchen doled out the pasta and covered it with thick red sauce and meatballs. The two of them moved to the living room, eating their meals on Gretchen's TV trays. Snow piled up on the windowsill outside. But inside, the house was warm. Alive with their laughter.

They indulged in several episodes of Gretchen's favourite show, followed by a rich helping of lemon berry swirl cheesecake. Jonie slapped his thigh while laughing. Television was new to him.

"Such a wonderful invention!" he said, wiping tears from his eyes.

Fuelled by good food, good company, and good television, Jonie lept up from the couch and whistled a happy tune while scrubbing the dishes until they were sparkling. All in all, a perfect evening.

"Do you have a place to stay?" Gretchen asked. The night was winding down. It was nearly time for bed.

"My book, back at the library," the old man replied.

"Oh…that doesn't sound too comfortable. You're welcome to stay here on the sofa, and have some more cheesecake in the morning," Gretchen said.

"Oh, I shouldn't." Jonie began to get up. Gretchen looked out the window. It was still snowing heavily. She would have to get up early tomorrow to brush off her car and shovel the walk before it froze. Her eyes lit up.

"What if I told you I thought of my third and final wish? Something to make my life a little easier," she said, still watching the snow.

The next morning Gretchen stretched as she sat up in bed. It felt good to sleep in. She got ready for the day, ate breakfast, and made a cup of joe to go. The snow had stopped in the night but had left its mark on the neighbourhood. People, dressed in their winter clothes, shivered as they scraped the ice off their cars and tried to shovel the snow from their driveways just as Gretchen had imagined they would the night before.

Warmed from the delicious breakfast and two cups of coffee she had indulged in, Gretchen made her way to her car. Her driveway was mostly clear, and her car was completely snow-free. Resting at the bottom of the driveway was Jonie, panting from his hard work.

"Thanks," Gretchen said with a smile.

"You know, you could have just wished the snow away," he said.

"I appreciate your hard work. There's cheesecake in the fridge and the coffee is still hot. Thanks so much for your help," Gretchen said before getting in her car.

Later that afternoon at the library, as Gretchen was putting books away once more, she overheard a family talking about the work they needed to be done on their house.

"But we can't afford to put in new flooring," the mother said, in an urgent whisper. "The car needs a new heater before winter hits."

"We can't afford to wait, or the water damage could spread," the father replied. Meanwhile, the two young children played in the children's area, unaware of the stressed whispers of their parents.

The most wonderful idea occurred to Gretchen. She pulled a certain book from the reference shelf before making her way to the financially strapped couple.

"I'm sorry to eavesdrop," Gretchen said. "But I know a guy who does great work. Pretty reasonable too," she said, placing the old book on the table in front of them. Without giving them a moment to respond, Gretchen walked away.

Curious, the couple opened the book. Gretchen heard the familiar stretch and yawn of her good friend. A sweet smile lit up her face. Turning to look behind her, she waved to the old man who was now sitting with the family. He looked back at her and smiled. With a song in her heart and a smile on her face, Gretchen went back to her aisle and continued putting books away.

About the Author

Stephanie Kvellestad is a fiction writer from Calgary, Alberta. She holds a Master of Arts degree from Oxford Brookes University as well as a Film and Video Production Certificate from SAIT. One day she hopes to have her own anthology television program, combining her love of writing with her passion for TV.

Her short stories can be found in Gypsum Sound Tales' *Thuggish Itch* and Dead Sea Press' *Shadows Beneath the Surface*. Three of her short screenplays, "Gertrude and Her Plant Steve," "I Swallow Your Secrets," and "Say Macaroni and Cheese," can be found on YouTube.

Instagram: @Kvellestadchaos

I Want My Kittens Back
by
Dana Bell

I Want My Kittens Back

Cadi had watched the humans drop things into the water place. The farmer's little girl had sacrificed her favorite ribbon, his wife the cheap ring he'd given her, the son his favorite knife, and the farmer, well, he'd drowned Cadi's kittens. Would have gotten her too if she hadn't hidden in the corn field.

She'd heard him yelling and his long blade slicing the dead stalks. The rains hadn't come, and he'd lost all his crops. From what dog shared, the farmer was going to lease his son to the landowner for the next year and his daughter to serve as the pastor's maid. Payment would be food for him and his wife.

Dog had vanished, as had the plow horse, and the milking goat. The chickens still laid eggs and every month one of them lost their head. Wife spent time pulling out their feathers and then cooking them for a fine meal. Cadi had stolen a piece more than once, careful not to be seen.

Turning her head toward the house, she listened as Farmer bellowed and his wife wailed. The children were leaving in the morning. Cadi suspected they would never come home. Just like her kittens hadn't when she'd gone hunting for a fat mouse. Their scent had stopped where she now stood.

Darkness stared up at her. Her jaws opened and she dropped the mouse head into the water. Faintly she heard a splash.

I want my kittens back. She'd heard the humans tell the well what they wanted. Seemed silly to ask water for anything besides a drink.

A loud slam alerted her Farmer had come outside. Cadi dashed into the bushes, startling a rabbit. It ran. She chased until they reached the dark woods. Darting into a hole, it escaped her.

Good thing she wasn't hungry or else she would have been disappointed. Jumping up on a fallen log, she watched the house. Farmer paced along the path leading to the barn, his arms raised above his head and his voice booming.

Not having learned the human tongue beyond her name, she had no idea why he was so angry. Slamming fists against the thick door, he didn't stop until blood ran down his arms and he sank to the ground.

Her tail swished from side to side. If she was larger, she would attack, using her claws to rip his back and any other part she could reach.

"Bad idea," a tiny voice said.

She bounced like the rabbit and hissed at the small creature hovering over a bright flower. Clear wings fluttered constantly, and the body was snake like with tiny front and back legs.

"He'd kill you."

The creature was not familiar to her, smelled like fire, and she hissed again.

"Stop that." Darting toward her, it hovered just out of reach of her claws. "You should come with me."

She took a long look at Farmer. He'd gotten to his feet and grabbed the fork he used for the hay. He'd killed many vipers with those pointed teeth.

"Come." The creature moved further into the woods. "Or don't you want your kittens back?"

Her kittens. What did this flying reptile know of them?

"Come." It waited, its long tail jerking up and down.

The house door slammed, and screams followed. Cadi had no idea what harm Farmer had inflicted upon the human family.

"There's nothing you can do." The creature sighed. "Humans should never make wishes."

What did that mean? Is that what she had done when she told the water place she wanted her kittens back?

Flames began to crawl up the side of the house, eating the boards like they were food. Cadi knew fire. Feared it, sensing the heat even here.

"What's done is done." Wings touched her fur. "Follow."

Thick smoke followed as she ran after the odd viper and into the woods. Animals darted out, going down paths she had never explored. A gurgling stream whispered close by, and she smelled sweet scents she knew. The blooms of white flowers, the needles under her paws, and faint prey animals like mice or others she hunted.

"Here." The flying serpent zipped to an open door.

Cadi stood outside, one paw up, using her nose to discover what strange place this would be. The outside looked like a tree with a door. Overhead, birds chirped, and one dropped foul smelling poop.

She ducked inside before it could touch her perfectly groomed brown striped fur.

"Look what I found!" her guide told the woman standing over a pot slung on poles and bubbling over a fire. The brew smelled like chicken and other good things.

"You did indeed," the woman returned, glancing at Cadi. "Welcome furred warrior." She bowed deeply.

With a blink she wondered how she could understand human speech.

"You are in a magical place." The woman wore a simple brown dress, a sash of green vines about her waist. Her hair had been pulled back into a long brown braid, tied with yellow flowers. No shoes adorned her bare feet.

Where are my kittens? She doubted she would be understood.

"They are safe," the woman promised. She poured some of the mixture she made into a bowl and offered it to Cadi.

She sniffed the contents. The mouse had very little meat, and her hunger took over. Watching the human and her odd flying companion, she ate her meal, washing her muzzle as she'd been taught by her mother.

Who are you?

"I'm one of the old ones." Sitting down, the woman drank her soup, keen green eyes observing Cadi as if she were prey.

"Ask," the winged one urged.

"All in its proper time."

Silence fell between them.

Darkness fell and those who hunted prowled past growling or sniffing around the door, but never daring to enter.

"The girl child survived," the woman said. "Hers was the only wish that gave to others."

Made no sense to Cadi. She draped her tail over her front paws and waited.

"Bring her to me, Cadi and you shall have your kittens."

I will have them now.

"They are safe I assure you."

Cadi considered the promise yet wondered if the old one told the truth.

"Should I go too?" the tiny one asked.

"Stay. You have a task to fulfill."

"Always. Always. Always. No fun."

"Cadi, take the path through the woods. You will find the girl child sleeping inside a log. Bring her here."

Farmer's daughter had been afraid of Cadi since the day she'd come into their lives. Not sure why, yet determined to get her kittens back, she left the odd house in the tree and started down the path. Not far away she could hear the wolves padding, no doubt looking for a fat hart to feed them. They darted away and she relaxed.

Long into the dark she travelled, following the path by scent and the faint moonlight filtering through the thick branches. Her nose led her to the child, snuggled into the tree like a bird in a nest.

The child turned, whimpering. Cadi smelled blood and knew the human had been injured. Perhaps the old one could help.

Slowly she crawled onto the girl's chest, lightly tapping the pale cheek. Eyes flew open and a scream escaped thin lips.

I wish I could help her understand.

"Hello," a cheerful voice greeted. The winged creature darted in. "There, there, don't cry. Cadi and I have come to help."

The old one said you had things to do.

"Done. Done."

The child raised a shaking hand to try and touch the viper. It darted away.

"Come, come." Flying outside it waited. Cadi followed, waiting to see what the child would do.

After a time, the small body crawled out, wobbling to bare feet. Again, fingers reached for the flying one.

"Follow." It disappeared into the dark.

She brushed against the child, urging the small human to follow.

Seemed to Cadi the journey back took longer than it had to travel before. The old one stood in the door and smiled when they finally reached the odd home.

"Welcome," she greeted the child, frowning at the wound bleeding on the thin arm. "That will never do." Taking the child inside, Cadi and her winged companion followed.

"Take care of wound first. Then talk." It flew to a perch on a small branch with leaves sprouting from it.

What are you?

"Dragon from the great land of China."

She'd never heard of China. Cadi found a spot to lie down near the fire, hoping she didn't get stepped on. Farmer had done that many times and always laughed when she yowled her pain.

"All better," the old one assured the little girl and smiled at her, her green eyes shining brightly.

"You witch!"

Cadi scampered to her feet, hissing. Farmer stood in the door, his bloody fingers wrapped around the long fork. "I'll kill you, her, and that cat!"

The old one whispered a word and Farmer froze. His blue eyes glared as if issuing a challenge.

"You were warned," the old one growled.

A deep silence settled over the warm room, the smell of chicken and vegetables circling around all. The child pressed against the old one's skirt.

The farmer's mouth tried to move as if he had something to say.

"You know the power of wishes, and yet you betrayed what you promised in return."

His eyes sought me out, anger blazing as hot as any blaze.

"Lucky for you I have those who watch."

Farmer's eyes widened and Cadi saw the first glimmer of fear.

"Child, there is a warm bed up those stairs," she pointed. "You'll be snug in the branches."

Without question the child took the steps, which had not been there before, vanishing from sight.

"I gave you a gift," the old one repeated, "and you betrayed me." She snapped her fingers.

"You gave me misery," Farmer snarled back. He tried to move his arm but couldn't. "Witch!" he accused.

"I have powers yes, but not as you understand them." Her head tilted to the side. "Why did you kill your wife and son?"

He snarled like an animal. "She tossed away the ring I worked hard to give her for our wedding. My son, the little liar, threw away the knife my father gave to me when I was the same age."

"Ah, so you think they betrayed you." She took as step closer to farmer. "And the girl?"

"Because of you."

With a shake of her head, the old one sighed. "Humans never appreciate what they have."

"You're responsible for the lack of rain and my crops dying. I did what I had to!"

"I do not control the weather, whatever you might think."

"Luckily, with the fire, the landlord will think us all dead. He'll take my property, and I will be free to start over."

"With no remorse over those who died?"

Cadi felt a chill.

"Had to be done." He bared his teeth like dog. "Now give me back the girl."

"I think not."

Overhead an owl hooted and close by the wolves howled, their song echoing through the woods.

"I release you Farmer of betrayal." She shoved him out the door. Cadi heard a thud. "When I close the door the binding I had upon you will vanish." The old one laughed. "Your future is in the hands of the pack."

A terrible anguished cry sounded as the old one closed the door.

"Pack eat well," the tiny reptile said.

"They'll run him to ground first."

Not truly understanding what had happened, Cadi watched as the old one kneeled down, extending her hand. "The affairs of humans is not your concern," she said quietly as if sensing the unasked question.

The winged one flew down. "Right you were. Taking back the girl child."

"I suspected he might go back on his word."

A paw scratched at the door. The old one opened it. A wolf walked inside, holding a basket handle in its mouth. Wiggling inside were Cadi's kittens. Gently they were put down and the wolf was given a bone before darting out.

"I had asked for one of your kittens," she explained to Cadi. "They are of great value."

Half listening, Cadi inspected each kitten. They needed to be cleaned since they smelled of wolf.

"I made you a warm place." The old one picked up the basket and set it inside a box. "You and they will be safe here."

How did you save them? I saw farmer throw them in the water place.

The image filled her mind. He dropped each of them, one by one, into the water place.

"I'm not always small." The flying reptile stretched to the size of Cadi. "I saved them."

"We left them in the wolves' care. They owed me several favors for saving their young."

The creature returned to its tiny size and zipped back up to its perch.

"You and your kittens are welcome to live here for as long as want." Her eyes travelled upward. "In the morning I will teach the child what she needs to know to become who she was born to be."

Settling beside her kittens, Cadi washed them, satisfied when they wanted milk. When next she looked up, the old one had gone.

Who is the child?

The creature fluttered down, hovering close to Cadi's head. "Not our worry."

A shimmering began and Cadi fell asleep, her kittens safe beside her. What the old one meant and what the future held, did not concern her. She had a safe place to live, a new human servant, and an annoying lizard snuggled in her fur.

About the Author

Owned by two cats Taj and Esther, Dana Bell often uses felines in her various tales. She is notorious for mixing genres and tying her various universes together. These include her Winter Trilogy, Five Systems/Borders and vampire cats. Currently she has three books released *Bast's Chosen Ones*, *Winter Awakening* and *God's Gift*. She is an editor as well with seven anthologies compiled and published. Belle Blukat is the pen name she uses for Paranormal Romances. Her first novel *Blood Bride* will be released soon. Hobbies include, flower arranging, making candle holders, soap, and building/decorating dollhouses.

.

The Monster in the Lantern

by
Ioanna Papadopoulou

The Monster in the Lantern

Parthena sat on her small market stool and brought out of her pocket the wooden lantern. It was warm to touch, and she pressed it against her belly to ease its ache. She rubbed with her thumb the wooden surface and the monster complained inside. The sun was high, and the heat radiated off the light brown walls. Few people walked by, looking lazily at each stall.

"How is work going today, Parthena?" Pambos asked as he approached. "We are slow."

Parthena put the lantern back into her pocket, securing it, and then brought her hands up on top of her small round table. "Nobody wants to learn their fortune, Pambos. These young people think they know everything, including what the future has set for them."

"Will you tell me something of my future, in exchange for a sweet, juicy pear?" Pambos asked and Parthena smiled at his words. She lifted her hand, offering her palm to the middle-aged man. He placed his on hers, palm open as well for Parthena to see the lines of his life, his past, present and future.

Her thin lips tightened, and her hand squeezed around his. "Make it a sweet, juicy pear and a bright, big red tomato for my dinner," she counter offered.

Pambos let out a throaty laugh. "You are a true veteran of the market, Parthena." He nodded his agreement, and she relaxed her hold.

She knew all the lines on his hand, having read it for years. In reality, she wasn't reading the hand. But the theatrics of the palm holding, and the projected symbolic power of the word 'reading,' was craved by Pambos and her other visitors.

She waited for the images to come to her mind, always the same since Pambos married Crystalia. The flow of his life had always been a sequence of plain happy moments, filled with his wife, his children, his future grandchildren with small interruptions of daily troubles. The images of his life began as Parthena expected. Crystalia giving birth to their last child, a daughter. Unlike past visions, the birth didn't bring joy.

Parthena's eyes widened and she let go of Pambos's hand. The images didn't stop. She saw a demon son, instead of an angelic daughter, destroy Pambos's family and his future with pain. "What did you see, Parthena?" Pambos asked her.

"A son," she said, and Pambos's face grew happy at the news.

"A son? Really? Finally, my prayers have been answered and my line will continue!" He leaned down and kissed her hands. "These are wonderful news! Crystalia will be thrilled when I tell her. She has been doing everything possible to ensure the success of this pregnancy."

Parthena smiled weakly at him.

The row of images of Pambos's future misfortune stained her mind until she couldn't take it anymore. She packed up her small stall and left halfway through the day. As she walked, she heard steps running behind her and turned to see Matta, Pambos's oldest child. "Auntie, hold on," she said, and Parthena waited for the young girl to reach her. "Daddy said to give these to you."

Matta offered Parthena a cloth bag with various fruits and vegetables. "This is too much, Matta. Your father and I only agreed for one pear and one tomato."

The child shook her head. Her dark brown eyes momentarily reminded Parthena of Matta's maternal grandfather. Parthena often felt that some of Cleander lived on in his granddaughter. "Daddy is very happy that he will finally have a true child."

Parthena sighed at the words. She took the bag from the girl's hands and put it over her shoulder. "You and your sisters are his true children. Your father is simply too stupid to express himself right. Don't ponder over his words too much."

Matta shrugged. "I don't care," she lied, and Parthena ruffled the girl's hair.

She watched Pambos's girl put her hands in the pockets of her pants and turn around to return to her family's stall. Parthena wanted to follow the girl, take her hand, and ease her discomfort, but the images of misfortune that awaited Pambos and his family stopped her.

She turned around and continued her way home.

Once she arrived, she left her bags on the kitchen table and took out of her pocket the wooden lantern. "Come out, monster," she called in the room and started rubbing the wooden surface furiously. The lantern grew warmer as the monster left its cage.

A puff of smoke leaked out of the object, coming out in all the colours of the rainbow until the monster materialized in front of her. As it happened each time she opened the lantern, she was struck by how white his skin was. Parthena had never before seen a man or woman as white and fair haired as the monster. He was strikingly handsome, but Parthena had long ago learnt that his good looks were only a mask of the bad luck he brought to those around him.

"You look terribly old, Parthena," the monster said.

"I am old," she answered his insult. "You haven't seen me in twenty years."

The monster let out a low growl. "That's because you have refused to use your remaining two wishes, you ugly hag. You have forced me to spend all this time by your side."

Parthena crossed her arms and walked to sit on her couch. The monster watched her, annoyed, as she stretched her legs on top of the small table. The monster scowled at the sight of her old and pained feet, full of bristles, bruises, and dry peeling skin. "Disgusting," he muttered. "Wish me to fix your looks and we will both be happier, you stubborn mare."

"No," Parthena refused. "I have a question for you."

The monster's light pink lips tightened. "I fulfil wishes. I am not an encyclopaedia."

"You and I will have a conversation, monster, or I will use one wish to give me a thousand years of healthy life and you will have to live them by my side," she threatened him. "I am sure after an entire lifetime with me you know that I would do it. Neither I, nor you, want that."

Parthena locked her gaze with his and dared in thought for him to strike her as he always desired. His face twitched as the thought formed in his mind. At that moment, the smell of smoky burnt flesh reached her nostrils from his wrists. It was the failsafe someone had long ago forced upon the monster.

He winced in pain until the thought of hurting her was forced out of his mind. He crossed his arms, hiding his new scars, and turned his back at her. "What is your question?" The monster asked after a moment of silence between them.

Parthena relaxed on her couch and wet her lips. "Can I make a wish to change someone's destiny? Not my own, someone else's?"

The monster turned around. Intrigue was clear on his face and Parthena bit her tongue to stop herself from ordering him back into his cage. The glee in his eyes made the hair on her neck rise. "Well, it depends on the change." His thin lips became a straight line but his eyes, his terrible blue eyes, told her that he was hatching a plan and Parthena, as his keeper, had to save the world from it.

Yet, the image of Pambos's future flashed through her mind and tore her resolve. It was unfair to be in such a dilemma. Cleander's father had passed the lantern to her because she promised him she would stay away from personal temptation. Her fingers twitched against the wooden surface. It was unfair. She had done so well for so long. She had refused to marry, to have children, avoided everything that could put her in temptation to use the wishes for gain and release the monster.

"No," she croaked word out. "I promised. No. Not again," she said and rubbed with her thumb the lantern. "Back! Get back!" she ordered and lifted the wooden lantern. The monster didn't look surprised. His eyes still shone with glee even as his body faded into smoke.

"You coward," he sneered at her. "Your filthy race has always been inferior." His mouth turned into smoke and his words were lost. He was pulled back inside the lantern and Parthena closed her eyes in relief that she had managed to avoid making another mistake.

The lantern was warm in her hand and eventually grew too hot to touch. She threw it on the couch next to her and she imagined the monster inside it laughing. She got up and went to her bedroom. She pulled the curtains closed and lay on the mattress. She placed a cloth over her face and breathed in its flower scent. It was supposed to help her mind relax but the strong scent did nothing to help her forget.

She threw it away from her face. It fell on the floor beside her. Parthena turned her gaze towards her hand. She lifted it and watched her fingers. They were old and very thin, betraying the skeletal bones under it which held the rest of her up. It was because she had used the wish once, that she was tempted again. If she had never wished for the actual ability to know the future, she wouldn't be torn.

She hugged her pillow and closed her eyes, willing herself to sleep, even though it was midday. She needed to ensure she didn't do anything that broke the promise she made to Drosos over fifty years ago. "You got to use two of the three wishes, Drosos. And yet, you made me promise to never use more than one."

Parthena suddenly wished she could push time back, find the man and ask him why he made such a rule. The smell of burnt flesh made her eyes snap open. She turned to see the wooden lantern on the bottom of her bed. It radiated heat and let out smoke, stinking of burnt meat.

"You prick," she cursed and kicked the wooden lantern off it. "You can't scare me, monster. And you aren't allowed to move on your own in my house."

Parthena stayed in her bed for the rest of the day. The wooden lantern was left on the floor, and she refused to look at it or pick it up. After the sun set, and a few repeated complaints from her stomach, she gave in to her hunger and got up. "Prick," she said to the wooden lantern as she passed it and went to her kitchen. She unpacked the bag of supplies Matta had given her. She placed all the vegetables and fruit on her kitchen table. "I don't deserve all this," she muttered as she watched the colourful food.

Her stomach growled in annoyance, and she picked a small sharp knife and one of the pears. She started eating by cutting small pieces of it. She walked towards her small sitting area, where the lantern had moved on top of her small table.

Her stomach, despite her hunger, suddenly couldn't accept the sweet, juicy food and she spat it out. She let the pear fall from her hand and it rolled on her rug, until it was under the table. "No," she said and grabbed the lantern. "That's enough of your bullying, monster." She dashed into her bedroom. She shoved it into her closet, where she stored her extra pillows for the rare occasions she had guests, making sure it was covered completely by them. "And stay there! I warn you!"

Parthena returned to her kitchen and stared at the rest of Pambos's produce. She couldn't eat any of it, not when she hid from him the terrible fate that awaited him and his family. Instead, she took some of the leftover bread she had, cut a small piece, and put it in her mouth. Both crust and crumb were hard. She softened it with her saliva and slowly the texture softened until she was able to chew and swallow.

The bread eased her hunger without any pleasure or joy of taste.

Her heart battled her mind as she tried to convince herself that Drosos would forgive her for breaking her promise, since it was for his granddaughter's good. Yet, she knew that the man who had passed the monster to her over his own son would never forgive such sentimentality. No matter how hard she tried to convince herself that he wouldn't writhe in disappointment and didn't risk his anger making him come out of his grave, she failed. She had already used the one wish she was allowed.

Some days later, when Parthena was trying to scrub the stain from her rug, there was a knock on her door. "Who the fuck is this?" Parthena muttered, annoyed at the interruption. She kicked the lantern away, letting her steam off at the monster, and walked to the door. Her one leg had gone stiff from the lack of moving, and she limped on it.

She stood in front of the door and there was another knock on it. "Parthena, it's me," Crystalia's voice was heard.

Parthena bit the inside of her cheek and took off the door latch. She opened the door and Crystalia pushed her way in. "How are you? We haven't seen you in the market for a few days."

"I had some clients that prefer to see me in their house." Parthena lied. She had avoided her usual spot in the market, preferring to go to a different one. Her desire to change the future clashed with her promise to Drosos each time she looked at Pambos and his family.

"I am glad. We were worried about you," Crystalia said and walked inside Parthena's small seating area. "Pambos told me of the news," Crystalia added. She placed her hand on her belly. "About our son. He is very excited."

"I am sure," Parthena said as she closed the door. "Can I offer you anything?"

Crystalia shook her head. "I want you to read my fortune and then to discuss the future," she said as she sat on a chair. The way she held her head up and her long neck struck Parthena. Her heart, despite its age, skipped a beat at the memory of Cleander. "What?" the younger woman asked when she noticed Parthena's gaze on her.

"You reminded me of your father," Parthena explained and walked with a slight limp to sit by Crystalia on another chair.

"I do have his colours," Crystalia said.

The younger woman took out of her pocket a coin and placed it on the small table. Parthena looked at it, seeing all her inner conflict reflected on the shiny object. Crystalia offered her hand, palm open, and Parthena tore her gaze away from the table towards Crystalia's face. Her eyes were the shape and colour of her mother, a woman who Parthena had learnt to love despite her initial jealousy, but the glint of life and spark in them was another reminder of Cleander. She took her hand and examined it.

Parthena let the images roll in her mind. They were similar to Pambos's, full of misfortunes but for Crystalia the pain was mixed with her intense love for her last child, her only son. That mixture would bring further misfortune to Crystalia as the son she carried would continually force her to choose between him and her daughters.

"I see a son," Parthena said, repeating what she said to Pambos, "who you will love very much. His arrival will not be easy though."

Crystalia nodded and leaned forward. "Do you see any misfortune?"

Unable to lie at the direct question, Parthena nodded. "I do. His arrival will bring strife in your family."

Crystalia sighed and pulled her hand away. "I thought so," she said. "It is why I needed to speak to you. About Matta. She told me of what you said to her. Thank you for calming her."

Parthena was momentarily confused over what Crystalia referred to but then she remembered her last conversation with the young girl. She puffed her cheeks and stretched her leg, moving it about to get the blood flowing. "I am very fond of Matta, you know that. I hate to see her sad."

"She is very upset that there will be a son. So, I wanted to ask you, if you could, to take her for a bit?"

Crystalia spoke slow, as if she was afraid to trip over her words. "What? Crystalia, why would you send your child away?"

"Not away. To you. You can teach her your craft and help her. The new baby is the future of our family. Matta is jealous, and you just told me you saw misfortune and strife in the future. Matta's emotions could be the source."

Parthena bit the inside of her cheek. Her eyes moved to Crystalia's belly. The images of the future already started coming true as the demon son started to create a schism in the family. She wanted to scold Crystalia, stamp her way to Pambos and slap him but she didn't. If she didn't take Matta, Crystalia might send her to another relative, if her fear of superstitious curses was so strong. "Ok," Parthena said. "If you are sure you want her to follow on my footsteps, then I will take her. Will you bring her tonight?"

Crystalia nodded. "I don't want to risk it. Matta was never jealous of a baby before, and this might be my only son," she tried to explain to Parthena. "It is hard, but I need to do what is best for the future."

Parthena didn't comment. "Will you help with her food?"

Crystalia nodded. "You can take some of our produce for her, and you, each day."

"Ok. Bring her and her clothes." Crystalia took Parthena's hands in her own and kissed them. The touch made Parthena have a roll of images again, this time showing clearer the pain that Cleander's daughter would face.

"Thank you, Parthena!" Crystalia said. "Pambos wanted to send her to his mother, but since she will be with you, we will be able to see her often." Parthena walked with Crystalia to the door and watched the woman dash down the road to her own house. The street was dark and the air chilly.

She closed the door and turned to her empty house. She didn't stand looking for long. She quickly took out from the closet the large pillows she had and made up a bed for Matta on the floor, next to her own.

After she finished, she remembered the monster. She found it under her small table, where she had kicked it out of spite. She took it out and placed it under her pillow. It wasn't a good enough hiding place. She needed to find a different, permanent one, to ensure that Matta didn't find the Monster.

Drosos had inherited the lantern during his old age, when his children had left the house and his wife was dead. Parthena had lived for decades alone. It was easier to keep the lantern in solitude.

As Parthena covered it with the pillows, a thought crossed her mind and she realized that she had found the solution to her earlier frustration. Matta was the answer to her dead-end dilemma.

Parthena, as she had promised Drosos, couldn't use another wish but Matta hadn't wished anything. If she passed the lantern to the young girl, making her its next Keeper, then Matta could use her one allowed wish to save her family. Parthena took the pillows off and stared at the lantern. She wanted to gloat at it, to tell the monster that she was going to trick one more wish out of him and he could do nothing to stop her. Instead, she stayed silent and walked to her sitting area. For the first time in her life, she placed the lantern on a visible corner, above a small stool.

She paced in her living room waiting for Matta. It was completely dark outside when Crystalia arrived with her daughter. Parthena opened the door, smiling widely at the girl. "Matta, my little dove, come in," she welcomed the young girl and pecked her on the cheek.

Matta's eyes were red and puffy, a clear sign of crying. Despite that, she pecked Parthena's cheek back and offered her a weak smile. "Hi Auntie," she greeted. "Mother said I am to live with you from now on."

Parthena nodded. "Yes, and we will have such a great time together."

"Yes, Auntie."

"Matta," Crystalia scolded her daughter. "Auntie Parthena is so kind to let you stay with her. Don't be so sad and make her think that you don't want to live with her."

Matta nodded at her mother's words. "I am sorry, Auntie. Thank you for taking me in," she said and took Parthena's hands and kissed them.

Parthena shook her head. "No need to be so formal, Matta. Come in. I have made your bed next to mine, and we will have a very nice time together. Did you bring your clothes and any of your toys?"

Matta shook her head. "Only clothes. I left all my toys to my little sisters."

"And little brother, too," Crystalia added. Matta refused to comment to her mother's words. Crystalia lowered her upper body to be eye level with her eldest daughter. She caressed her hair, kissed her cheek, and inhaled deeply Matta's smell. "Can I have a hug?" she asked her child.

Matta didn't say anything. She walked farther inside her new house without looking back at her mother. Parthena grabbed Crystalia's hand and smiled. "She will be ok. It is just the change.

Next time you see her, she will shower you with love. She needs some time."

Crystalia nodded. She lingered at the door, looking at Matta and waiting for her to turn around, but her daughter, so much like her grandfather and great-grandfather in pride, didn't even flinch. Eventually, Crystalia sighed and gave up. "Well, goodnight! Thank you again, Parthena." She glanced at Matta again. "I will see you two tomorrow at the market?"

Parthena shook her head. "No, I still have some clients to see in their houses. I will take Matta with me, but we will try to come and see you on our way back."

"Yes, that will be lovely," Crystalia said and turned to leave. Parthena didn't miss the pain in the woman's eyes nor each slow motion that hoped for Matta to turn around and offer a small sign of love. Yet, Matta refused to give in.

Parthena closed the door, put the door latch back, and approached the little girl. "Matta? Are you ok?"

The little girl shook her head and turned to face Parthena. Her eyes turned redder and new tears rolled down her face. "I hate the new baby," she cried. "I hate that everyone will love him more than me, more than anyone else."

Parthena sighed and opened her arms. Matta walked towards her and let her head bury against her belly. Parthena lifted the girl in her arms and carried her to one of the chairs. She curled her small body against the older woman and continued crying. It was in that position, after hours of sobbing and weeping and multiple failed attempts to convince her that it wasn't as bad as the girl feared, that Matta fell asleep.

Parthena glanced at the lantern and closed her eyes. Matta had to wish the misfortune on her family away soon, but the little girl wasn't ready to take on the monster. She lifted the child in her arms again and moved her into bed. She lay by her side and gazed admiringly at her little face. Parthena had sacrificed all attempts of family to honour her promise to Drosos. A small part of her warmed at the unexpected chance to raise a child.

She fell asleep looking at the girl.

The next morning, Parthena woke up to find Matta missing from her bed. She entered her sitting room to find the little girl sitting on a chair and staring at the lantern. "How did you sleep, Matta?"

"Good, Auntie," Matta answered without tearing her gaze from the wooden lantern. "What is this? I have never seen it in your house before?"

Parthena let out a chuckle at the blunt question. "Yes, I usually keep it hidden. But I have had it since your great-grandfather died. He gave it to me, and I think I might give it to you. Do you like it?"

Matta pushed her lips in thought. Parthena bit her lip to stop another chuckle as the girl crossed her arms, leaned back, and continued studying the lantern. "But what is it? A box?"

"A lantern," Parthena answered.

"But it is wooden and has no glass. How do you light it?" Matta asked.

"You don't light it. A monster lives inside it."

Matta snapped her head to Parthena. Her small eyes widened open. Parthena waited for the girl to work through the information. Matta stood up and approached the lantern. She kept her arms clasped behind her back and eventually went close enough and took a sniff.

"Are you sure my great-grandfather didn't trick you. Auntie? Mummy always says he could sell anything."

Parthena let out a chuckle again. "No, he didn't, Matta. Would you like to meet the monster?"

"Is it dangerous? Like in stories?"

Parthena nodded solemnly. "Far more dangerous than any monster in any story. But it cannot hurt you or me. I am its Keeper, and while I have unused wishes, the monster is bound."

Matta nodded, finding everything Parthena said completely logical. "But what will happen when you use all your wishes? Will the monster hurt us then?"

Parthena sat on a chair facing the lantern. "Come here. Sit on my lap," she instructed the girl. Matta obeyed. "I will never use all my wishes. I promised your great-grandfather to only use one wish. He also never used all his wishes." Parthena explained. "That way the monster will never run wild. It changes hands from Keeper to Keeper. Drosos gave it to me, and I will give it to you, and you will find the next person."

Matta nodded again.

"Shall I take the monster out for you to see?" Parthena asked again.

"Yes, Auntie," Matta said and jumped off her knee. Parthena picked the lantern up and returned to her seat. She patted her knee for Matta to hop on again.

"Monster, come out!" she commanded, and smoke escaped the lantern until the monster appeared in the middle of her sitting room.

"Are you ready to make another wish, Parthena?" he asked.

"No," Parthena refused. "I just wanted Matta to see you."

He moved his eyes to the girl and his lips stretched into a smile. "Will you give me to this child?"

Parthena shrugged her shoulders.

"You don't look like a monster," Matta stated, interrupting their conversation. "It's just a man, one of the light ones that come from the West. We see them in the market sometimes."

"That's because Parthena and her predecessors are prejudiced against me," he said.

"No, it is because he is such a terrible creature and has done so many terrible things that he only deserves to be called a monster," Parthena explained. "One of our wise magus trapped him in the lantern and forced him, as penance, to grant others' wishes but never his own. We need to make sure he never gets to grant all the wishes and escape his penance."

The monster gritted his teeth and offered a wide big smile. "Oh, boo hoo! Occupiers and bullshit. I did what any man would do. I saw a chance and I took it. And I won. If it wasn't for your dark occult practices, I wouldn't be here. You are the evil demonic ones, not me. I was showing you how to evolve," the monster ranted.

Matta stood up from Parthena's knee and approached the monster. "But if it is penance, shouldn't he have the chance to change? Shouldn't we help him, Auntie?"

Parthena stamped her foot on the floor and grabbed the wooden lantern. "In. Get back!" she ordered the monster who slowly formed into smoke. As he did, he winked at Matta and half raised his hand at her.

"Why did you do that, Auntie?" the young child asked.

"Because you are too young," she said and went and placed the lantern in her bag. "Now, go and get dressed. We need to leave to visit some clients. I will explain what you need to do on the way," she instructed.

She watched Matta go into their joint room and take off her night clothes. Parthena, still wearing her previous day's clothes, took some of her rose water and sprinkled it over her hair and face, to cover the sweaty smell. She put the lantern in her bag. A few minutes later, Matta appeared again wearing a pair of baggy black pants and a loose purple shirt. "Good girl," Parthena said and the two of them put their shoes and made their way out of the house.

Matta didn't mention the monster throughout the day and Parthena felt the hot lantern in her bag. She hadn't expected for the child to find excuses for the Monster nor question the Keeper's role. Her plan was too risky. Matta was still too young to understand.

Parthena guarded the lantern from Matta, and, to her surprise, the girl never mentioned it to her. She wondered if the child thought it was a dream or a story. Matta gazed at it in curiosity, but never spoke a word. Parthena wanted to question the girl, to understand what she was trying to figure out when she looked at it, but the opportunity never arose to start the conversation.

Matta swung her legs as she sat on top of her stool next to Parthena. They watched the people passing by. Parthena met any wandering gaze eye to eye, daring and inviting them to hear their fortune. Some took the bait. Parthena was glad that none of the ones stopping had a terrible fate. She hated giving people bad news.

"Matta?" Pambos asked. "How are you, my daughter?"

The girl shrugged her shoulders without answering. Parthena stood up from her stool and opened her arms wide to hug the man. "You were late coming this morning. Is everything all right?"

Pambos gazed at Matta again and then motioned for Parthena to follow him aside. "Crystalia was bleeding last night."

Parthena lifted her hand to her mouth to cover a gasp. "Is she alright?" she whispered.

Pambos nodded. "Yes, thankfully. We had to get the doctor. She needs to stay in bed for the rest of the pregnancy. Our son is very spirited it seems and is already demanding all her attention."

Dread rose in her stomach. She knew that the son they were expecting wasn't simply spirited but ill fated. "And your other girls? Will they stay with her? Tally is only two. Shouldn't you take them with you?"

"The girls went to my mother, in Iskaria. They will come back when Crystalia has given birth."

211

"The misfortune," Parthena muttered.

"What?" Pambos said. "What did you say?"

Parthena shook her head. "Nothing, Pambos. I will take Matta to see Crystalia if you want. We can help cook something for her."

He put his hand over her shoulder and lowered his head. "I am already in your debt, Parthena. You foretold me a son, you took Matta in, and now you will help Crystalia through the pregnancy. I don't know if I will ever be able to repay you."

Parthena let out a loud laugh. She turned to Matta and snapped her fingers to grab her attention. The girl stood up from her stool and approached. "Matta, I was speaking with your father, and he said your mummy is sick and we might need to help her. Wouldn't that be lovely?"

Matta shrugged her shoulders again. "I don't care."

Pambos's eyes sharpened and, before Parthena could react, he struck Matta's cheek. "You insolent girl. You have caused so much grief the last few weeks and now you don't care about your own mother? Have you no shame?"

Matta lifted her hand to touch her reddened cheek. Parthena watched her bite her lip and her eyes fill with tears. She glared at her father and then stamped her foot and walked away.

"Matta!" Parthena called and hurried after her. "Matta, come back!"

The girl didn't listen, and Parthena feared she would be lost in the crowd. "Keep an eye on my staff, Pambos," Parthena said as she grabbed her bag and hurried after her. She squeezed through the crowd of people, barely able to keep an eye on Matta.

Parthena followed Matta to her old house, where she climbed through the window and entered. "Matta!" she yelled between ragged breaths. "Open the door now!"

To her surprise, Matta obeyed, and the door of the house opened from the inside. Parthena went inside to see her disappearing into her parents' bedroom. She closed the door and followed the girl.

Crystalia looked weak and ill, as if years of hardships had passed through her, even though Parthena had only seen her a day before. "Oh, Crystalia." She rushed to her side. "How are you feeling?"

Matta sat by her mother's bedside. "Painful," the woman admitted. "But less so now that my first daughter has come to see me. How are you, my girl?"

"Is it the baby, Mummy?" Matta asked. "Is the boy making you ill?"

"He is just a very strong boy and plays too rough with his old mother. He will learn to be nicer when he gets older. You and I can teach him manners, what do you say?"

Matta glanced at her mother's belly. It was just a tiny bump, as if Crystalia had eaten heavily. The girl lifted her hand and slowly placed it on the belly. She didn't caress it, just touched it, and then pulled away. "Will you die, Mummy? Will the new baby kill you?"

Crystalia let out a laughter. "Of course not, silly. I have birthed four children already. It is nothing to worry about. I just need to rest for a bit. It's just a tiny baby, right Parthena?" the mother said and took the older woman's hand and placed it over her stomach.

At that moment, the fortune telling gift sparked alive and she saw not only the mother's future but also the baby's. It would bring pain and misery to his family. Crystalia's body would never fully recover from the birth, and the son, who Parthena had initially seen as a demon, would lead a sad life himself. She saw his future loneliness and pain at the misfortune he would bring to his family. The lost love between him and his sisters, who blamed him.

"Just an innocent little baby. You are right," Parthena said and pulled her hand away from the woman. "I will make you some soup, is that ok?"

Crystalia nodded. "You are an angel, Parthena."

"Matta, stay with your mother and keep her company while I cook."

The girl didn't say anything, and Parthena was glad that she didn't attempt to disobey her. Matta moved slightly closer to her mother, taking her hand in hers.

Once the food was ready, and Crystalia had eaten and was back into bed, Parthena and Matta left. They walked in silence under the hot setting sun until they reached their house.

"Matta, I need you to be a big girl," Parthena said. "I need you to promise me that I can trust you with this. If I give you the Monster, you will never let it go. You will never use all your wishes."

The girl's eyes stayed impassive. "The monster in the wooden box?"

"The lantern, yes. I will pass you the lantern and then you will be the Keeper. You will never use all three wishes. Can you promise me that? Promise me on your sisters' lives?"

Matta didn't nod. She looked at Parthena as if she didn't understand what the words she heard meant. "The monster might appear beautiful and can pretend to be kind, but it is evil. Can I trust you that you will never let it go? That you will be as strong as I and your great-grandfather and so many others before us were?" She shook the girl, holding at her shoulders.

The girl still didn't respond. Not matter how many times she tried to make her promise, Matta stayed silent, until Parthena, in a midst of anger and despair, sent her to bed for punishment. She paced over her sitting room, wondering, and weighing Crystalia's life against her promise to Drosos until she was dizzy and sick and fell asleep on a chair.

The next morning Parthena woke up by Matta's poking. The girl standing next to the chair holding the wooden lantern. She offered it to Parthena. "I promise that I will never use all my wishes, Auntie."

It took a moment for the meaning of her words to register in her mind. "I knew I could trust you, Matta." She placed the lantern on the floor and kissed the girl's forehead. "You sweet and blessed child." She showered the girl's face with kisses, tickling her, and then hugged her tightly. "Ok, I will pass you the lantern and then you can wish your whole family good fortune. That will help your mother get better, your sisters will come back, and everything will return to normal."

Parthena didn't wait for Matta's answer. She rubbed with both of her hands the hot lantern and the monster leaked out. She was stricken again by his beauty. This was her last time calling him out, the last time she owned him. His eyes, full of hatred and contempt for her, seemed to know that their relationship, which had lasted for over forty years, was coming to an end. "I will use my next wish, Monster," she announced him. "I wish for the lantern and its ownership to pass to Matta, restarting the clock and letting her have three wishes you are bound to fulfil."

As she said the words, she handed the lantern to Matta. The girl held it in her small hands. It was too big for her to hold, and Parthena hated herself for asking a child to take such a responsibility. She wished she could reverse the wish, take it back, but it was too late.

She felt the warmth of the lantern leave her insides, as the wish was fulfilled.

Matta let out a gasp. She dropped the lantern, and it made a loud thumping noise as it collided with the floor. She put her hands over her chest and her neck, gasping for breath. "It burns, Auntie. The fire. I am burning."

"Shhh," Parthena said, remembering how the warmth and heat felt the first time. "Command the monster back to its cage and it will feel easier."

Matta lifted her eyes to the monster, who without any words from her, went back inside his cage, understanding her need. As he disappeared, Parthena saw Matta's eyes close in relief. She still inhaled deeply and sharply, as if there wasn't enough air.

"Let's get you to bed," Parthena said and lifted her.

For the first time in her life, Parthena felt the weight too much, and her body too weak, but she persevered and carried the girl to bed. She returned to her sitting room and picked up the wooden lantern. It was cold to touch. She felt nothing inside it. She placed it next to Matta's pillow, who gazed at it.

For the next two days, Matta burnt with fever. Parthena didn't let her father see her nor called the doctor but allowed time for the girl learn the fire. She stayed awake by her side as she sweat and cried in pain. The monster came in and out of the lantern as the fever spiked and studied his new Keeper.

Parthena wondered if she had made a mistake, the one responsible for the pain, if Matta was too young and the fire would kill her, freeing the monster and failing Drosos, but on the third day, Matta woke up feverless. "Oh Matta! You won! You beat it! Well done! You blessed child."

Matta watched Parthena as if she were a stranger and then turned to the wooden lantern. She folded her legs in a basket, placed the wooden object in her lap and cradled it as if it was a doll. She caressed it with her fingers and slowly the Monster came out. He appeared older than Parthena had ever seen him. His hair had turned grey, and his face was full of wrinkles. "Matta, are you ready for your first wish?"

The girl nodded. "I wish for the baby inside my mother's belly to die."

Parthena let out a gasp and tried to snatch the wooden box from Matta's hands. The Monster nodded. Nothing happened apart from Matta grabbing her chest in pain. She let out cries and gasps. "Please," she begged, and the Monster returned to its cage.

The older fortune teller watched the young girl in confused horror. "Why did you do that? We agreed to wish good fortune for your family."

"Because I hated the baby. He was the reason I was sent away."

Parthena knew, watching Matta's pain filled eyes, that she had sealed her own fate. She would carry the burden of her kin's death all her life. Parthena thought of Drosos, who had never told her why he chose her over Cleander. She glanced at Matta's eyes again, and she had the answer to her question from decades before.

The Monster was too big of a burden to pass to your loved ones.

About the Author

Ioanna Papadopoulou is a Greek author, currently residing in Glasgow. She studied Art History and Heritage Visualization and has worked in museums, libraries and community centres. She is currently on a Museum studies course. Her work can be found at places like Hexagon Magazine, Idle Ink, Piker Press and Nymphs.

Twitter: @IoannaP_Author

Eyelash
by
Thomas Nicholson

Eyelash

You know what that means?" said Marla. She wiped her son's cheek, and a curl of stiff black hair came away on her fingertip. "What?" asked Danny. He tried to wriggle free of her clutches, but she held a firm grip around the back of his head.

"It means you get a wish. Anything you want. Then you blow, and it'll come true."

Danny's eyes widened and his body stilled. "Anything?"

"Anything you can think of."

Before she could stop him, Danny had blurted out his deepest desire.

"I wish I was a vet and I got to play with the animals every day! And I want to be a superhero!"

He blew, and a wad of wet breath washed the lash off his mother's finger.

"Ah-ah!" she said. "You can't tell me, or it won't come true! And you only get one. Don't be greedy."

Danny scanned the floor, sighing as the hair absconded among the cream and mauve carpet patterns. He rubbed his eyes, hoping to shake another loose, but Marla yanked his hand away.

"Don't do that, or you'll go blind."

So, he waited patiently. His mum wouldn't lie to him. Not about something as important as this. It didn't take long for more to fall out. He shed lashes like snakeskin. They regrew overnight, thicker, and longer than ever, dense forests surrounding twin lakes, obscuring the corners of his vision.

Every day he tried to make his dreams come true. Never the same wish. Simply whatever was in his mind at the time. They started big. His mum buying him a dog or getting the train to Southend to play at Adventure Island. When these didn't work, he lowered his expectations. Pizza for dinner, or an extra long breaktime at school.

Someone must have heard him. It was the only explanation. God was everywhere, after all. That was what Mum said. His thoughts never stayed inside his head. The words always left a flicker across his lips. If God was everywhere, he'd have been there, too, his ear pressed to Danny's mouth, listening to any squeak of sound that leaked out, and killing his wishes before they could shape into reality.

He couldn't control the noises, and they were worse when he was sleeping. Sometimes, if he was having a particularly vivid dream, he'd wake up to Marla standing over him, squeezing his wrist.

"Please, Danny. I've got to be up in the morning. Just try to be quiet, OK?"

Yes, that would be it. He wasn't quiet enough, but try as he might, the magic constantly slipped away. Something always went wrong, and nothing about his or his mum's lives ever changed for the better.

Still, a seed had been planted. The idea that there was power in his eyelashes lingered, waiting for a flash of light to help it grow. With how often the hairs came out, there had to be a point to them, didn't there? Not a day went by when he didn't scrape a fleck of mud from his cheek and dislodge another perfectly spiralling bristle, dyed white at the root. A tiny matchstick, fire hidden within, eager for him to release its energy.

"You can't tell me, or it won't come true!"

The promise was a hint. A cryptic riddle for him to decipher, like the puzzles they gave him at school when he finished his worksheets early. His brain flared, the seed twisting and turning each night while he dreamed, until one morning, over breakfast, its shoots broke through the surface. Another fine wire rested on the back of his hand, and he shouted across the table.

"I wish when we play football at lunchtime that my team loses!"

Marla looked at him over her coffee. She frowned, heavy lines digging into her forehead. Steam crested over her cracked lips and blew away as she breathed out heavily.

"Why would you wish for something like that, my love?"

"You said if I tell someone my wish, it won't come true. So, if I tell you, that means we'll win, right?"

His mother closed her eyes. She tried to smile at him, but the expression died on her teeth, never quite making it to her cheeks.

"That's not really how it works, dearest."

But Danny wasn't convinced, and when he scored the winning goal seconds before the bell sounded for afternoon classes, that was all the proof he needed. He'd beaten the system. He'd found the secret to keeping him and his mum happy. The seed had snuck through the earth and bloomed. It didn't matter what he wished for now. As long as someone was in earshot to tell, anything bad coming his way stopped dead in its tracks. Anything at all.

Every day Danny rushed home to tell Marla about the wonderful things that had happened at school. They hadn't been given homework! He had been chosen to help his teacher give out the textbooks! The goldfish had gone to live with the headmaster and they were getting a new tank to keep the replacements in! Life seemed a whole lot easier with this aura of protection around him, and with a healthy supply of lashes dropping off his face like fruit from an apple tree, there was nothing to fear for many years to come.

After saying goodbye to his friends for another evening, he skipped along the pavement, whipping his head back and forth, trying to provoke another detachment to wish for an earlier bedtime. A screech from the road made him trip over his laces. The noise was followed by a squelch like melting ice cream pressed down under a spoon. He turned in time to see the cat's ginger paw disappear under the car's tyre, and his future plans to become a vet went with it.

He walked the rest of the way home with his head focused on the pavement in front of him. When he got to the door of their flat, he reached for the handle and found a cluster of damp hairs stuck to his palm. Most uncoupled as he jerked the hand back, but one stuck fast, gripping on to the curving scar that encircled his thumb. He tiptoed carefully through the kitchen, pulling out the chair at the Formica dining table with his left hand, all the while keeping a careful eye on the lash, praying that it would stay with him until his mother finished work.

The sun receded from the tabletop, crossed the tiled floor, slithered up past the water-stained sink, the rusty tap, the paint-peeling wall, before creeping out of the cracked window. Danny was just thinking about getting up to flick the light switch when the front door clicked open. He ran to greet his mother, nearly knocking over the chair in his haste. She stood on the welcome mat, her shoulders hunched, slipping off her dirty black trainers with a grunt.

"Mum! I wish that tomorrow I get hit by a car!"

She took him to the doctor that weekend. It was an open clinic, and they had to wait several hours of her only day off before the queue diminished. The haggard GP looked less than thrilled when she described Danny's symptoms.

"Daniel," he said. "Do you really believe these things are going to come true?"

Danny wasn't sure what the question meant. Of course he didn't believe. Why would he wish for things like that? Maybe this was a test. Someone trying to break the loophole he'd found. If he said he believed, then all his awful wishes would come true.

"No," said Danny.

The GP sat back in his chair and stared at Marla. The square of LED lighting embedded in the ceiling turned the dark circles around his eyes a deep purple.

From then on, Danny's wishes became more defensive.

"Mum! I hope *you* get hit by a car today!"

"Mum! I hope someone robs our home while we're asleep!"

"Mum! I hope someone poisons our breakfast cereal!"

Each time he declared a wish, Marla nodded along, massaging her temples, and with each time nothing happened, Danny blew away the next lash with a bigger smile.

Marla started coming home late from work not long after their visit to the doctor. Danny sat on the threadbare sofa, one finger held in front of his face, checking the hair hadn't flown away, lost in the dusty carpet. He watched a lot of TV news while he waited for her. He saw far away countries exploding in balls of flame. He saw people crying outside houses that had been pulled down the street in flash floods. He saw kids his age separated from their families and stuffed into cages. He wished for it all to happen, running up to greet his mother with requests for the latest terrible crisis before it befell them, too.

She stopped nodding after he wished for their neighbour's flat to catch fire. Danny didn't mind. She couldn't understand, and he couldn't tell her. That would ruin the magic.

"You can't tell me, or it won't come true!"

He was trying to keep them safe. He was helping out around the house, like she always asked him to. This was more important than sweeping the floors or washing the dishes. He was a hero, keeping evil at bay. As long as she was around to listen, nothing could go wrong.

The news started up, as it always did. Hundreds of people stood around a barbed wire fence. They jumped, catching their sleeves or their arms on the hungry metal teeth. In the background, dust kicked up and large cars hurtled towards the crowd, tyres yearning to squash like they'd squashed the cat. The camera zoomed in on a baby being lifted over the fence. At the top of the fence stood a soldier with a large rifle. He scooped the baby up out of the arms of a young woman, her face flushed with exhaustion, her hands barely strong enough to lift the infant by its harness.

Danny rubbed his eyes furiously. Never would he let that happen to them. Never in a million years would he let anyone separate him and his mum. He dug his fingers into his tear ducts, scraping along the wet cuticles, desperate to free one more hair. One more wish to keep them safe before bedtime. It didn't matter if he went blind, as long as they were together.

"Mum!" he called as he uprooted a microscopic thread. "Mum!"

He struggled to rise from the sofa, nearly dropping the eyelash as the cushion slid under him, but he held his finger up high like he was celebrating another goal on the playground. This couldn't wait a second longer. Before he got to the hallway, he shouted his wish, as hard as he'd ever wished for anything.

"Mum! I wish that someone will take you away from me!"

He barrelled into the hallway, careening past his school bag lying abandoned on the floor. A gust of wind blew through, ruffling the collar of his uniform. The front door banged off its stopper, the stairwell ahead empty. The bland, slap-brushed wall of the neighbour's flat greeted him, unburned and intact. Danny dashed to the welcome mat, the hard bristles knitting between his toes. There was no pair of dirty trainers beside him. Marla was nowhere in sight. There was no one around to hear. No one to tell. No one to cancel out his final, crucial wish.

About the Author

Thomas Nicholson is a teacher and UX designer from the UK who has spent time living in Spain, Colombia, and Vietnam. His short stories have appeared in anthologies and magazines around the world, including recent publications from Madhouse Books, Thuggish Itch, and Scare Street.

He is currently in the process of finalizing his first full length novel and is actively seeking representation. When not working on this, he spends most of his free time thinking about new darkly comic horror stories while trying not to lose his grip on everyday reality.

https://www.instagram.com/tom.nich/

Goat Girl Stamps the White horse

by
Diana Benedict

Goat Girl Stamps the White Horse

Tiki Jo's cocoa brown fist flew out, like a ramrod, middle finger bent at the knuckle so it made a point. It moved so fast Estela couldn't dodge. The punch landed on Estela's right bicep, the force of the blow knocking her sideways.

Estela was skinny, *que flaca*, her mom said, so it hurt right down through the stringy muscle into the bone.

Pain blossomed in her arm, and it suddenly felt numb and useless. She would have a bruise for sure. But she didn't cry. At sixteen you didn't cry. In public anyway.

"Aintcha gonna cry, little goat girl, little wetback shit kicker?" Tiki Jo crooned as she smirked that hateful smile, the gaps between her teeth like uneven fence pickets. She bent over, slapping her thighs as she laughed, brown ringlets jiggling like springs. "Mebbe you should go back to your farm. That's where you belong, right there with all the chickens."

Why Tiki Jo still talked like a *pendeja* from a bad gang movie, Estela didn't know. Christian Donaldson had come to the tiny town on Colorado's Eastern plains after the hurricane, and he hardly had a Southern accent anymore.

Estela hadn't cried since Tiki had hit her the first time, in eighth grade, but the *culera* still tried to make her, four years later. And how juvenile was that?

She stared down at the ground, waiting to see what else Tiki Jo had in mind.

Distant shouts and whistles from the football and cheerleader practice floated across the warm fall breeze. Estela looked up at the field and straightened, her acrid sweat rising up around her as her ass tightened in shame and humiliation, helpless fury making her grit her teeth.

Estela's family was Mexican, but they had been here since the 1600s, and Tiki Jo's mother's people had only come in the late 1700s. So, who had a wetter back?

She lived on a farm out of town and raised goats, that was true. Plus, she rode horses. That might make her a shit kicker. She even wished sometimes she could kick the shit out of Tiki Jo. But those were just idle dreams, her anger speaking. She didn't really want to hurt anyone or anything. Besides, trying just got Tiki Jo to double down and smack her down worse.

That didn't make Estela a chicken. It made her…civilized. Tiki Jo didn't even qualify as an animal. Animals had a pecking order, but they didn't go around beating up on others like Tiki Jo did.

Over Tiki Jo's shoulder, Estela saw Mrs. Crestwell, the PE teacher. She had noticed the clump of kids, who had also seen her, and they headed off, away from Tiki Jo and Estela.

Estela didn't need a teacher or anyone to ask her what had happened. Tiki swaggered off. Estela walked stiff-legged, trying not to meet anyone's eyes, up the hill from the football field and toward the school.

When she reached the front of the long, one-story concrete school, The Garnett Prison, the kids called it, she hitched herself up onto the low wall along the sidewalk. She bounced her heels off the wall while she waited for her mom and thought the two more years till graduation seemed like forever.

Her mother's beat up little blue Toyota Camry pulled up in front of her. When Estela opened the door, perfume fragrance flowed out of the car. Not just one perfume; that wouldn't be so bad. But this was a mix of half a dozen. The back seat was filled with boxes of cosmetic products.

"How was the party?" Estela asked, rolling down the window a crack, enough to let air in, but not all the dust when they hit the county road.

"I got twenty-three orders," her mom said jubilantly. "I'm getting closer to driving for free. Won't that be great, driving around in a pink Cadillac Navigator?"

The only good thing would be she got this car. Her mom was *loca por* Mary Kay, just like her *Tío* Cruz said.

"Better to pamper women," her mom told her brother, flipping her black hair over her shoulder, her dark eyes sparkling, "than crawl around on the floor all day breathing glue fumes, *mi hermano*."

Her uncle had shrugged and cracked that silly smile.

Estela wished she had a brother who would kid her like that, but Dad had gotten sick when he came home from Desert Storm and then died of a heart attack three years ago.

The tiny town of Garnett slid away behind them, and the asphalt gave way to dirt county road. She thought about Tiki's latest attack. She just didn't understand why the girl insisted on being such a *pendeja* to anyone she could intimidate.

The first time, Estela told the counselor about the attack. Mrs. Whitney, the middle school principal, had called Tiki Jo to the office. Then she'd called Tiki's mom.

"Can't stand and take it, little pussy?" Tiki Jo had growled when she caught Estela down by the Music Room after she got back from suspension. "Think I assaulted you, pussy? I'll show you assault."

And she had, knocking Estela down on the ground. Then she sat on Estela and pummeled her. Her nose had bled and her hair had been full of dead grass and twigs and dirt, not to mention grinding dirt into her brand-new jeans and white shirt.

She'd slunk away after Tiki let her up and cleaned up as best as she could, making excuses when her mother asked on the ride home after school.

After the third time, Estela asked her mom if she could take Karate or something, but her mom said, "It's that or riding lessons."

Estela had been a barrel racer since she was eleven and she wasn't going to give up a chance for a championship with Salbatore, her quarter horse. So no help there.

Maybe she'd get lucky and Tiki Jo would run away from home or be sent to Juvie.

A person could always dream.

If Estela could only be as brave as her dad had been. *Tío* Cruz always referred to him as *muy muy*, a bad ass.

He'd gone to Desert Storm and come home with a Purple Heart. "Never let 'em see me scared," her dad had told her uncle. "I just did what had to be done."

She didn't want to kill Tiki Jo. No, she just wanted the harassment to stop. But Estela wasn't brave, and while she could handle a quarter ton horse, she was helpless against the girl.

Right before their turn Estela saw a horse in the field out her window; a white horse with a delicate Arabian face, mane and long tail flying as it galloped along the fence line.

Everything was suddenly magnified and slowed down by half. The light shone super bright and intense, etching everything clearly, like when she was little and outlined everything in the coloring book in black.

Every toss of its graceful head and every step of his shiny black hooves said pure joy and love of living.

She could hear the thud of his hooves in the turf over the wind that sang through the rolled down window.

"*Sello del caballo blanco*," her mother said suddenly. It meant "stamp the white horse," and it was a way to wish, like pulling wishbones or blowing out candles. They'd wished on white horses since she was little. "Hurry, before he's gone."

The memory of Tiki Jo's knuckled fist and her cackling laughter leaped into Estela's mind. Yeah, that was a wish.

Estela licked her right index finger and pressed it into her left palm, feeling the nail dig into her flesh. She would never hit anyone, but she hoped that karma would come around. Yeah.

I wish someone would hurt Tiki Jo really bad, so she knows what it's like.

Estela remembered the sharp pain of the punch, the way her arm felt, how it hung loosely engulfed in pain, practically useless.

Stamping the meaty part of her right hand into her left palm, once, twice, three times, because Mom said three was a power number, Estela put all the anger and hurt and determination she could muster into the action. The sore spot on her arm echoed the pain of the punch with each smack of her fist.

Yeah, take that, Tiki Jo. You see how big a pussy you are when someone hurts you for no reason.

The horse looked right at her as they drove past, then it tossed its head, which shone with a halo from the afternoon sun behind its head. Estela clearly heard a *ting!* like the triangle in the school band, and felt, not a shiver, not a shock, but something between the two run through her body.

The white mane waved like a glorious flag as the horse tore over a hill, flicking his tail high, and he was gone.

"I hope you got a good wish. I hope it makes you happy," her mom said.

Suddenly uncomfortable, Estela looked back toward where the horse had disappeared.

It was just a silly game anyway.

She had smacked her fist three times.

It was done.

Estela settled back in the seat and stared out the window all the way home.

They pulled up into the yard and, as always, Estela smiled at the house, a totally green, recycled, small carbon footprint building, her *abuelo*, her grandfather, had built in the late Seventies.

The Life Ship looked like a stranded upright ark, a main sail of silvery solar panels facing the prow to the south, the stucco bleached peach-colored by the sun.

"I've gotta run," her mom said, leaning over to kiss her. Estela offered a cheek. "*Te amo, mi hija.* I left elk chili in the crock pot for you and Cruz. You can make some cornbread to go with it."

"Okay. I love you, too." Estela pulled her bag out and slammed the door.

Two dogs ran up to greet her. "*Hola*, Moscado, Ladrón," she said to the two brownish shepherd-mix dogs.

Her mom created a cloud of dust as she turned and headed back down the dirt road, driving through the settling rooster tails they had made coming in. She disappeared down the hill, and Estela didn't stay to watch her come up the other side.

The dogs trotted after Estela, their tails wagging happily as she walked up to the house past *Tío* Cruz's ratty white work van, stuffed with carpet pad from whatever job he did today.

Estela opened the storm door and stepped into the foyer. The house was dim and cool even with the sun shining from the west. Mom said she was imagining it, but Estela always swore she could smell the dirt-packed tires that made up the thick exterior walls, even slathered in plaster and covered with three generations of paint.

Estela made her way through the parlor filled with old-timey furniture that had belonged to her *gran abuelita*, her great grandmother. Her mother insisted that it be polished every week, and the room always smelled of lemon oil. Estela sneezed once, twice, three times, as she passed through and headed for the stairs.

Upstairs, the fans hummed and whooshed, creating a pleasant breeze. Her tennis shoes squeaked as she walked over the reclaimed barn wood toward her room at the southern end of the house.

Her mom had finally gotten rid of Estela's little kid twin bed last year and given her a bed set that had belonged to Estela's Gran *Tía*

Conchita. She loved the furniture, the way the cherry wood had turned dark reddish-brown with age. The bed had delicate chains of flowers on the head and footboards, and swirly trim on the legs and brass knobs on the uprights.

The matching vanity and dresser, and the little mahogany secretary, with its dozen drawers and slots, made the room tight, but she didn't care. She felt grown up and regal just being in there.

A set of French doors opened onto a little balcony. When she stared out, she was rewarded with the sight of a hawk coasting in the late afternoon, watching for bunnies, likely.

The white wrought iron lounge and the small matching side table called to her, and she promised herself some time on it after chores and homework were done.

Quickly, she stripped off her clothes and hissed as she raised her arms to take her shirt off. Sure enough, there was a purple bruise the size of Tiki Jo's pointed knuckle forming on her arm.

She changed into work clothes and pulled her hat on as she headed back downstairs to slip her paddock boots on. Then off for the barn where *Tío* Cruz, wearing his beat-up Aussie hat, spread chicken feed for the birds that crowded around him.

Moscado and Ladrón caught up to her as she slipped through the big red gate on the fence that marked the end of the yard and the beginning of the pasture. The white, steel barn, with its copper shingles, was another fifty yards down the hill.

She saw the horse trough about to overrun and shut off the water. Cruz looked up and waved.

"*Hola, Tío,*" Estela said when she got close enough to not shout.

"*Hola, Estela. ¿Qué pedo?*"

Estela giggled at the slang. It meant "what fart," but he intended it like "what's up."

"*Nada.*" The chickens pecked at her feet hopefully, and she moved away.

"You wanna do the goats and hay the horses?"

"Sure." Estela headed down to the barn. Inside, she took a deep breath of air laced with hay, manure, leather, and Murphy's Oil Soap. *Heaven.* The interior was dim except for patches of light made by the skylights and a beam of late afternoon sun shining through the dust from the open door.

She filled a bucket with the goat chow and grinned when she got a glimpse of them in their pen, standing on the little house, the platforms, and the dead tree that was concreted into the ground—*jugeutes de cabra*—goat toys her mom called them.

Estela got a red ribbon at the county fair last year and hoped for a blue with this year's kids.

She squeezed in through the gate, and they jumped down from their various perches. "Whew," she said. "You need to have the pen mucked."

The dozen goats crowded around her trying to get to the bucket. She petted them as they bumped her.

"Now, *mis hijos*, be patient. I'm going to feed you right now," she said to the three kids who were the most persistent.

She poured out the food into the troughs and pulled up the spigot to refill their water. Stashing the bucket in the tiny shed in the corner, she got her tools and went to work.

After she put everything away, she went to feed the horses. She whistled as she put a bale in the feed stand, and a black quarter horse, a leggy dapple gray, and an appaloosa pony came trotting over the hill.

She gave Alfredo, the pony, and Pancho, *Tio's* aging horse, a piece of horse candy, and laughed as Salbatore nuzzled her pocket for a piece of his own, bumping her chest with his head. She scratched his chin and ran her hands over his flanks after feeding him the treat. "We'll practice tomorrow, *mi caro bonito*."

She glanced over to the practice ring with its barrels set at either end, feeling the surge of energy and excitement that came from riding him as they rounded the last barrel and pounded toward the finish line, the seconds ticking.

That made her think of the white horse she'd seen on the way home. She'd love to ride him, give him his head, the wind in their ears, as he ate the ground with his hooves.

Her wish flitted through her mind, and she pushed it away as she headed back to the house, her boots scuffing in the dusty ground. The sun was just kissing the hills to the west when she met up with her uncle.

"I'll wash up, check the chili, and get the cornbread going."

"*¡Que bueno!*" he said. "I'm going to take a shower."

The weekend flew by in a haze of chores, homework, and barrel racing practice.

Tío Cruz dropped her off at school Monday on the way to his jobsite.

Clots of kids stood around, heads leaned in toward each other, talking quietly.

Miriam, her Chem Lab partner, sidled up to Estela as she opened her locker.

"Didja hear?"

"Hear what?"

"It's all over the place. How could you not have heard? Oh, that's right, you live out yonder." She gestured limply south of town.

"So, what's up?"

"Tiki Jo's in the hospital."

"How? Why?" Her heart skipped a beat as she thought of the white horse and how it had seemed to toss its head acknowledging her wish.

"She was headed home. Somebody pulled her into the alley between Carson and Monroe, raped her, and kicked the shit out of her. Janie Hanson found her layin' on the ground when she took out the trash, her pants all pulled down."

¡Lo terrible! How horrible.

Had she done this? Estela remembered the connection she felt between her and the white horse when she smacked her hand with her fist.

I wish someone would hurt Tiki Jo really bad, so she knows what it's like.

It was the same as the monkey paw story her mom told at Halloween. An old couple bought the magic paw and made wishes on it. The results got them what they wanted, but in the most awful way.

Be careful of what you wish for.

No. It was just a stupid game, it didn't mean anything.

"Why look so down? Tiki Jo treats you like shit. She walks all over you and knocks you around. You should feel happy that she got some of her own. Everybody else is."

Estela stared at Miriam, not able to stop from remembering her wish.

But this was worse, way worse than any verbal humiliation or pummeling in the school yard.

She remembered her satisfaction as she made the wish and how the horse had tossed his head, how she heard the bell and felt the shock as the wish settled into reality.

Her face flushed in shame at the memory and turned away from the girl, digging in her locker for nothing until the girl left.

The rest of the day went by in a haze. Tiki Jo was all anybody could talk about, and Estela just mumbled whenever anyone asked her about it.

Tío Cruz came after to school to pick her up.

"Could you drop me by the hospital? Someone I know got hurt and I want to see her."

"Sure, I could go over to Jesus' for a while. You wanna walk over there when you're done? I'll buy subs for dinner, and we can hurry up with the chores before your mom comes back tonight."

"Thanks. That would be great."

He dropped her at the small hospital on Cannon Street, and she went to the florist next door and bought a tiny bouquet. Tiki Jo would probably hate them and bad mouth them, the idea, and Estela for doing it. But it was what you did when someone was hurt.

She ignored the small voice that said it was also what you did when you did wrong and you were guilty about it.

The hospital was an old red brick building, just two stories, but clean and bright with new faux wood flooring, compliments of Uncle Cruz. Interspersed with the smell of coffee and donuts from the kiosk across the way, she could still smell the mastic he used to set the wood-like vinyl planks and colored tiles in lines for people to follow to various areas in the hospital, spreading out like a board game.

Do not pass Go, do not collect two hundred dollars.

She stopped at the front desk and asked for Tiki Jo's room.

Her tennis shoes softly clunking on the floor, she followed a green line. The smells changed from glue and coffee to antiseptic and sick people. She found Tiki Jo's room and paused. She could hear the TV, some talk thing with lots of clapping and wooting.

Her mouth was dry and her heart fluttered. Switching the flowers to the other hand, she wiped sweat on her pants.

What would she say? What would Tiki Jo do?

Nothing for it but to go in and see her. Tiki Jo wouldn't hurt Estela here. At the most, she would make fun of her, say rude things.

In which case, Estela could just give her the flowers and leave. No harm, no foul.

Except that was a lie.

She stepped into the pale blue room with bland prints of mountains and flowers on the wall. The window on the far wall offered a view of the main square, the old Episcopalian church, and the Veterans of Foreign Wars Hall.

Estela looked at the bed and stopped, her breath hissing out in dismay.

"Whatchu want, goat girl? You take a wrong turn on the way to the chickens?"

Tiki Jo's face was puffy and purple. Her right eye was completely swollen shut. Her arms, where they lay on the blankets were a mass of bruises, handprints, she realized, from whoever had clutched her.

Estela's throat grew tight. *Yeah, take that, Tiki Jo.*

She had done this. The horse had granted her wish.

She had wasted a magical moment, spending it on petty revenge that put this girl in the hospital.

Oh, she could tell herself it was a silly game, but she had seen the horse look at her, heard the bell ring, felt the shock of the wish shimmer into reality.

"I...I just came to see how you are."

The monitor in the corner beeped quietly, the TV erupted into wild applause and cheering. Estela glanced at the screen.

"Came to gloat, huh?"

Estela looked back, afraid to meet her face, thinking she would think she was staring. "No, no. I was worried about you."

Tiki Jo sat up, making a melodramatically disbelieving face. "Why you worry about me, goat girl? What did I ever do that you should worry about *me*?"

"Because a terrible thing happened to you, Tiki Jo. And no matter what you've done to me, this is awful, and I feel bad about it."

"It's not like you hit me up alongside the head and drug me down the alley. Didja? Didju pull my pants down and shove me up against the garage? Didju? Didja punch me in the face? Didja call me a slutty bitch?"

Her eyes narrowed. "Mebbe you got that guy to go after me. Didja pay him?"

Estela flushed in shame at how close she came to the truth and felt horror wash over her at the very idea that someone could do such a thing. "No, no, Tiki Jo. I didn't get anyone to attack you." Which was technically true.

"I didn't pay anyone," was definitely true.

"I just worried about you." Which was absolutely true.

She paused, feeling the sweat on the plastic around the bouquet. "I brought you these." She held out the flowers. When the girl didn't take them, Estela stepped forward and laid them on the rolling table.

Tiki Jo just turned away and stared at the TV.

"Look, Tiki Jo, I have never understood what I did to make you want to bully me all the time. I just wished you'd stop. I'm really sorry this happened to you. Really, I am."

The girl turned back to her. "And what? You want me to think this is how you feel when I rag you?" Her voice turned hard. "You don't do anything to deserve it. You're just a little whiny goat girl. And you wear the fancy boots and the hat and ride that fancy horse around and around the arena," she said in a mocking voice. "Who does dumb shit like that? A dumb wetback goat girl. That's why I rag you," she said derisively. "Now get out of here." She flicked the flowers off onto the floor.

Estela didn't know what else to say so she left, following the green line back to the front door. As she walked to Jesus' house on the other side of the church, she thought about what Tiki Jo had said. It didn't make any sense. She beat Estela up because she rode Salbatore in her Westernaire's outfit?

Except how would she know about the Westernaires' drill show unless she'd seen it? Ah, at the county fair. The Westernaires always carried the state and American flags to open the rodeo.

Was Tiki Jo jealous? Did she wish she rode a horse? Estela didn't know much about the girl's family. They'd moved from Denver when Tiki's dad took over at the highway department after Janie Hanson's grandpa retired. Tiki Jo's mom worked at the Garnett Grocery Store. They lived in a little house a block behind the tractor supply store. It wasn't a bad house, but it had clearly seen better days.

What was Estela supposed to do now? She felt responsible, knew she had caused Tiki Jo's situation, which meant that she had a debt to pay. What could she do? Go see her again?

How did she know if that was just a way to make herself feel better or if it was really the right thing to do?

In the end she decided it didn't matter whether it was to make herself feel better or to do the right thing. She just had to do something.

Something turned out to be a batch of cookies and Tiki Jo's homework. If Tiki Jo didn't like the cookies, well, *podía ir a la chingada*, and the devil could deal with her.

Tiki Jo went home the next day, so Estela got her mom to drop her off while she went grocery shopping. Her heart pounded as she walked up to the front door, a plastic container of cookies in her hand and a bag of homework slug over her wrist.

She felt stupid and would have turned away, except that someone might see her and think she was a coward, and she just kept hearing her dad tell *Tío* Cruz, "I never let 'em see me scared, just did what had to be done."

Well, this had to be done.

She squared her shoulders and took a deep breath. She could smell something spicy cooking. Whatever it was it made her mouth water. The traffic from the highway hummed in her ears as she struggled to gather the courage to knock. She hadn't realized how loud it must be to live in the city. Just as she raised her hand, the door flew open and a little boy of about six stood there. He looked like a miniature Tiki Jo—same brown eyes, same cocoa skin, same picket fence teeth, except for the gap in front where his front teeth had fallen out.

"Wayull," he drawled. "You gonna knock or stand there all day?"

"Actually, I was enjoying the smell of whatever's cooking."

"Mom's ribs. Dinner's in a bit, so you can't stay."

"That's okay. I just brought Tiki Jo's homework."

"And more'n that it looks like." He motioned at the container.

"Yeah, that, too. Can I see her?"

"She's on the couch. Beat up bad," he whispered as he led her through a hallway cluttered with coats and shoes and bags.

The first thing Estela saw was the flowers arranged in a nice vase on the coffee table in front of the couch where Tiki Jo lay propped up so she could watch TV.

When she saw Estela, she shook her head. "Goat girl, again. Din't you get enough yesterday?"

Estela took another breath and her tummy rumbled. "I just thought you'd like your homework, so you don't get too far behind."

"Oh, yeah, thanks. That's exactly what I want, my homework. Thanks, really. Yeah. No."

Unsure, Estela laid the bag down next to the coffee table and offered the container.

"Oh, you made me cookies, too? Aren't you just the nicest goat girl?" Tiki Jo waved them away

Estela set them down on the coffee table next to the flowers.

"Tiki Jo, don't call her names, and be nice," her mom said, bustling out of the kitchen. She had Tiki Jo's teeth and the same springy hair. Tiki Jo must have got the hair color from her dad. "This girl's gone to all the effort to bring you these things. Thank her," she commanded.

"No, that's okay," Estela said. "And I really am a goat girl. I raise them."

"You do? Make cheese?" she wiped her hands on a dish towel.

"No, just confirmation, uh, the way they look."

"You wanna sell milk? I like goat cheese. My great aunt used to make it."

"I suppose I could. I never tried to milk them."

Tiki Jo's mom laughed. "I know how to milk 'em. Spent all my summers on that farm."

"Well, sure." Estela didn't know what else to say.

"Okay, then. We can set something up. You live off the county road?"

"Yes. Out past Bayberry's ranch."

"Good enough. Come on, Ezekiel. Let the two talk in peace."

"That's good, goat girl," Tiki Jo said. "You come to my house, get my mom excited about cheese. What, you tryin' to go all BFF on me?"

"No. I—"

"That's what it looks like. You never gave a shit about me before now. You never tried to be my friend before. What's going on? You sure you didn't have anything to do with the other night?"

Anger and shame made Estela's face burn. "Look," she said. "I didn't get anybody to do it, but, yes, I wished someone would hurt you so that you knew what it was like to be on the receiving end of what you dish out."

Tiki Jo stared at her and smiled crookedly. "You wanted me to know what it was like? How the hell do you know I don't?"

Estela looked toward the kitchen where Tiki's mom was.

"No. Don't you even think it," Tiki Jo snarled softly. "You don't know nothin', goat girl."

"So, okay, I don't," Estela said, keeping her voice low, anger making her words come out hoarsely. "But I know there's no need to take it out on someone else. And I may have wished it, but when I saw what happened to you, I felt bad. What happened to you was awful. And I'm sorry. I really am."

"So you bring flowers and cookies to make yourself feel better. That's good. You just keep telling yourself that."

"Whatever. I am sorry I wished it. I'm sorry it happened to you. But I still think there is no need to take it out on anyone else. I never did anything to you. I would have been your friend, even."

"You would've been my friend?" Tiki Jo laughed and laughed until it sounded like she was sobbing.

Estela left then, not knowing what to do.

Tiki Jo came back to school the next week. As Estela waited for her mom, she came up to her. "Here," she said, pulling the plastic container out of her bag. "They weren't as good as my mom's, but my brother ate 'em anyway."

Estela shook her head. Could she never be nice? "I'm glad you're back. You look better. I hope you're feeling better."

"You don't have to worry about it anymore. They caught him. He's in jail right now. Some limp-dick-over-the-road-truck-driver, can't get it up except for raping and beatin' girls. Now I just have to go to court. Yeah. No."

Estela wasn't sure what was better, not knowing who did it or having to go face him.

She sighed, not knowing what to say. "I am sorry. I would do something if I could."

Estela's mom pulled up. She stood to go to the car.

"And my mom asked if she could come milk a goat this weekend," Tiki Jo said. She offered a piece of paper. "Here's her number."

244

"Sure," Estela felt relief at the change in topic. "You can come, too," she said. "Your brother, too, if he wants. I could saddle Alfredo, and he could have a ride." Realizing she had just excluded Tiki Jo, probably insulting her, she hurriedly added, "Alfredo's just a pony. But I could saddle Pancho, and you could ride, too, if you want."

"I ain't never been on a horse. I'd prob'ly fall off and break my neck." She stared at Estela. "I might come. But don't think we'll be BFFs or anything."

Her mom pulled up. "No, no. I would never think that." She opened the car door and slid inside."

"Is that a new friend?" her mom asked as she pulled away from the curb.

"No, nothing like that. Her mom wants some goat's milk so she can make cheese. They're going to come out this weekend.

"Hmm. Well, that's nice I 'spose."

"Yeah, I 'spose." She could wish. That she could wish for.

Saturday afternoon Estela had four doe goats and their kids tied up in the barn. She'd also corralled all three horses in case Tiki Jo changed her mind. She saw rooster tails of dust just making the curve before the hill to her house and started toward the house, Moscado and Ladrón at her heels.

Ezekial jumped out of the car as soon as the car came to a stop in front of the house.

She gestured the dogs to heel as the boy raced toward her.

"Tiki Jo says I can ride a horse. That true?"

Estela grinned. "Yup. Alfredo's all ready to be saddled."

Tiki Jo opened the passenger door.

"Pancho, too," Estela said. "If you want to ride, Tiki Jo."

Tiki Jo shrugged as she got out.

"Hey, can I pet your dogs?" Ezekial asked.

She introduced them and Ezekial scritched them, then ran around, the dogs trying to herd him. She called, "That'll do," and the dogs left off and returned to her.

When Tiki Jo's mom got out of the car with a pail, a bottle, and a collapsible stool, Estela greeted her.

"Call me Bernis," she said.

"Okay, Bernis, come on down to the goats."

Tiki Jo reached out to stroke one of the dogs as they walked.

The boy ran off as soon as he saw the chickens. "I wanna pet one."

"Watch out for the rooster, he'll chase you," Estela shouted.

"Why's your house so funny looking?"

"Tiki Jo," her mom said.

"It's okay," Estela said. "My grandfather was really into the whole 'be light on the Earth' thing. The house is totally green and efficient."

Tiki Jo snorted. "It's your whole family. Is there anything you don't do?"

"I don't rope calves. I don't type very well. I hate math."

"Math's easy. You just gotta know the rules."

Estela gawped at her.

They came around the corner of the barn where the goats were in their pen.

"What is that, a jungle gym?" Tiki Jo asked.

"Yeah. They like to climb and be high, and there's not a lot of places out here. My *tío* and I built it.

"Horses," Ezekial cried, giving up on the chickens and heading for the corral.

"Quiet, there, buddy," Estela said. "You don't want to spook them."

She chuckled as Ezekial got cartoon quiet and tiptoed toward them.

"Alfredo's the little one?" he asked.

"Yep. He's a pony. And Pancho's the gray and white one. Salbatore is the black one. Let me get your mom started and we can give them a treat and saddle them."

"Have they ever been milked?" Bernis asked.

"No, but I have four nursing does right in the barn for you."

Tiki Jo followed her mom into the barn. They got everything settled and the girls watched as Bernis crooned to a goat and started milking. The doe wasn't sure and wanted her kid, but pretty soon, she settled down and the milk started hitting the bucket.

"You girls go on now and enjoy yourselves. I'll tell you when I'm done."

"You wanna help me get the tack out?" Estela asked Tiki Jo.

"What's tack?"

"The saddles and stuff. We can get horse candy, too."

"Horse candy?" she said dubiously.

"Yeah, they're molasses and grain."

"No apples or carrots?"

"Yeah, I just don't have any of that handy."

"We brought some. Ezekial had Mom bring some home from the store."

"Oh. That's cool. They'll like that."

Tiki Jo shouted for Ezekial to get the bag for the horses, and he tore past, the dogs on his heels.

Estela opened the door to the tack trailer and gust of leather and grain scents whooshed past them.

"Ew, what stinks?"

"Stinks? It's the leather and the grain and stuff."

"Gross." She wrinkled her nose dramatically.

Together they got tack for the pony and Pancho.

As they walked to the corral, Tiki Jo asked, "You ever fallen off your horse?"

"Sure. And I've lost races cuz I made mistakes."

"Wayull. I'll be."

The horses crowded up along the fence nickering in greeting. Estela showed Tiki Jo how to balance the tack on the fence.

"Can I pet one?"

"Sure, but I'll show you how to introduce yourself first." She leaned in toward Pancho's face and blew gently across his nose. The horse snorted and whickered.

"That's like shaking hands with a horse. They get your smell. Then they know you."

Ezekial returned, tiptoeing again.

"You can walk, buddy, just no loud noises or abrupt movements."

"Do they freak out easily?" Tiki Jo asked, looking at them dubiously.

"No, but if you're calm, they're calm. Better all around."

Tiki Jo leaned in and blew her breath at Pancho. "Hey, horse, Pancho," she said.

Tiki Jo explained to her brother about meeting the horses. He huffed at Alfredo, who was more interested in the bag. Estela showed them how to feed them and while the horses crunched, she got Alfredo saddled.

Once the boy was mounted, Estela gave some instructions and they watched him go around the corral for a while, Tiki Jo stroking Pancho all the while.

"Wanna try it?"

"Yeah. Yeah, I do."

"Good, you can help me saddle him."

Together, they got the horse saddled and the bridle on. Tiki Jo looked uncertain.

"He's so tall."

"He's very experienced. He'll know you've never ridden, and he'll be careful."

She gaped at Estela. "He will? How will he know?"

"Because you won't have a good seat."

As Tiki Jo's face hardened, Estela shrugged. "How could you yet? But I'll show you and you'll learn. I can lead you if you want."

Tiki Jo looked at her brother, trotting around the corral, his elbows flapping as he bounced up and down in the saddle. "I don't want to look like a scarecrow in a storm."

"You won't."

"Okay." She got a foot up in the stirrup and managed to pull herself up.

Estela gave her directions. Tiki Jo did well. She gave Ezekial some instruction while Tiki Jo went around the ring, talking gently to the horse.

"His ears are back, that means he's listening to you. You're doing great. Sit up a little straighter, remember, push your heels down, and let your butt settle into the saddle. Easy on the reins. He's trained for neck reining, so just light touches and he'll go. Look where you want to go. He'll sense it."

"They're smart," Tiki Jo said, reaching out with one hand to pat Pancho's neck.

"They are. More like partners when you get the hang of it."

"I see why you like it, goat girl." Tiki Jo smiled at her as she said it.

Estela smiled back at the friendly jibe.

By the time Tiki Jo's mom came down to lean on the fence with Estela, they were both doing pretty well.

248

"I think we have time to get cleaned up. I want to get the cheese going."

Ezekial complained but his mom insisted, so they came over to the fence. Tiki Jo groaned as she dismounted, but she stroked Pancho's head and rubbed his ears, whispering to him. The horse nickered and huffed, lipping her hair.

They gave them each another apple after they curried them, and Tiki Jo opened the gate for them to go back into the pasture.

"Bye, Pancho. Thanks for the ride," she called.

As Tiki Jo opened the car door, she turned to Estela. "You aren't so bad for shit kicker. And horses are cool. Thanks for the lesson."

She stared at Estela for a long moment. "Come by after school if you want, and I'll help you with Algebra."

Then she got in and closed the door.

Estela stared as the car turned onto the road and headed down the hill, plumes of dust rising up behind them.

Well, beat that with a stick.

Tiki Jo had offered to help her with math.

And she liked the horses.

She thought of the white horse racing over the prairie. That was a bad wish, but maybe they could both make something good out of it.

About the Author

Diana Benedict's fiction has appeared in *Midwinter Fae*, *Doorway into Faerie*, *Beauty and Wickedness*, and Fiction River's *Editor's Choice*, *Tavern Tales*, *Sparks*, and *Alchemy and Steam* anthologies.

Her first novel is *Perils for Portents*. Find more of Diana's work at www.dianabenedict.com.

Amanda's Christmas Wish

by
Rob Nisbet

Amanda's Christmas Wish

I t was the same every Christmas Eve. It wasn't until she came to make the Christmas pudding that Amanda realised, yet again, that she hadn't got around to buying a steamer. Still, she'd managed to reach her early fifties without the help of a fancy steamer and, no doubt, after Christmas she'd forget all about it again till the following year.

But what was Amanda to do about the pudding? She rummaged to the back of her disorganised kitchen cupboards till she found her large casserole pot. She placed a sturdy bowl inside, upside-down, and covered the base of the pot with water an inch deep so that the bottom of the bowl broke the surface like a ceramic island. She remembered as a young girl watching her mother do much the same thing. Amanda hefted the pot up onto the hob and placed the lid on top—*there*, she thought with some satisfaction, *an instant pudding steamer*. All she needed now was the Christmas pudding mixture.

An hour later Amanda had a smudge of flour across her furrowed forehead where she kept pushing back a lock of her unruly greying hair, but at last the pudding was ready to be stirred. She'd sifted, peeled, and chopped a mixing bowl of sweet-smelling ingredients, pounding them into a spicy dark mound of fruit, nuts, and sweetness. That would please Malcolm; he liked a rich pudding. Then in another bowl was the rum, the barley wine, and a generous glug of stout all thoroughly beaten with a couple of eggs. If they had this with a dollop of brandy butter, they'd all be tipsy after Christmas lunch. Then they'd collapse round the TV and probably fall asleep.

Amanda wiped her hands on a tea-towel. It was time for the traditional stirring of the pudding. She had fond childhood memories from when her mother had let her stir the mixture, and, of course, she had always made a wish. Amanda wondered what she should wish for and was pleasantly surprised that she couldn't think of anything. She had found a good husband in Malcolm, and the twins had grown into well-balanced young adults; she was very lucky.

Amanda's eyes wandered to the window running with little streams of water from the constant winter drizzle outside. Perhaps she'd just wish for snow, then Christmas would be perfect. She stood at the kitchen door and called to her family that the mixture was ready.

Carla and Max appeared almost instantly at the kitchen door, together as usual.

"Mmm, smells great, Mum." Carla held back her auburn curls as she leant over the mixing bowls for another sniff.

"As usual," said Max, dabbing at the mixture with his finger and licking it with relish. "A little raw though," he said with a grin. "Not quite done."

Carla gave her brother a friendly dig with her elbow. "Max, you're disgusting."

Max mock-smiled back at his twin, as if he'd been paid a compliment.

Amanda smiled too and shuffled to one side as Malcolm, her husband, also came into the small kitchen. Malcolm leaned over the bowls and nodded approvingly. "Smells nice," he said.

"Too late, Dad. Carla's already done that," said Max.

"And Max has already done that disgusting licking-his-finger-thing," said Carla. "He obviously doesn't know it has to be cooked."

"That's enough, *kids*," laughed Malcolm. Being called 'kids' was the one thing he knew would stop the twins in their tracks. They were nineteen now, and they scowled their disapproval at him in unison.

Amanda poured the alcohol over the pudding mixture and produced a wooden spoon. "Are we ready?" she asked. "Stir it clockwise for luck, and don't forget to make a wish." She handed the spoon to Carla.

Carla smiled at the thought of making a wish. "Honestly, Mum," she said with a meaningful glance at her father. "We're not kids you know." Carla gave the mixture an exaggerated stir. Wishes were stupid, kids' stuff, they never came true, but still she closed her eyes, just as she did every year, stirred the pudding—and wished.

A few years ago, like most teenagers, Carla had been obsessed with her looks, spending her meagre allowance on medicated preparations that promised to rid the world of spots, and she had tried practically every cream and paste to conceal the small birthmark at the side of her right eye. These days it didn't really trouble her, but her wish was always the same. "I wish I had been born without the little birthmark," she thought. "And, while I'm at it, my eyes could be a shade larger and my cheekbones more pronounced. Straighter hair would be nice—blond too, I'm fed-up with auburn curls. Oh, and a bigger bust…"

Carla opened her eyes, passed the spoon to her brother, *and the world changed.*

Max took the spoon and stepped up to the bowl. This tradition of wishing was all a bit embarrassing now. He could remember back to when he was about five, his gran had made the Christmas pudding then and he'd always wished for sweets—as if he didn't get a sweet overload at Christmas anyway. Still, Carla had gone through with it. Max wondered what Carla could possibly have wished for; perhaps she'd just closed her eyes and stirred to keep Mum happy. Knowing Carla, she'd probably have wished for world peace or some other altruistic fancy, she certainly didn't need the wish for herself. Carla had always been the better-looking twin. Max thought of her long blond hair flowing straight over her shoulders, her perfect eyes and curvaceous figure. Carla ought to become a model—perhaps *that's* what she had wished for.

Max stirred the Christmas pudding. It was all nonsense of course—but, if he *could* wish for something, there was always that new bike he'd seen in the showroom window last summer, all sleek and chrome. It wasn't the most powerful bike in the window, but he had often imagined himself roaring past the cars on the motorway, perhaps with the latest of a string of girlfriends on the seat behind clinging tightly round his waist. Some hope, he thought. He handed the wooden spoon to his father, *and the world changed again.*

Malcolm took the spoon from his son, and they shuffled round each other as if performing the steps of some bizarre dance in the small space of the kitchen. "What shall I wish for?" he wondered.

"You mustn't say it out loud," Amanda said reproachfully. "The magic won't work."

Malcolm gave his wife an amused glance under raised eyebrows and began to stir. Christmas, Malcolm thought, was a time of reflection and, if he was honest, there *were* a few things he would like to change—if he could make a wish that really would come true. He loved his children dearly, but he wasn't so blinded that he couldn't see their faults.

Carla now, she had always been a looker and that had made her popular at school and at college. The trouble was that having the constant attention and adoration of her peers hadn't made her a very pleasant young woman. Most people made friends by being friendly themselves. Carla had grown up to *expect* friendship and attention with no effort on her part. She had become—if he were honest— lazy, vain, and demanding.

Max, Malcolm thought, had fared a little better—until recently. Malcolm traced the change back to the summer when Max had brought that motorbike. A car had been out of the question, they were too expensive, and the bike itself wasn't the problem. But the bike had led Max into what Malcolm thought of as the 'wrong crowd'.

Racing and drinking, never at home. And the girls he'd been seen with were hardly the type Malcolm had hoped for in a daughter-in-law. No wonder Max never brought them home, often staying out all night and shredding his mother's nerves with worry.

It was hard, Malcolm thought, to decide what he might have done differently. Money had always been tight of course. He glanced around the small kitchen. The house wasn't really big enough for them now that the kids had grown-up. Perhaps if he'd had enough money the house wouldn't be so cramped, perhaps Carla would have grown-up to be a bit more generous and pleasant, and Max could have had a sensible car rather than that bike.

Malcolm knew that money wouldn't solve everything—but it wouldn't do any harm, would it? He stirred the Christmas pudding, *the world changed*, and he held out the spoon to his wife.

Amanda stepped across the wide tiled floor, around the granite-topped breakfast bar to take the spoon. She remembered stirring the pudding when her mum used to make it. Things had been different then; she hadn't got a shiny modern kitchen or an electric steamer for a start—her mother would have made do with a casserole pot. But though space had been cramped in those days and money a bit tight, Amanda was sure that they had been happier. She tried to force back a sob that threatened to catch in her throat.

This would be their first Christmas without Max. A part of their family had been cruelly ripped from them and like an unhealed wound it opened and hurt every time she thought of him. It hurt so very much.

Naturally, it was Carla who missed him most of all, missed their companionship and sibling banter. Not that Amanda could tell much of what went on in Carla's head. She'd grown even more sullen and withdrawn recently. She'd always been vain as a child, now she spent her time behind a mask of make-up, feeding her ego with designer clothes and expensive 'bling'—was that the word? Malcolm had tried to help by giving Carla and Max—before the accident—everything they wanted. What, Malcolm had said, was the point of all the sacrifices he had made, the effort of working his way up the hierarchy of the business, if he couldn't lavish a bit of his earnings on his children.

Amanda sighed. Perhaps, if they couldn't have afforded it, Max wouldn't have insisted on the biggest most powerful bike he could find; perhaps he wouldn't have been travelling quite so fast when the accident happened. She and Malcolm had argued about it on many occasions. That was no surprise; they argued now about most things. Malcolm drove himself too hard, never relaxed, always the businessman, always earning—but always working, always stressed. Amanda glanced round her spacious kitchen. They'd achieved a very comfortable lifestyle, but, for all their gadgets and possessions, she couldn't honestly say that they were happy.

That's what she would wish for. Amanda stirred her Christmas pudding mixture and wished for them to be happy.

Malcolm took the lid from Amanda's improvised steamer. "Resourceful as ever," he said with a smile. "You certainly take after your mother."

"I shall take that as a complement," Amanda said, covering the bowl with a tea towel. "The mixture needs to stand for a while then it has to steam for about eight hours, all ready for tomorrow."

"Come on, *kids*," said Malcolm waving his arm. "Give your mother some room to work."

"We're not kids," said Carla absently playing with a curl of her dark auburn hair. She turned in the doorway. "I'll be back in a minute Mum. I'll help prepare the sprouts. If we leave it to the men, they'll get it all wrong."

While his mother was distracted, Max stuck his finger under the tea towel for another taste of the pudding mixture.

"I saw that, Max," said his sister. "You're still disgusting."

"And a merry Christmas to you too," said Max with a grin.

Left alone in her little kitchen, Amanda smiled to herself as she placed a pile of sticky utensils in the sink below the window. It was at occasions like this that she really appreciated the closeness of her family—how happy they were. Yes 'happy', that was the word.

A movement outside caught Amanda's eye. There must have been a change in the wind; the drizzle had been transformed as if by magic into silent swirls of snow. Her eyes widened in surprise. Snow for Christmas. Perhaps wishes did come true after all.

About the Author

Rob Nisbet, as befits his age, lives in a bungalow on the English south coast near Brighton. He has won three international writing competitions and has had over 70 stories printed in anthologies and magazines ranging from romance (under his wife's name) to horror. His wife has recently turned to crime!

He is a member of the IAMTW having written several audio scripts produced by Big Finish for their Doctor Who range. He also keeps chickens.

The Well

by
Peter Sartucci

The Well

I've heard bad things about you." Ernie shuffled around the waist-high stone ring, trying to look inside without actually leaning over the rim. The Juke's pasture fence curved around the back side of the old well, guardian blackberry bushes trying to claw him. A couple crows peered down from winter-bare trees with barbed wire grown into their gray bark.

"Some of them are probably true," whispered a damp voice out of the depths, slick and chill as an icy brook. "Yet here you are."

"Uh, yeah." Ernie dragged his injured leg the other way, dislodging a clot of half-decayed leaves. Their pungent aroma remined him of winters past, of rain and decay. He moved slightly closer to stare at the weakly-lit inside of the stone-lined shaft. How deep was it? He hesitated, shifted from foot to foot as the nape of his neck prickled in the March breeze. "My Aunt Edna says you caused that heart attack that stopped her husband when he was beating her the last time."

"He ate a lot of greasy food and had unhealthy genes. He might have died anyway." The voice rustled like something heavy sliding over wet moss. Maybe chuckling?

Ernie swallowed, his Adam's apple bobbing. "Then she had that bad car accident and had to spend all his insurance money just getting well again."

"She shouldn't have run that stop sign."

Definitely a chuckle this time, the sound of water over rocks. Ernie shifted a little closer, he could almost touch the rim now. His leg throbbed the way it had after the Juke boys took turns kicking him, even though it had mostly healed. *Gawd* that had hurt so much. He hadn't been able to kick a soccer ball since. Goodbye scholarship, hello leg brace.

Ernie swallowed hard. Temptation was every bit as powerful as Father Muloney said, and his resolve was weaker than the winter sunshine. "I . . . need something."

"Everybody does. That's why they come to me."

Ernie reached out, brushed fingertips against the rough sandstone. Pulled his hand back, clenched it, then reached out again. The stone was bitingly cold. How far down into the old well did the sunlight reach anyway? He shifted closer.

"I . . ." He stopped, started again. "The Juke boys broke my leg and left me lying there in the high school parking lot. It didn't heal straight. I can't play. I can hardly walk." It had taken him an hour to hobble here, his resolve shredding under pain and cold and growing numbness.

"You want them to suffer? How much? Illness, crippling, death?" The voice sounded eager. Gleeful, even gloating.

"Um, n-n-not death." Ernie swallowed even harder. "I don't want to kill nobody."

"Pity." This time he was sure the voice laughed. "Maiming, then. They could each lose a leg to a surprise accident on their dad's farm. Tractors are dangerous."

"No! Not that either." Visions of the Juke boys, humbled and screaming in pain, washed through him. So, tempting. "No," he repeated more firmly, gripping the sandstone rim. This was harder than he'd thought it would be. "I don't want to maim them either." Though there'd been a time when he had wanted it, very badly. Visions of their cruel faces danced in his head.

"Then what?" The voice sounded disappointed. "Suffering? How about leukemia? It's curable, after months of pain. Could be many months. Humiliating too, as their hair falls out and they lose control over their bodily functions. They might both end up sterile and impotent. Last of their line, no more Jukes after them."

"No." Ernie took a deep breath, leaned his good hip against the stone wall, and looked directly down into the darkness. "I want them to become better people; good people."

The shaft of sunlight pinched out only a few feet down. Ernie could dimly see the stonework continuing down, down, at least thirty feet to a gleam of water in the darkness. Water that rippled as if something agitated moved under the surface.

"Why should I do such a thing?" The voice was harsh now, like wet stones grating against each other. Ernie wondered if the wall would part and dump him down the shaft headfirst into the cold, cold water. People whispered that there was always a price. So many dark prices were rumored to have been paid here.

"Because I ask it," Ernie answered, hoping his voice didn't quaver. "It is my wish that the Juke boys become good people."

The stone wall shook and the ground heaved. Ernie found himself pitched backwards head over heels. His soccer reflexes hadn't faded completely, but he couldn't stop himself before rolling into a tree. His brace snapped, a line of fire striped his calf, and the wrench to his crooked leg put stars before his eyes. For a moment he lay there stunned. Had his wish been rejected? He looked toward the old well.

It was gone, not even a dimple to mark where it had been, and the Juke's vine-covered fence ran straight now. Ernie bowed his head.

Wheels crunched gravel at the road's verge, car doors slammed.

"Ernie?" Bo Juke's voice. "Are you all right, man? That looked like a bad fall."

Cole Juke knelt by Ernie's leg, found the snapped aluminum ends of the leg brace poking out through his ripped pants. "Jesus love you, Ernie, looks like your leg's broken. You're bleeding too. Bo, grab that plank out of the truck, let's get him onto it and take him to the clinic."

"We don't have any insurance left," Ernie protested through the pain. "I can't pay!"

"Don't worry," Bo assured him absently, using his own belt to strap Ernie's leg to the rough plank. "We got a check from the oil company for the new well."

"Dad split it with us," Cole added. "We'll cover your bills."

They lifted him as tenderly as a child. Ernie gritted his teeth against anticipated agony, but it wasn't nearly as bad as he expected. Bo called ahead and the clinic had a gurney ready for him. As the paramedics loaded Ernie into it, he looked up at the Juke's malice-free faces.

"Why are you doing this for me?"

Bo Juke looked at his twin. Cole answered for both.

"Shucks, Ernie, we're neighbors. Just trying to be good people."

About the Author

Peter Sartucci lives in Colorado with his wife and special-needs daughter and three cats that believe they own this house. By day he is disguised as a mild-mannered real estate appraiser, but after sunset he transforms into that most fearsome of creatures, a Writer. Don't worry, he doesn't bite, and he barks very little. He likes chocolate, books, wine, fantastical imagery, pasta, and too many other things to list here.

Additional Copyright Information

Don't Annoy the Genie © 2022 Emily Martha Sorensen

The Girl from the Well © 2022 Kay Hanifen

The Wishing Cat © 2022 Sylvia Son

The Price of the Pool © 2022 Kara Race-Moore

A Wish Well Spent © 2022 Laura G. Kaschak

Waxing, Waning © 2022 Remy Allen

Katie and Kyle Forever © 2022 Alyssa Beatty

Death Stopped for Florencia © 2022 C.B. Calsing

Best Wishes © 2020 Edward Ahern

Wish for Ebony © 2022 Katie Kent

Where Wishes Come True © 2022 J. L. Royce

Clever, Little Mortals © 2022 Daniel R. Robichaud

What Do I Want? © 2022 Stephanie Kvellestad

I Want My Kittens Back © 2022 Dana Bell

The Monster in the Lantern © 2021 Ioanna Papadopoulou. Originally published by Piker Press as the Cover Story on 5/7/2021

Eyelash © 2022 Thomas Nicholson

Goat Girl Stamps the White Horse © 2022 Diana Benedict

Amanda's Christmas Wish © 2011 Rob Nisbet

The Well © 2022 Peter Sartucci